Praise for *Of Memories and Mirages*

"*Of Memories and Mirages* is a masterful exploration into the themes of identity, diaspora, migration, love, and war through the intimate stories of a rich array of characters navigating their place in a world that was not of their choosing. The reader is given a glimpse into the travails of South Asian Muslim students in a post-9/11 America before being transported back in time to the Partition of the subcontinent, and then forward in time to the effects of America's ongoing war in Afghanistan, bearing witness every step of the way. Each one of these enormous historic events is refracted through the ordinary lives of the book's protagonists, who prove to be more than just the sum of their experiences and emerge in their full vividness as agents of their own stories. A wonderful and captivating read."

—Asad Dandia, Brooklyn-born Pakistani-American
writer and organizer

"Though deceptively straightforward, *Of Memories and Mirages* is a masterful display of the intricacies in the vocabulary of love. Throughout— while the stories are separated by time, mood, and forms of love— Rafique is devastatingly delicate, yet painfully precise. Before you know it, you ache with the characters as the tragedy of the human condition artfully makes itself known. It sneaks up on you, tender tendrils gripping your heart from behind. A wonderful read for all connoisseurs of love and loss out there."

—Elia Rathore, writer and journalist

More praise for *Of Memories and Mirages*

"*Of Memories and Mirages* is Abu B. Rafique's finest work. In this novel comprised of letters, recollections, and lush, descriptive writing, characters grapple with love, loss, grief, hope, and uncertainty. Events that are writ large on the world stage are brought into sharp relief through their impact on this close-knit Karachi neighborhood. Rafique deftly draws a straight line from war to romantic relationships, playground bullies, and family recipes. Each vignette is painted over with love and romanticism, such that even the most gruesome accounts are underscored by an empathy that is rarely afforded to characters such as these."

—Tori Mumtaz, visual artist and writer

"A beautiful amalgamation of stories and characters, interwoven yet individual at the same time. Moving, cinematic, and deeply philosophical, this is a treasure I cherished wholeheartedly. The stories are etched in my soul, and I am still feeling the pain and grief that Rafique has evoked through his poignant words. An important and magnificent novel, and a must-read for all."

—Rekha Bhardwaj, singer and seeker

"Abu Rafique writes with honesty, precision, and compassion. He understands the frailties and strengths inside the hearts and minds of his characters and writes with great awareness and empathy toward the human condition."

—Michael Imperioli, author of *The Perfume Burned His Eyes*

ABU B. RAFIQUE

Of Memories and Mirages

Brandylane
Publishers, Inc.
Publishing books since 1985

ISBN: 978-1-953021-02-1
LCCN: 2021914916

Cover art by Bhavneet B.

Designed by Michael Hardison
Production managed by Haley Simpkiss

Printed in the United States of America

Published by
Brandylane Publishers, Inc.
5 S. 1st Street
Richmond, Virginia 23219

Brandylane
Publishers, Inc.
Publishing books since 1985

brandylanepublishers.

For my Mehrnoush Jaan, whose watchful eyes and unending insight helped me construct this story properly when I first began writing it years ago.

For my Bhavi, who took the time to comb through this manuscript time and time again to help me form a vision for what these characters and their world looked like.

For Khizra, my Joonam, without whom I would never have been able to construct the character of Suraiya, and who provided all the patience in the world when it came to providing me feedback three years ago when I was writing this novel.

And for my Khursheed Khala, whose home I was in when the idea for this story first struck me—who would sit in the bedroom next to the kitchen and pray through the night while I wrote. Who inspired the character of Khursheed in this novel, beyond just the name. Who passed away the night this novel was accepted for publication. I did not have the chance to tell her it had happened, but I'm sure she somehow knows.

I see a horizon lit with blood.

And many a starless night.

A generation comes and another goes.

And the fire keeps burning . . .

—Iraqi poet Muhammad Mahdi Al-Jawahiri

PART ONE
AASIYA & ASHFAQ

Chapter One

July 2, 2017

Aasiya hurried along the street leading to Salim's Teashop. It was still early in the morning, and people were slowly and sleepily emerging from their houses, on their way to school or work. The shop would not be crowded right now. If she was early enough, Aasiya knew she could get a table in one of the corners, where nobody she knew was likely to notice her once business picked up. Even with this thought in mind, she pulled her dark blue scarf a little tighter around her head and glanced around quickly to make sure nobody familiar was out and about. Her parents were under the impression that she had gone to the university with some friends for a study group, even though it was her day off from classes. If anyone who knew her family saw her going this direction, word was sure to get back to her parents, and although Aasiya was certain she could come up with some sort of lie to placate them and ease any suspicions, she preferred to avoid it altogether.

After a few more minutes of hurried walking, Aasiya at last cleared the streets where lived the people most likely to recognize her, and she was finally able to relax. She loosened her grip on her scarf and let it rest lightly around her head, drawing in a deep breath of early morning air. As it was in most big cities, the air in Karachi carried the burnt tinge of industry. But it was familiar; it was home. She could tell by the taste of the air that the day would be very hot and humid. Later, when the power went out at its scheduled time, she would soak her clothes in a bucket of cold water and put them on to keep cool. A rickshaw rushed past at the corner, the driver beeping his horn loudly despite the fact that nobody was in his way, and a milkman rode by on his motorbike in the opposite direction. He nodded at Aasiya as he passed, and she smiled politely before turning to her left and going up a few paces to stop at the entrance to Salim's Teashop.

It was a relatively small shop, but well-kept and clean, with a couple dozen tables crammed inside and six more situated out front. A few old, sticky, faded posters were taped up in the front windows, advertising the chai and a few of the snacks sold inside. When Aasiya walked in, old Salim greeted her with a big smile.

'Subha bakhair, azizam!' he said. Aasiya smiled back as he strode around the counter and placed a gentle hand atop her head.

'Asalam walaikum, Uncle,' she said.

'Walaikum asalam!' he replied, 'You know, I was thinking of you earlier, meri gul.' Salim had called Aasiya my rose since she was a girl. When she was little, whenever she visited his shop with her family, he would lower the vase he kept on the front counter to her and say, 'Go ahead. A rose for a rose—pick one! Any one you'd like!' To this day, if anyone in her family brought home sweets from Salim's, they would come with a rose taped on top of the package, always. 'When I was a young boy in Afghanistan,' Salim had explained to Aasiya once, when she was eight years old, 'my mother told me that I had had a sister who had passed away very young from some sickness. Amma would describe this sister to me all the time, and everything that I can remember about what she was like, I see in you. Ah, how the old project their silly imaginings onto the young, hain?'

Aasiya smiled at the old man again. 'Why were you thinking of me, Uncle?' she asked.

'Well, I had a customer early this morning who was asking about you. You might know him?' Salim tilted his head toward one of the back corners of the shop, where a young man was sitting at a table, looking in their direction with amusement in his eyes and a steaming cup of chai resting in front of him.

'I don't think I know him,' said Aasiya with a grin.

'Maybe you should go and make sure,' said Salim, his eyes twinkling. 'I will bring another cup for you in a moment.' He patted her shoulder and returned to his place behind the counter.

Ashfaq stood and came around the table to embrace Aasiya as she approached, and she buried her face in his chest, taking in the familiar scent of his cologne and his skin beneath it. He kissed the top of her head and held her like that for a moment, before they pulled apart and sat down across from each other. Salim's Teashop was famous among the young people in this part of the city, because they knew they could go there without worrying about the disparaging eyes of an elder bearing down on them. The tables in the corners of the shop were known unofficially as 'lover's corners.' In these corners, couples could hunch over cups of chai and plates of snacks to have some time together to talk, drink, eat, flirt, and just generally enjoy some time to themselves. Upon request, the old man would even hang sheets up from any of the numerous clotheslines that crisscrossed the ceiling, offering privacy to any couple who wanted it.

'Your parents think you're in class right now?' Ashfaq asked.

'Mhm.' Aasiya reached over and grabbed his cup, taking a sip from it as he watched. 'I should head back in an hour or so. I told them it wouldn't take very long.'

'I leave tomorrow, and you can only spare one hour for me?' asked Ashfaq with mild surprise. Aasiya felt a jolt in her stomach, and she touched his wrist gently. 'That's not how it is. Besides, I'm seeing you tonight, aren't I? I told Amma I'd be working on a project with Haniah after Maghrib.'

'I told you, I can't be sure about tonight yet. I just finished packing last night, and my parents want to throw a final daawat today before I leave. All my relatives will be there too, to say goodbye. You're more than welcome to come. They said I can invite friends.' Aasiya winced and immediately, he knew he had made a mistake with his choice of words.

'Friends?' asked Aasiya. 'You haven't told them yet?' Ashfaq stared at her hands in his for a moment.

'I haven't had the chance to yet. I've been meaning to, but there hasn't been a good time. They've been so caught up in my leaving, Aasiya, I told you that.'

She pulled her hands back a bit, frowning.

'Yes, you did. And you also told me that you would tell them about us before you left. And that you would speak to my parents before leaving as well. I suppose that won't be happening either?'

Ashfaq sighed and opened his mouth to respond, but before he could Salim returned with a cup and a pot of chai in hand.

'Here you go, children,' Salim said as he set the cup down in front of Aasiya and poured the creamy, light brown brew out for her. He then reached into the front of his apron and pulled out a small tin of biscuits, setting it down between the two of them.

'Salim Uncle, please . . .' Ashfaq reached into his pocket to pull out his wallet, but the old man smacked him on the shoulder.

'Put that away!' he said. 'You know my rule: if you're here together, you don't pay. I'll square it up with you next time you're here. You'll be a big American-educated man by then!'

Ashfaq laughed and said, 'That won't be for almost another year!'

'Well then I will wait. But I can't guarantee that others will be so patient.' Salim nodded his head at Aasiya and smiled. 'Consider this your gift from me,' he added. He set the pot down in between them on a little wire rack and bowed his head before going back behind the counter.

Ashfaq watched him go. 'I love that man,' he said. 'I'm going to miss him.' He turned his attention back to Aasiya, who was blowing gently on her cup to cool it down. 'I'm going to miss you too, Aasiya,' he said.

'Will you now? For a whole year? All the way over there in America?' The hint of annoyance in her voice did not go unnoticed, and Ashfaq sighed. She leaned forward. 'I'm sorry if I'm adding to the pressure, Ashfaq. I don't mean to. But you must understand where it's coming from. Amma wants to get me married soon, or at least engaged. The only reason she hasn't been putting more pressure on me is because Abba and I convinced her to at least let me finish college first. She says plenty of girls get married and still go to university, that it's a new day and age. She doesn't like that every time some auntie tries to bring her bloated and balding self-assured son around, she has to turn them away because she knows that I wouldn't be interested.'

'Ah, so you're using me as a deterrent for these bloated, balding types, then?' Ashfaq said with a chuckle.

Aasiya glared at him and slapped his wrist. 'I'm not interested in them because I love you. And you know that.' She turned away after saying this. They'd only said those words to each other two times before then. It burned her to have to say it again.

'Aasiya, I'm sorry,' said Ashfaq. He leaned forward and took both her hands in his. 'I'm an imbecile. A moron. A wrinkled old donkey.'

She glanced up at him. 'Don't stop there. Keep going,' she said.

He laughed. 'I will speak to your parents; I promise I will. I've never broken a promise to you before, have I?'

Aasiya sighed and squeezed his hands. 'I know you've never broken a promise to me before. But you have to realize, Ashfaq, I can't wait for you. Or anyone else. It isn't fair for me. If all this talk of going to my parents doesn't go anywhere, then I'll have to tell Amma that I just don't want to get married—not right now, anyway. And you and I will have to stop seeing each other.'

'This is not how I thought things were going to go today.' Ashfaq sighed, and then he smiled. 'Although, I suppose if you didn't address the looming issue right off the bat, you wouldn't be you.'

'I'm sorry. I don't mean to pile on when I know what's on your mind already. I've been worrying about you. I'm always going to worry about you no matter what. But I need to know where we stand before you leave for a whole year, Ashfaq.'

'I understand. I promise, I understand. And if I can somehow manage to come home during the winter break, I'll go straight to your house to talk to your parents. If not, I'll do it when I'm back next May.'

Aasiya held his gaze as he spoke, trying, as she sometimes did when feeling particularly vulnerable or uneasy, to spot some sign of a lie— any glimmer of insincerity. But of course, as per usual, she found none. Ashfaq meant what he said. He always did. And she was suddenly overcome with guilt at having brought any of this up to him during one of the last times she got to see him before he left for a whole year. 'I'm sorry,' she said, 'I should've spoken to you about this sooner. Or maybe later. I know you're stressed already.'

'It's okay, jaan. I'm glad you brought it up. I've been absentminded about it. And you're right, that isn't fair to you.'

Aasiya didn't know how to respond right away, so instead she took a sip of her chai and nibbled on a biscuit. 'You've finished all your packing, you said?' she asked finally.

Ashfaq nodded. 'That's right. All the clothes, books, and other little things that I'll need. New laptop as well. A couple pictures of you tucked into the small pocket on the inside of one of my suitcases. Everything a young man could ever need.'

Aasiya shook her head with a laugh. 'Lovely. Yes, I think all of that should make sure that your life in a new country is full of comfort.'

She waited for Ashfaq to say what she expected him to say next, as he played with the ring on her thumb and stroked the inner crest between her index finger and thumb, distracting himself for a moment, trying to hold back the next part of their conversation for as long as possible. 'I didn't think I'd fall asleep, but I did. For a couple of hours,' he said at last.

'And?'

'I had another nightmare.'

'The same one?'

Ashfaq nodded. 'Exact same one. You know, it's strange how I didn't even know I could remember their voices until I started having these nightmares. But I hear them clearly now every night. It's like they're right there in my ear. . . .'

Aasiya watched his face closely. 'Are you okay?' When he didn't answer, she shook the hand that he was still holding gently, and he looked up.

'Oh. I'm sorry. I was just thinking; just remembering,' he said.

Aasiya smiled and held a hand up to his cheek. 'You're allowed to talk about it sometimes, you know that, right? I know it's hard, and not something you like remembering, but you can talk to me, Ashfaq.'

He sighed and leaned back in his chair. 'I know. I know I can. But it's nothing you haven't heard before, Aasiya. And I don't see a point in repeating it. I just don't want to sound like a broken record.'

She raised an eyebrow and smiled at him. 'Wah! What an American expression. You haven't even left yet, and you're already talking just like them,' she said with a laugh.

Ashfaq blushed. 'You know what I mean,' he mumbled.

Aasiya squeezed his hand again. 'If something bothers you, you can talk to me about it as much as you'd like. I thought that was obvious.'

He smiled. 'You can come to me too, even when I'm gone. You can call me. You can WhatsApp me, message me on Facebook. Whatever it is, I'm always going to be there for you. Besides, we'll have to get used to communicating like that for a while.'

'Oh, what difference will it make, Ashfaq? I see you sparingly already! Here, when you live only ten minutes away from me!'

'That is true, but we do still see each other. And spend time together. I can see you up close. I can touch you, and hear you, smell you. I can feel what you do, or what you feel. And the same goes for you with me. It won't be the same.'

Aasiya sighed. 'Yes. No more meeting on campus.'

'Or in markets.'

'The mall.'

'Or the alley behind the masjid.'

'That was one time! And it was stupid, and risky. And I could've killed you for it!'

'Uncle would've killed me for it first,' said Ashfaq with a smile. 'The whole neighborhood might've helped him kill me for it.'

'Yes, well, we learned that day at least that real life is not a Bollywood film,' said Aasiya with a chuckle.

'No. Not at all. In real life, if your desire to fight for your secret romance becomes too stupid, you get murdered.'

'In the films, if you love enough, you have the strength to take on one hundred men, including the girl's father himself!' she laughed.

'Forgive me if I don't find the strength to do that.'

'It's the effort that counts.' Aasiya looked around the teashop, taking it all in for a moment, and then said, 'No more meeting in Salim Uncle's shop.'

'In the lovers' corners.' Ashfaq looked around at the shop as well. 'I'm going to miss it.'

'Jab tum wapas aao ge agle saal toh hum idhar ayeinge. When you come back next year, we'll come here,' Aasiya spoke quietly.

'Haan, we will,' said Ashfaq.

The two sat there for another hour or so, talking quietly and sipping their chai. Once or twice they exchanged a kiss and sat with their foreheads pressed together. Salim pretended not to notice, busying himself with brewing more chai, or yelling at the boys in the kitchen to get the meat out so he could make pulao later. Anytime a customer at the counter eyed the corner where the young couple sat, Salim would politely, but firmly, direct their attention back to himself.

Before they left, Salim came up to Ashfaq, pulled him into a big hug, and kissed him on the cheek. 'You take care of yourself in Amreeka!' said the old man. 'And study hard. Make us all proud! You've plenty of people here who will always be supporting you, zergai.' At this, he glanced at Aasiya and smiled. 'Young people always find ways to keep themselves busy, and young lovers find ways to make all time shrink into one moment. They make it last, or they make it pass by in the blink of an eye if they need to.' He directed his next words at both of them: 'He will sit and say to himself, azizam, thinking he is speaking to you: Look how incomplete I am without you, my love; how incomplete you must be too.' The lyrics stirred up the faint sounds of a familiar song somewhere in Aasiya's brain and brought a smile to her face. They both bowed their heads slightly, so Salim could brush his hand over them, and then they said their goodbyes and left the shop.

Together, Aasiya and Ashfaq walked back in the direction of her house, keeping a slight distance between them. Aasiya wore her scarf drawn across her face again, held lightly between her teeth. Every few seconds, she swung her hand back as she walked, and Ashfaq stepped forward and brush his hand discretely against it, causing her to smile. When they turned onto her street, they stopped. Aasiya looked around quickly to make sure none of the neighbors were peering out at them before she hugged Ashfaq tight.

'I promise I will see you at least one more time alone before I leave,' he whispered as he pressed his lips to the top of her head, closing his eyes and breathing in the faint scent of the almond oil that had recently been washed out of her hair.

'I won't let you leave without that,' she spoke into his chest, smiling to herself wistfully.

They pulled apart, and as he watched her walk toward her house, he shouted after her, 'Call me later!'

She glanced back and grinned at him. 'Maybe!'

Chapter Two

Ashfaq was born in America. His mother gave birth to him in the Children's Hospital of Los Angeles in 1996, and his family lived quite happily in America for a few years, until the attacks on September 11. In the months that followed, they were subjected to the same bigotry that many, if not all, brown people in the United States fell victim to during that time. One of their neighbors, a Sikh man, spent a month in the hospital after a group of young men attacked him behind the restaurant where he worked. He'd been hit in the back of the head with a pipe and left in the alley while blood pooled under him. The attack left the man partially blind in one eye.

Following this, Ashfaq's mother, Roop, had stopped covering her head when she went out, and did her best to dress as "American" as she possibly could. For a little while, the worst their family had to deal with was the occasional slur shouted on the street, telling them to go back to their country. And one evening, someone threw a rock through the living room window and punctured the tires of Ashfaq's father's car. 'This will pass,' Farhan, Ashfaq's father, had said to a sobbing Roop in their kitchen that night. 'America is a good country. These people are just afraid. In time, this will pass, my love.' Farhan had no clue how wrong he was.

A few weeks after that incident, Ashfaq was walking past a park on his way home from the bus stop after school, when a boy on the soccer field shouted, 'Terrorist!' Ashfaq froze and turned to look at the boy, who was approaching the short fence with a few other boys. As he watched them approach, a dozen alarms went off in Ashfaq's head, telling him to run, to head home, which was only a few houses up the street. 'You don't belong here, you fucking terrorist,' said the same boy.

One of the other boys, this one a bit taller and with longer hair, laughed and said, 'Your towelhead mom stopped wearing that shit on her head, but we all know what she is.' Ashfaq's eyes darted from one face to the other, and his eyes welled up with tears of anger and hurt. Their words stung.

'Aw, the little haaji is going to cry,' said another boy, who laughed before hopping over the fence and landing in front of Ashfaq, blocking his path. Ashfaq took a step back.

The boy who had yelled first leapt over the fence as well, landing behind Ashfaq, and grabbed his bag. Ashfaq tore it out of the older boy's hand and tried to run, only to be stopped by the boy in front of him. The two boys grabbed Ashfaq and hoisted him up, then dropped him over the fence onto the soccer field. Their friends laughed and pushed him as he tried to stand up. Somehow, Ashfaq managed to scramble to his feet before a fist hit him square in the face. Although he couldn't recall the sound of his own screams, Ashfaq knew that he had curled up and cried as the boys beat him, doing his best to cover his head as their fists and feet punched, kicked, and clawed at every part of him they could reach. One of the boys spit on him after they'd finished, and Ashfaq lay there crying and bleeding for a moment before rolling over and vomiting onto a patch of dirt beside him.

He lay there, his head throbbing and spinning, his eyes bursting with bright lights and tears, until he heard the distant thud of footsteps running toward him. Some of the other children at the park had seen what happened, and they'd run to get his mother. Roop ran up the street and fell to her knees beside him, crying out in panic. She clutched him to her breast and lifted him up as if he were still a baby, crying and swearing in Urdu, wishing a thousand curses upon the monsters that had done this to her boy. She wet her scarf once they were home and used it to wipe the blood, tears, snot, and vomit off Ashfaq's face, before using her hands to splash him with warm water to wipe away anything she had missed. She stood him in the bathtub and had him take off his clothes. His shirt had been torn, and his pants and underwear were stained with urine where he had lost control of his bladder. Roop threw the clothes into a corner and, very carefully, she washed Ashfaq's body, gently cleaning every cut and running the warm washcloth over the ugly bruises on his torso and back. Throughout the entire process, Ashfaq didn't say a word.

Afterward, she dressed him in clean clothes, put anti-septic and band-aids on all his cuts, gave him a cup of warm milk with turmeric and a painkiller, and finally put him to bed. Still, the boy didn't say a word, beyond whimpering a little when the antiseptic was applied. Once he was in bed, Roop ran to the kitchen to grab the phone, stepped outside the front door, called the school, and began yelling the moment someone answered. The school secretary, who had been getting ready to leave for the day, was taken aback as Roop shouted, cursing the school, the bus driver, and the students, crying hysterically all the while. A few minutes passed before the secretary could calm her down enough to get her to explain what had happened. 'MY SON WAS ATTACKED! HE WAS ATTACKED AS HE GOT OFF YOUR SCHOOL BUS!' The secretary took down what details Roop could give, promised she'd pass it onto the principal, and told her to come in the morning with her husband and her son. Reassured that the school would get to the bottom of it, Roop strode back into the kitchen in a panic and finally called Farhan at work.

She explained to him quickly what had happened, whispering in gasping breaths while cracking the door to Ashfaq's bedroom just a bit to check on the sleeping boy, and Farhan told her he was on his way home.

When Farhan came home, he immediately ran to Ashfaq's room to see his son, with Roop close behind him. Reassured that Ashfaq was asleep, Farhan went to the kitchen, grabbed the phone, and called the police. He explained that his six-year old son had been attacked on his way home from school. 'Did you take the boy to the hospital, sir?' asked the operator.

'No, my wife cleaned him up the best she could and then put him to bed.'

'You might want to do that. There's no telling how badly he was hurt. There is a unit on the way to your address as we speak; they'll be there soon.'

When the police arrived, Roop woke Ashfaq up and carried him to the living room. He was still silent, but he responded with a shake of his head when Roop asked him if she could get him anything. There were two officers standing in the living room, talking to Farhan. Farhan strode over to Roop and immediately took Ashfaq in his own arms and kissed his face, which was now swollen and bruised.

'Ashfaq, beta, we need you to tell these policemen what happened when you were coming home from school. Do you think you can do that?' asked Farhan. Ashfaq still didn't say a word.

One of the officers stepped forward and introduced himself to Ashfaq, before gently asking him if he could tell them what happened so that they could make sure that whoever had hit him would get in trouble and not be able to do it again.

Ashfaq stared at the officer silently, and then said in a very quiet voice, 'I didn't know them. They were bigger than me, and they don't go to my school.' At this, both officers took out their notebooks and wrote down what he was saying.

'Had you seen them before?'

'I don't know. I think they always play on the soccer field, but I didn't know them.'

'Could you recognize them if you saw them?' Ashfaq shook his head.

'I didn't get to see their faces before they hit me.' A bit more questioning led to Ashfaq repeating some of the things the boys had said to him as they'd beaten him. Farhan went stiff, his fists clenched. Roop cried silently as she listened.

'Is there anyone else who saw what happened, son?' asked one of the officers.

'I don't know. Maybe someone did. But I can't remember. I can't remember anything else.'

'Okay. That'll do fine for now. We'll ask around the neighborhood and see if anyone saw what happened,' the officer told Farhan and Roop. He looked down at Ashfaq again. 'If you remember anything else, you tell your mom and dad and they'll call me, okay?' Ashfaq nodded. The officer smiled and patted Ashfaq's head gently before pulling out his card and handing it to Farhan. He and his partner shook hands with Farhan and Roop in turn and gave them a polite goodbye before leaving.

Ashfaq was taken to the emergency room once the police left, and there he was given a full check-up. He had no severe injuries, no concussion, no broken bones, no internal bleeding. But his ribs had been bruised, and a tooth had been chipped. 'It'll be awhile before the swelling on his face goes down, but he should be okay. Ice his face and all the other swollen areas, keep his ribs bandaged, and the cuts clean and covered. Maybe take some time off from school to rest. He'll be alright in no time,' said the doctor to Farhan, who almost sobbed with relief.

The whole family went to the school the next morning to meet with the principal, Ashfaq's bus driver, and the guidance counselor. The police had contacted the school that morning to inform them that they were investigating an attack on one of their students, and the trio spent an hour apologizing profusely and promising to launch their own investigation. 'I swear to you, it wasn't any of the students on the bus!' said the driver. 'I would have noticed that. They'd have picked on him beforehand or something, that's how these kids treat each other. It's never sudden!' The weak explanation offered little comfort.

The guidance counselor asked, 'Has Ashfaq said anything about who it was? The police told us that he said he didn't recognize his attackers, but if he's remembered, it would make it easier for us.'

'He said they were older, and didn't go to his school,' said Farhan quietly. The bus driver visibly relaxed.

'But he could be lying! He could just be scared!' said Roop.

The principal nodded knowingly. 'We'll ask some of the other students on the bus if they saw anything.'

'The kids won't say anything,' Farhan said to Roop in Urdu.

'What was that?' asked the guidance counselor.

'Just saying how much we appreciate your help,' said Roop.

The investigation lasted all of three weeks, and both the police and the school informed Farhan and Roop that they could not find out who had attacked Ashfaq. That same day, Roop finally spoke to Farhan of what she had been thinking since the incident; something that he himself had also considered once or twice.

'I want to go home,' she said. 'I can't stay here. We can't stay here. Not when we know this can happen again; not when we know they won't be able to help us.' Farhan placed his hands on Roop's shoulders and tried to calm her down.

'Jaan, listen—' he said.

But Roop shrugged him off and shook her head.

'No, Farhan. You listen to me. This is not our country, and if we stay here, it could ruin us!'

'We came here for a better life, Roop. This is just a bad thing. It's happened to others we know, and they—"

'I don't care about others, Farhan. We want a better future for our son, but our son might not have a future if we stay here! What happens if they do it again? What happens if they have a knife or a gun next time? What if they just don't stop beating him? Would you like me to run to that field again and see our son's broken body waiting for me? Would you have me clean the piss and vomit and blood from his face and body again? I can't do that, Farhan, I can't wait for that to happen. I'll go crazy waiting for it to happen!'

Farhan grabbed her gently and pulled her close again, shushing her and kissing the top of her head. 'I won't put you through that again, Roop. I don't want that either. I'm as scared as you are. But let's plan this out first, if you're serious about it.'

'I am,' she said. 'I know I am.'

'Okay, let me talk to my brother. And my manager. I will see what I can do.'

'Should we send Ashfaq back to school in the meantime?' asked Roop. Farhan gave the matter a moment's thought, picturing his son riding home on the bus all alone again. He imagined him trying to walk that same path home, and a group of faceless strangers stopping him once more. He imagined a crowd of onlookers turning the other way as his son was beaten.

'Farhan?'

He snapped out of it and shook his head. 'No. Tell him the doctor said not to go back yet and tell the school we're pulling him out.'

Ashfaq remembered in flashes how quickly that last month in America went by. One night his father came home and told him they were moving, and he would bring home boxes the next day so they could start packing. 'I want you to help your mother when I'm not at home!'

he had said. In a haze, Ashfaq could recall their little home on that last day, stripped down to nearly nothing, with everything they owned sitting in a van outside. He could recall the long plane ride, jammed in between his mother's right elbow and the window, eating scrambled eggs and watching bits of a movie, or two, or three, maybe more. And he remembered coming out of the airport to be blasted by the hot Karachi air, and being received outside by what seemed like a small army. Aunts, uncles, cousins, grandparents—all the people he had never met before, but the labels he'd heard time and time again. All pulling him into tight embraces, planting wet kisses on the cheeks and forehead, shaking his hand and tousling of his hair. But he couldn't remember much past that. He could not remember when, in his mind, Pakistan stopped being new, and started being home.

Chapter Three

Aasiya's father, Bilal, was just coming down the stairs into the sitting room when she stepped inside, pulling the door shut behind her. 'An early start like always, beti?' he asked.

'And a late one for you, like always,' she said with a smile as he ran a hand over her head.

'That new medicine the doctor put me on has me sleeping even longer than usual.' Bilal pulled up the hems of his shalwar as he sat down on the couch.

'You need the rest, Baba. You were the one who kept saying that you weren't able to sleep properly anymore.' Aasiya peeked up the stairs again as she sat down across from Bilal, who gave her a knowing look.

'She'll be down in a second. She was having a bath when I woke up. And by the way, I never said I wanted medicine to help me sleep. Once one grows old, everything starts going. Hair, teeth, eyesight, hearing, and yes, even the ability to sleep normally. Sense of smell will be next probably, and strength. It'll happen to you too, beti. One day, you'll be as gray as a raincloud, and all the years when you were young will seem like a very old dream.'

Aasiya laughed and shook her head.

'Baba! You're talking like someone who is thousands of years old. You're only fifty! Don't be dramatic!'

Bilal chuckled. 'What hurt it brings to a father when his own daughter downplays the pain of aging. Although, I suppose it might not play out for you the same way. You are too much like your grandmother. You will age just like her too, I bet.' At least once a week, Bilal remarked on how much Aasiya was like his own mother, Suraiya. When she smiled a certain way, or sported a certain hairstyle, or wore a certain dress, Bilal would stare at her for a moment and then say, 'You are so much like your grandmother, meri jaan.' Aasiya's mother, Fatima, sometimes did the same thing, although it was not always complimentary. When they argued about grades, or chores, or whether Aasiya got to go out with her friends on a certain night, Fatima would throw up her arms and say, 'Why is there so much of my mother-in-law in you? You're my daughter!'

Good or bad, Aasiya could not say whether the comparisons were apt, since she had been only five years old when Suraiya passed away. In truth, Aasiya sometimes had a hard time remembering what her grandmother had even looked like. At least, when she was awake. When she was asleep, she sometimes saw the woman clearly, every feature as bright and vibrant as a film on a big screen. Something in her dreams would tell her silently to commit her grandmother's face to memory, to look at later. But for whatever reason, Aasiya was never able to hang onto it all. She would wake and still see the woman in her mind's eye, but the details faded right away. It was like water slipping through her fingers; she could never hang onto enough. Lately, she'd been seeing Suraiya in her dreams more often than ever.

'Did you have anything to eat at the college?' asked Bilal as he pulled out his glasses to look at his phone.

'Just a few biscuits and some chai, Baba.'

Bilal clicked his tongue.

'How are you going to stay healthy eating like that? You kids these days are strange. All this work you do for your schooling and you eat worse than dogs! Burgers, pizza, biscuits, all these sweets, pah! How will your body or mind be strong eating like that?'

Aasiya laughed. This was another constant with her father. Bilal had been a pehlwan, a wrestler, in his youth, just like his own father was before him. And although he hadn't formally trained or competed in nearly thirty years, he was still a very fit and health-conscious man. Aside from all the chai he now drank, and the bowls of halwa he had on the weekends when Fatima took it upon herself to make more desserts than she did meals, Bilal still adhered to a relatively strict diet. Aasiya could recall him making plane sounds as he piloted pieces of roasted chicken dipped in curd, or some roti slathered with ghee to her mouth when she was a child. She could also remember hoarding the chocolate bars that Fatima snuck to her when Bilal wasn't home and eating them in her room. The muscles of his chest and shoulders bulged and stretched his shirt a bit when he readjusted himself on the couch.

'Why are you laughing? I'm not joking!' he said.

'Okay, okay, Baba, I will go make some food. Would you like anything?' asked Aasiya, still chuckling to herself.

'One roti and whatever you're having,' said Bilal without looking up from his phone.

Aasiya went to the kitchen and busied herself slicing onions, tomatoes, cilantro, and green chilis before tossing it all into a bowl. She cracked a few eggs into the bowl as well and added a pinch of salt, some black pepper, half a spoonful of chili powder, and a fourth of a spoonful of turmeric. As she was beating the mixture together, she felt a hand on her shoulder and turned to see her mother standing behind her, a light pink scarf drawn loosely over her head.

'Asalam Walaikum, Amma,' said Aasiya.

'Walaikum Asalam,' said Fatima cheerfully as she brushed past Aasiya to get to the cabinets above the counter. 'Did you make rotis yet?' she asked.

'Not yet,' Aasiya said as she put a pan on the stove and heated up a dollop of ghee.

'Will you make them, or shall I?'

'I can make them, Amma. Just make the chai and go see Abba. I think he's waiting for you.'

Fatima laughed and grabbed an old pot from under the counter, filled it with milk and a little bit of water, and put it on the stove while Aasiya began frying omelets. She then went over to the fridge and pulled out a large mixing bowl that was covered with a towel and set it out on the counter.

'The dough is right here for the roti,' she said. Aasiya mumbled a word of thanks while prodding gently at the eggs in the pan. Fatima added a few spoonfuls of black tea to the milk in the pot once it came to a simmer, along with a palmful of sugar. While waiting for the tea to come to a boil, she watched Aasiya turn over one omelet and put it onto a plate before pouring more of the egg mixture into the pan. The kitchen was filled with the smell of the sweet cardamom steeped chai and the frying eggs.

Once the chai was ready, Fatima carefully poured a cup out for herself and one for Bilal. On her way out of the kitchen, she stopped behind Aasiya. 'Let us know when it's ready, jaan,' she said, and kissed the back of her head. Aasiya smiled to herself as she felt her mother's lips make contact. In the mornings, there was always peace between them. She loved being around Fatima then. They cooked breakfast together, and if Bilal was sleeping in or if he'd left for work early, they would sit with cups of chai and exchange the gossip of their respective worlds. Fatima would tell Aasiya about whose daughter had gotten engaged, or fallen out of an engagement; she would tell her about whose son had been caught doing what, and about the weak excuses that were given to justify the behavior. She would talk about what she had seen in the news while Aasiya was out, especially if the story was anything centered around a young woman in the vast realm of politics, which Aasiya hoped to enter into herself someday. In return, Aasiya would tell Fatima about the latest drama at her university, who was dating, who had broken up, who had been caught with their lover by their parents, who had gotten engaged, who had gotten their heart broken, and much more. And in between the big gasps and laughs, Fatima would always ask, 'And where do you fit into all of this, beti?' And Aasiya would always respond, 'Removed from it all to avoid the headaches that come with.' And they would laugh together. As far as Aasiya knew, Fatima did not know about Ashfaq. She only knew that they were friends and had been such since childhood.

But the bliss of the mornings always got lost on its way to the rest of the day. At some point during the process of dishes being cleared and washed, and foodstuffs being put away, it would slowly fade. A silence would settle in between Fatima and Aasiya, and it would break only when Fatima yelled at Aasiya to do something, or else brought up a topic that led them to an argument. Nowadays, more often than not, that topic was marriage. A particularly heated argument had taken place the previous week. 'I don't want that right now, Amma!' Aasiya had said, and Fatima countered with, 'Nobody is asking you settle down and start raising children, Aasiya! You can get married and still finish school. Things are different in today's world!'

'They are not that different if you're pushing for your daughter to get married when she doesn't want to!'

At this, Fatima had slammed the plate that she was holding down onto the table, causing it to crack in two. She didn't notice; she was too focused on yelling. 'I'm not forcing you to marry just anyone! I want you to pick! I want the choice to be yours!'

'Yes, but only if that choice ends in me marrying! Have you ever considered that maybe I don't want that? Not just now, but ever?!' Aasiya yelled back.

The argument had ended at that, and the two spent the rest of the day avoiding each other, or else ignoring one another if they happened to be sharing the same space. Bilal had come home hours later to find tension still hanging in the air like a thick curtain; he was used to this. He did what he would usually do, which was to kiss Fatima on the cheek and call Aasiya down from her room to kiss the top of her head. Then he stretched, took off his shoes, pulled out a seat at the kitchen table, and said, 'Have my two tigresses stopped warring for the day?' Fatima had glared at him and set his cup of chai down in front of him a bit too hard, causing some to spill over the edges of the cup. Bilal didn't take it personally; he never took anything personally. In fact, he spent the next half hour or so talking to them both, making the same little jokes he always did, slipping in little tidbits about his day: 'Oh yes, my lunch was fine, thank you very much. I should eat your rotis a bit sooner in the day, my love, they are as stiff as boards by the time I do. Through no fault of yours, of course. I don't know why I don't use the damn microwave to heat them up.' Or, 'Yes, yes, the manager must have been clubbed over the head by his wife before leaving home, or kicked out of his daughter's room like a buffoon. He was extra cruel and buffoonish today. I'm lucky he likes me, or he'd fire me just to ease his own frustration!'

Eventually, Fatima and Aasiya both began to laugh and talk freely, the bitterness of the day forgotten. Instead, their home was filled with sounds of happy conversation, and the smells of dinner being cooked. Bilal could always fill the gaps between mother and daughter with a warmth that they were unable to maintain on their own—and never more so than in recent months.

For her part, Fatima desperately wished she could just say aloud why she wanted what she did for Aasiya's future. Every day after Bilal left, she glanced up from the courtyard to look at Aasiya's bedroom window next to the terrace and considered going up there, throwing open the door, and saying to the girl point blank exactly what was on her mind. But she couldn't. Even during their most heated arguments, the words she wanted to call forth failed to show up. They weren't there. She couldn't, for whatever reason, bring herself to speak to Aasiya so directly. She felt the need to be tactful and clever; to convince her, sway her, with the manipulations she felt should be instinctive to any parent.

The fact of the matter was this: one night, just a month or so before, Aasiya had gone to a study group with Ashfaq and a few other school friends. Bilal was taking a nap before dinner, and Fatima was out on the terrace, having a cup of chai. She was about to head back inside to start cooking when she saw two figures moving up the dimly lit side street leading to their house. It was a man and a woman—she could tell by the scarf that billowed behind one of the figures. The two stopped a couple yards away from the gate and embraced, remaining in each other's arms for far too long to simply be friends. Once they pulled apart, Fatima heard the girl laugh at something the boy said as he walked away. And then, she watched as the girl turned and walked the remaining distance to their gate, unlocked it, and stepped into the courtyard.

Fatima had spent the following week considering dozens, if not hundreds, of possibilities. How many people discussed Aasiya and Ashfaq's affair at their dinner tables? How many of the vulture-like neighborhood women, who starved for scraps of gossip and tall tales to spread amongst each other whether they had a hint of truth to them or not, had her daughter's name in their mouths? How many daughters shared morning rituals with their own mothers like the one she shared with Aasiya, telling them the latest gossip about Aasiya and Ashfaq over morning chores?

As far as Fatima knew, her daughter did not yet understand the lengths to which some people would go to tear a girl down. How they longed to find one thing to hold against her; to have one innocent action to blow out of proportion and turn into a label for life, as it was done for them years before. To create a story for her, even knowing that no matter how true or false it was, the story would become her reputation and the reputation would follow her through her life. A box to stick a woman in. The tale would be whispered as a warning to potential suitors, told to young girls and boys of the next generation as a warning, something to avoid. It would become something they could spit out at the merest mention of her name for as long as she was alive. And upon that woman's passing, there could be no ill speaking of the dead, and so her name would be spoken with reverence and longing. A crocodile tear would be shed; the most talented might even sob. And then, the cruel cycle would start anew with another girl. Never a boy, for they were tempestuous and slaves to their desires; they were bound to make mistakes. They could be easily forgiven; any number of reasons could be conjured up to excuse them. A mother with loose morals, or a father who hadn't been entirely present, and if nothing else, they were boys, after all. Allah had created them differently, and whatever they did, well, it must surely be a necessary step on the journey to becoming a perfect man.

Chapter Four

Once breakfast was ready, Aasiya called both of her parents to the table. They walked in, lightly holding each other's hands, Bilal one step behind Fatima.

'Omelet?' he asked with a hopeful glance at the table.

'Yes, Baba. Omelet and roti,' replied Aasiya.

'Ah! See how wonderful our daughter is?' Bilal said to Fatima as they took their seats at the table. 'Now why can't you cook like this for yourself, meri jaan? And eat right? Instead of stuffing yourself with biscuits and chai at your school's canteen?'

Fatima swatted his arm playfully and said, 'Well, you seem to have trouble resisting halwa or any sweet when I make it. Why trouble the poor girl when you yourself can't stay away from such things?'

Bilal shook his head as he grabbed a roti and put it on his plate, along with some of the eggs. 'Listen. What I eat is made by you. If she were to gorge herself on what you make at home, I wouldn't complain.'

Aasiya and Fatima both rolled their eyes and exchanged a knowing look, but they decided to humor him.

'Why wouldn't you complain, Baba?' Aasiya asked casually.

'When you eat something made by someone you love, regardless of what it is, there is no way you can get sick or fat or unhappy,' he said, not looking up from his plate as he began to eat. 'They must make it with love, and you must eat it with happiness. You'll never need another diet again.'

Fatima smiled and placed a hand on his arm. Bilal looked up at the two of them and shrugged. 'It's true. They say ghee is bad for you if you aren't active. I'm not so active anymore. And you have cooked this in ghee, Aasiya, like you always do. I can taste it. But I'm fine. I'm always fine—I'll always be fine. And it is because I love eating what you cook.'

Aasiya smiled at her father and gave a small nod. 'Well, I'm glad you do, Baba.'

The three of them talked just as pleasantly for the rest of breakfast, a bit about the news, about plans for the day, etc. Once they were finished and Fatima had cleared away the dishes, Aasiya made to head upstairs to her room while Bilal went to go get ready for work. As she began to climb the stairs, Aasiya heard Fatima call her from the kitchen: 'Just a moment, Aasiya!' She went back downstairs, where Fatima was putting the leftover omelets in the fridge.

'Yes, Amma?' she asked.

'Will you be going with me to Khursheed Auntie's house tomorrow morning?' Fatima asked.

For a moment Aasiya was confused, but then she remembered. 'Oh! I didn't realize the date. . . .'

Every year on the third of July, Fatima and Aasiya would visit Khursheed Auntie's home in the morning, to drop off some food, say a prayer, and wish the family well. It would be ten years now since the death of her eldest son, Irfan. Aasiya had been young when it happened, and she couldn't remember the boy much. But she could recall sometimes seeing him, a tall young man with a beard, a wild head of dark hair, and a thin but strong physique. She hadn't ever fully understood how he died. There were rumors of course, but as far as she knew the truth was not in any of them. One day, when she had come home from school, she'd announced that some other students had said he was a militant. Fatima and Bilal had both yelled at her to never say that again, especially not around Khursheed Auntie or anyone from her family. The younger boy, Sameer, was Aasiya's age. They had been school friends as children, but he had changed a bit after the death of his brother—grown more withdrawn. He and Aasiya still exchanged polite hellos and smiles if they saw each other. Once in a while, he would even bring over some food Khursheed Auntie had made, and they would exchange pleasantries. But other than that, nothing of the childhood friendship remained.

'Did you have other plans?' asked Fatima.

'Well . . . Ashfaq's flight leaves tomorrow morning. All of our friends and I were going to see him off at the airport first thing.'

'Hm. What university is he attending again?'

'George Washington University. It's a very good school,' Aasiya said, trying to read Fatima's face for any signs of an impending argument.

Fatima considered what she wanted to say for a moment, and then: 'Hmm . . . he is your friend. You should go see him off. And give him our best too; he's got a good family. We've always gotten along well with them.'

Aasiya blinked. 'Really?' she asked.

'Yes. Really. But we will go to Khursheed Baji's house afterward.' Aasiya struggled to contain her joy. Usually in a situation like this, Fatima simply imposed her will and told Aasiya that whatever plans she had made on her own could wait. 'Did you have any plans for today?' asked Fatima.

'I'm a bit tired since I had to leave so early this morning,' said Aasiya. 'I was going to go lay down for a little while. And then maybe study some more once I wake up. I think Jamila said she wanted my help on her paper tonight, so she might come and pick me up to go to her house for a little while after Maghrib prayers, if that's alright.'

'That would be fine. Just remember to eat after you wake up. And clean the chicken for me before you go please, so I can cook it for dinner,' said Fatima.

'I will. Is there anything else you'd like me to do?' asked Aasiya.

'Just fold and put away the laundry after you wake up, please.'

'Okay.'

And then they both stood there, Aasiya at the foot of the stairs, and Fatima a few feet away near the kitchen door, both staring at each other without making direct eye contact, just a few feet separating them. Aasiya strode over suddenly and kissed Fatima on the cheek, pressing her cool palm to the side of her mother's face. A look of mild surprise flickered across Fatima's eyes for a moment before she reached up and pressed her hand onto Aasiya's, holding it against her face. Underneath her palm, Aasiya could feel the slightest of lines running across Fatima's cheeks. In just a few more years, they'd be visible—deep markers of lost time stretching across her face. Those years would show in her hair too, stripping it of color and leaving an exhausted gray. Perhaps Fatima would do what so many older women did and use henna paste to dye the white into a deep orange-red color. Or perhaps she would embrace her age with a collected grace, resigning herself to the fact that nobody could slow down, stop, or reverse the steady decay of all things.

All of this passed between mother and daughter in a moment's eye contact, and both felt a pang of regret for the tensions that had built up between them over the past few months. Once again, the desire to say what was eating away at her rose within Fatima. The girl was standing right there. 'Say it . . . say it . . . say it,' went a whisper in her head. But Fatima's tongue couldn't form the words. Instead her mouth, unsteadily at first, curled into a smile.

'No warring today?' Bilal said as he reappeared downstairs, fully dressed for work with a big smile on his face. 'Now I know my day will be great.' He walked over and embraced both women, kissing the tops of their heads. 'If there can be peace here, who's to say there can't be peace all over the world?' he said before throwing his head back and laughing loudly at his own little joke. Fatima and Aasiya chuckled along politely.

'You go out; I'll be there in a moment. I wanted to say something to Aasiya first,' Bilal said to Fatima. Once she left the kitchen, Bilal put a hand on Aasiya's shoulder and smiled. 'Try and be easy today, meri jaan. Whatever your mother says and does, it doesn't come from a bad place. She never had your mentality—she can't always understand it. But she knows that this world tries hard to run it out of young girls. She just wants to avoid that. She wants you to keep being you as long as possible.' Aasiya mumbled a few words in agreement, and Bilal kissed her forehead. 'See how nice and easy this morning was? I want things between you both to be like that always.'

'I know you do, Baba.'

Bilal gave Aasiya another smile before placing a hand on her head, turning around, and heading out into the courtyard where Fatima was waiting by the gate, her scarf drawn partially over her head. Once his hand was on the door handle, she pressed herself against his chest and lay her head on it; he wrapped one arm around her waist and squeezed her gently. 'We raised her too well, my love," he told her. "She will stay true to herself and what she wants regardless of what anyone else pushes for. Even us.'

At this, Fatima laughed.

'Why did we leave her around your parents so much?' she asked.

'It isn't just my mother in her, you know,' Bilal said. 'She takes a lot after you as well. Perhaps that's why you fight so much.'

'I don't enjoy fighting with her,' said Fatima.

'I don't think Aasiya enjoys it either,' Bilal said with a smile. And then he rested his forehead against hers for a moment and kissed her cheek before dipping his head to step through the gate and onto the sidewalk outside.

❧❧❧❧

Once Bilal left for work, Fatima went to the living room to watch TV, and Aasiya was finally able to go up to her room to be alone for a while. As soon as she closed the door behind her, Aasiya went over to her bed and fell face-down on top of it. She sighed heavily and then breathed deep, taking in the smell of clean sheets, and the hint of the lavender air freshener she loved. She spritzed her room with it every morning, and the scent had settled into the fibers of her sheets and curtains and carpet.

The day had barely begun, and already it had been incredibly draining. Aasiya felt her muscles relax and ease into the softness of the mattress. She was always tired lately, but she could not sleep. At least, not well. She dreamed too much; or were they dreams? She couldn't be sure anymore. When she was younger, she had thought so. But now they seemed like something more. Dreams were a part of sleep, were they not? One would still be rested after having one, wouldn't they? Unless it was a nightmare. But Aasiya's dreams felt like long trips. More often now than ever before, Aasiya found that closing her eyes only meant that she was leaving for a place where nobody else could follow her. As she began to drift off, she could feel it happening once more. . . .

Aasiya had been Suraiya's first and only grandchild, so the old woman had been given the honor of selecting the baby's name. 'Aasiya,' she whispered over the baby girl two days after her birth. She leaned down and let her lips hover above the pale little face for a moment, murmuring six different prayers and six different blessings, before blowing into the girl's face lightly and kissing her forehead. Almost immediately the little eyes sprang open, and Suraiya smiled at their deep brown color, watching as they quickly darted around the old woman's face, taking in the strange new visual. After a moment of analysis, the girl opened her little pink mouth, yawned, and then began to cry. Suraiya laughed at this, letting Bilal step past her to tend to his daughter. 'Come! Come! Oh, she'll be healthy, this one! And smart too!'

Perhaps it was the fact that the old woman's lips had spoken her name for the first time, or perhaps it was something else. Whatever the reason, Aasiya was never more attached to anyone in her early years than she was to her grandmother. For five and a half years, if Suraiya was nearby, Aasiya's eyes sought only her. She would fidget, cry, and scream until someone handed her off to the old woman in defeat.

'My! Why do you make such a fuss for me? Your ammi is right there! And your baba! He's my son, you know. I held him like I'm holding you now.' The girl would giggle, as if she understood exactly what was being said; as if she very well knew that her father had once been as small as she was and had been held within the same strong and gentle hands. And then she would reach up and her hand would tug on a lock of Suraiya's hair, or knock off her glasses, and she'd squeal with excitement. Suraiya never scolded her for it. Instead, she would laugh and bounce the girl on her knee, insisting to Bilal and Fatima that it was the mark of an intelligent child. Suraiya took Aasiya with her everywhere she could; to the market, to afternoon tea at a friend's, to her husband Iqbal's grave, to the fabrics shop, the neighborhood park, and so on. Aasiya was five years old and crouched next to Suraiya's pillow on the day that she died. Her voice was little more than a cracked whisper cutting through her dry, gray lips, but Aasiya moved in very close to hear what her beloved grandmother had to say. 'Sing me a song, jaani.' Aasiya straightened up and gulped, and then very steadily began to sing the words to a very old Bollywood song that Suraiya had liked to play in the kitchen when watching Aasiya.

'I won't remain forever,
You won't remain forever,
But still our marks will remain.'

Aasiya could not remember how she had felt immediately after Suraiya died. The days after were a stretch of blank canvas in her mind. There were the last days in the hospital, the morning of the funeral, and then nothing. According to Fatima, she had stopped eating for three days.

But in the years since then, Aasiya had begun to feel more and more as if Suraiya's presence were still around her. The first time the thought occurred to her, she was ten years old. She had gotten into a fight with some girls at school, and they had pulled on her pigtails and called her an "oily witch."

As she sat on the edge of her bed, staring into the mirror with tears flowing down her face, she had reached up to undo them, silently swearing that she'd never sport the hairstyle again. But suddenly, the words to that old song Suraiya had liked so much had sprung to her lips. It happened out of the blue, but it didn't feel like she was singing them. It felt like someone else was. Even though her own lips were the ones moving and the sound was coming from her mouth, Aasiya felt as though the song was being sung by a warm figure behind her. When she spun around to look, nobody was there, but the song still echoed in her ears. Daadi was singing, she thought for a moment, but of course, the thought passed when she realized how ridiculous it was. Daadi was dead; she was gone. There were no songs for her to sing anymore.

But as the years went on, Aasiya began to think more and more that maybe Suraiya wasn't completely gone after all. She began to see the old woman in her dreams whenever she felt particularly stressed or upset about something. She'd step out into the light behind Aasiya's closed eyes, as if she'd been waiting there the whole time, her eyes sparkling, her expression pained and panicked. Why do you hurt? she seemed to ask

Aasiya. What has gone wrong? And Aasiya didn't know how to respond. She only knew that whatever pain or overwhelming stress she felt in her waking life had aggravated her grandmother somehow—wherever she was.

In the ground.

In the lowest level of heaven.

Waiting.

Maybe she was just in Aasiya's head. Or maybe, somehow, the old woman's soul had latched onto her granddaughter as it was leaving her body. When she was eleven years old, Aasiya had asked Bilal if spirits could feel pain.

'Of course they can, Aasiya! A spirit is as real as flesh and blood and bone! It can't feel the way we can, but it can feel,' he said.

'What about . . . people we love? Their spirits, if they aren't here anymore, would they be able to feel what the people they used to love feel, somehow?'

Bilal considered the question for a moment, scratching at one of his mangled ears as he did. 'I think they can,' he said finally. 'There's certain bonds that aren't ever severed, my love. You will learn that when you are older. But there are certain connections that have existed far longer than we have. And there's something else too. Something that we are born around, created around. It's there before the blood, and the bone, and the flesh. It feels for us, it feels for who we love, for those who love us. Maybe it's what some people call a soul, but my mind isn't big enough to try naming things like that, jaan.'

With that in mind, Aasiya came to expect a visit from her grandmother every time she was troubled or upset, and she always got one. The old woman was always waiting for her in the darkness. Why do you hurt? What has gone wrong? The two questions every time. Aasiya would talk to her, not with words, but something else. Something that seemed to hover in the space between them; some means that could only be used away from the waking world. Suraiya would listen, and in turn she would impart some sort of comfort onto her granddaughter—reassuring her that everything would be alright even as she paced back and forth, agitated by the girl's discomfort. Aasiya tried to be as happy as she could be, as often as she could be, because she didn't want to cause Suraiya discomfort. She wanted her to rest, to be at peace. But often, especially in recent months, after waking at the call for Fajr prayer, Aasiya would walk over to her window in her thin cotton nightshirt, and she would stare at the sky outside. In the darkened reflection, she often felt she could see Suraiya, like a gentle shadow, the kind and tired face smiling wistfully in her direction. The twinkling in her eyes gave the impression that not only could Suriaya see her, but she had been there the whole time.

Chapter Five

About an hour passed before Aasiya woke up. She had managed to roll onto her side in her sleep, and her hair had created an untidy half curtain over her face in the process. She sat up, brushing it back out of her eyes, and stretched before laying back and trying hard to remember what she had seen in her dreams. Once again, Suraiya had been there, and Aasiya knew that she had somehow communicated to her grandmother her worries about Ashfaq's leaving, as well as the state of things with her mother. Now, inexplicably, she felt the strong urge to call Ashfaq and speak to him, and then to go downstairs and speak to Fatima right after. It was as if she could hear a voice that wasn't her own in her head, telling her to call him. In the same part of her brain, the words of that old song echoed faintly.

Aasiya shook her head and then closed her eyes, reaching up to press both palms hard into her eyes. Bright orange burst behind her eyelids, and she thought to herself how utterly insane her line of thinking was. 'I'm taking advice from a dead woman in my head,' she said out loud. She didn't get a response, aside from the whirring of her ceiling fan. But she hadn't truly expected one. Aasiya sat up again, pulled out her phone, and found Ashfaq's number in her contacts list.

Can I call? she texted him.

His response came a moment later: Yes.

Aasiya called, and after a few rings, Ashfaq answered. 'Are you okay?' he asked immediately.

'I'm fine! I just wanted to talk,' she said.

'Are you sure? You never ask to call in the middle of the day.'

'I know, but I didn't want to text. And I wanted to hear your voice.'

She felt that she could hear him smiling before he said anything.

'Acha. Okay. That's fine. I'm glad I get to hear yours too,' he said.

'Who knows how often you'll be able to hear it when you're all the way over in America? Busy with all your work, the friends you'll make, and that's not even taking into consideration the time difference there'll be between us. . . .'

'I won't be hearing you anywhere near as often as I'd like to, that's for sure. And you'll be busy too, jaan. Don't you start applying to schools next year?'

'Don't remind me. I've been trying not to think about it on top of everything else,' groaned Aasiya.

'Well . . . George Washington is a great school, you know. And if you went there, we would be together.'

'Ha! Like my parents would allow that. Or yours, for that matter.'

'They would if we were married, Aasiya.'

'And you think they'd let us marry before we finish school? You're not that much of a dreamer, Ashfaq.'

Again, the smile had a sound. 'No. I'm not. A more realistic dream is us just leaving school and running off together to marry, and then coming back home afterward.'

Aasiya laughed at this. 'No. I couldn't do that, and you know it. I want my parents at my wedding. I want yours there as well.'

'I know, I know. I'm only joking,' he said.

There was a moment of silence, and then Aasiya asked, 'How are you feeling?'

'I'm okay. Still thinking. Why do you ask?'

"I thought I should. I had a feeling.'

'What was the feeling?'

'Just a feeling, one that I should talk to you. Needed to talk to you.'

'Did you have another one of those dreams, Aasiya?'

She had only spoken to Ashfaq about the dreams twice before. She liked that he remembered, and that he took her seriously. But she didn't like that he could guess about them so accurately. 'Yes. I did,' she said after a moment.

Ashfaq chuckled. 'How am I meant to hide anything from you if you've got a sense like this?'

'You'd like to hide things from me?'

'Not forever. But there are some things I might not want to reveal right away. What am I supposed to do about that now?'

Aasiya laughed and said, 'I can't tell if something is on your mind at will, Ashfaq!'

'No. Just when you fall asleep.'

'Mm. You're deflecting.'

'It's nothing I haven't told you already, Aasiya. We just talked about it this morning anyway.'

'I don't care, Ashfaq. Tell me again,' Aasiya said firmly.

Ashfaq considered it for a moment, and then he began to talk. He talked about how he could not shake the memory of the boys and what they had done. How their voices were louder in his head now than they ever had been before. 'I can't even tell anymore if that's what they actually sounded like, and if those things are what they actually said, or if it's all just become this thing I've imagined so much over time just to frighten myself that I think it's real!' He talked about how even though every part of him knew that he wouldn't run into them again, and that he was a grown man now and could take care of himself, something about the memory still made the hairs on the back of his neck stand up when he thought about it.

And then he stopped talking. Aasiya could hear him breathing a bit heavily; she heard him sniff and realized he might be crying. She didn't acknowledge it. Instead, she let a few moments pass by in silence before saying, 'Ashfaq?'

'Hm? I'm sorry, I'm okay. I just need a moment.'

'That's okay. You don't have to say more if that's all you can say right now.'

'I told you it was nothing you didn't already know, Aasiya.'

'It's alright. I don't mind hearing about it. I don't want you keeping it in, Ashfaq. You have to let things out.'

'Yes. I'm sure spilling irrational fears to my girlfriend makes me all the more endearing to her.'

Aasiya smiled. 'The same way me telling my boyfriend about the visions or weird dreams I have make me all the more endearing to him?'

Ashfaq laughed at this. 'It doesn't have to make you endearing, jaan. That's not the point. It's something real about you and that's all that matters,' he said.

'The same can be said for everything you told me, Ashfaq. And I know I've said this to you before, but it will pass once you're there.'

'I know it will, and that's what makes me stupider for feeling this way.'

'It's okay to be anxious. Especially when you consider what you went through, it's not stupid to feel that way.'

Ashfaq silently mulled this over, and she let him. She could practically hear his thoughts crashing over one another through the phone, the same way she felt she could hear the sound of his smile.

'You're still going to be there tomorrow morning, yes?' he asked suddenly.

'Yes.' Aasiya decided not to call him on the change of subject. 'I almost forgot to tell you, Amma said I could come.'

'That's great, Aasiya! I'm so glad to hear that. Maybe this is things getting better between you two.'

'I hope so. But don't think that means you're free from what we talked about this morning.'

Ashfaq laughed. 'I won't forget, don't worry.'

They made small talk for a little while longer, until Ashfaq heard his father calling him downstairs. 'I have to go,' he said. 'I'll text you in a little while, and I'll see you in the morning, yeah?'

'Theek hai, alright,' she said.

'I love you, Aasiya,' said Ashfaq.

'I love you too, Ashfaq.' He smiled at her words before hanging up, and she hung up as well, feeling much better than she did before the phone call.

Aasiya didn't know it, but Fatima had been standing outside her bedroom door for the past ten minutes or so, and she had caught a bit of the conversation with Ashfaq. It pleased her to hear her daughter sound so happy talking to the boy, and a jolt of both shock and concern shot through her when she heard Aasiya profess her love for him. But these things happened, she knew, especially at that age. Fatima pushed the concern to the back of her mind. You weren't going to keep her away from it all forever, she said to herself for what seemed like the thousandth time in recent months. And again, the urge to speak to her daughter plainly about it all rose up in her, and Fatima began to push it back down into the pit of her stomach as she always did. But this time, her hand seemed to move toward the door handle of its own accord. She held it for a moment, then turned it, pushed the door open, and walked in.

'Aasiya?'

ﻢﻤﻤﻤ

Ashfaq came back to Pakistan the next summer, like he had said he would. His first year of university in America had gone incredibly well. He had adjusted to his new life better than he ever could have imagined. After the mandatory few hours spent with his family, Ashfaq was finally able to get away, and headed straight for Aasiya's house, just like he had told her he would.

PART TWO
SURAIYA & IQBAL

Chapter Six

November 1947   **Lahore.**

Suraiya was sitting in the chair she had moved closer to the living room window, looking down at the street below. Despite the late hour, there were still many people moving around outside; but there was a quietness to them, very different from the swollen sounds of rage and rioting that had echoed through the streets of Lahore over the past few months.

She was careful not to make a sound. A thin curtain was draped over the gaping hole in the window, which had been created when someone in the streets below had thrown a brick through it two weeks ago. Despite the quiet of the crowd below, Suraiya did not want to attract attention to herself. She simply wanted to see what was happening. The past months had been hardest on the women in so many ways. With too many horror stories floating around of women and girls of all ages being raped and butchered, their corpses hung up on display, or thrown into wells, or burned in massive piles, her father, Jalal, like so many others, had begun keeping the women of the house completely confined to their flat. Partition had revealed the full extent of the rage and hatred harbored by so many.

The word "Pakistan" still felt funny on everyone's tongues. It had a different sound, a different taste, a different feeling. And with the way things were going, nobody was sure that it was going to last. Which wasn't to say that the new Hindustan was any better. The borders running through Punjab and Bengal had become gaping wounds, the division of land causing the blood of thousands upon thousands of people to spill over onto either side of the new borders—the newly independent people reduced to nothing more than fertilizer for the split earth and food for the crows.

During the day, the family stayed away from windows and doors. Jalal stayed at home as much as he could. His office had closed indefinitely, so he only left to get supplies, and before doing so he would always put an extra padlock on the bolt locking their door. He would sit Suraiya's younger brother, Yusuf, who was only thirteen years old, down in a chair in front of the door, and press a polished revolver into the boy's hands.

'If anyone knocks or tries to come in, don't say a word. Pretend nobody is here. If someone tries to force their way in, you shoot,' he had instructed the boy, the first time this happened. 'If it's me coming home, I'll call out your name, and if I tell you nobody else is out here, only then do you unlock this door. Understand me?' Yusuf had nodded. A mixture of fear and excitement flickered across Yusuf's face whenever their father left, and it turned Suraiya's stomach to see the imagination whirring behind his eyes. A chance to play the hero! To shoot a gun the way he saw heroes doing in films. But what if someone really tried to force their way in? And what would they do if they managed it? Every time they heard footsteps running up or down the steps in the corridor, Yusuf would shudder and grip the pistol tighter.

Suraiya thought about what she would do in that situation as well, while watching the people milling about in the street below. She had heard the horror stories too—fuel enough for a lifetime of nightmares. An old Hindu woman who lived a couple of streets away had been savaged just the other month by a mob of Muslim students who broke into her home. They took all of the money and jewelry they could get their hands on and killed her son, who had been visiting with his wife and kids. The wife had taken the children to her parents' house before the incident. Nobody knew where she was. The old woman was said to have wandered around her home, mad with grief, before finally succumbing to her injuries.

There were stories of other women; Muslim, Hindu, Sikh, Jain, Christian, young and old alike, forced to jump into wells or take poison or hang themselves to avoid the fates that awaited them at the hands of their attackers. Sometimes the men of the house were forced to take care of the task themselves.

Occasionally, Suraiya caught herself watching Jalal as he moved through the day, wondering if her father could bring himself to do the same to her. She shuddered at the thought.

When she had asked her mother, Mohsina, what she thought, the response was a slap across the face. 'Don't ever think that! He loves us. He loves us too much. He would kill himself before laying a finger on us! He believes his family to have a fighting chance,' the woman had said, with an expression of utter pain on her face.

Suraiya hadn't meant to upset her mother. She only wondered if the woman shared her concerns. Deep down, Suraiya felt sure that Mohsina wondered the same thing. Just like she was sure that all those other men loved the women in their families as well, right up until the last second, when they had to stop and lie to themselves, tell themselves that it was the only way. . . .

Before pulling a trigger.

Or swinging a sword.

Or poisoning the water at home.

One night, some weeks ago, Jalal had come into Suraiya's bedroom and sat at the foot of her bed, smoking a cigarette. Suraiya watched as he blew out little clouds of smoke. After a moment of this, he turned to her and said, 'Tumko kya lagta hai? Humein kya karna chaiye? What do you think? What should we do?'

'We should stay, Abba,' Suraiya had said. He nodded knowingly. This was the answer he had expected. Jalal had a cousin in Peshawar who had written to suggest that they come and stay with him and his family until things settled. Things are a little bit easier here, he wrote. They're bad all over, I'd say, but at least we would all be together. Who knows when all of this insanity will finally end?

After talking to Suraiya and Mohsina, who had also elected to stay, Jalal wrote back, saying, My family and I appreciate the offer. But traveling is not the safest thing to do right now. You live on the other side of the country. There is too much road between here and there, too much that can happen. It is not a risk I can take. Inshallah, this will all end soon enough.

Suraiya's family had had a family of Hindu neighbors who lived right across the hall. They always exchanged sweets on holidays and during any sort of celebration. When they had fled Lahore three weeks earlier, Mohsina had given them a large bag filled with blankets and tiffin lunchboxes nestled in between. Jalal also tried to give money to Aakav, the patriarch of the family, but the man politely declined. 'Who knows what value this will have there? Everything is bound to change,' he had said with a sad smile.

'It already has. Otherwise you wouldn't be leaving your home,' Jalal responded quietly.

'We can't call it home anymore,' Aakav said. 'Home is on the other side of a new border.'

Suraiya had said good-bye to their daughter, Asha, whom she had always been friendly with. They used to oil each other's hair on weekends from time to time, and work on homework assignments together, since they went to the same school and shared a few classes. She wondered where the girl was now; whether her family had safely arrived in Amritsar or not.

A shout from the street below interrupted Suraiya's thoughts, and she instinctively moved away from the window. Her breathing was shallow as she stared straight ahead, watching the signboards on the buildings across the street swing in the nighttime breeze. Giant shadows flickered on the walls, thrown up by the light of streetlamps and torches in the crowd below. Suraiya caught her breath and slowly moved back toward the window, peering down again. Two bullock carts had come close to colliding, and the drivers were shouting at each other.

She sighed and stepped back again. It was late. Jalal could wake up at any moment to check and see if everything was okay. He had developed a habit of doing that in recent months; waking up in the middle of the night and going to every room, making sure everyone who was supposed to be there was still there, and making sure nobody else had managed to break into their home.

Suraiya felt a chill go down her spine at the thought of someone managing to break in. She looked over her shoulder into the dark space of the sitting room, and the hallway leading to the dining area and kitchen beyond that.

Very quietly, so as not to make a sound and wake her father, Suraiya crept through the darkness all the way back to her bedroom, where only a sliver of light made its way in through a crack in the drawn curtains.

Mohsina had been telling her for weeks that they would soon have one of Jalal's old friends staying with them for a little while. He and his family were coming from Hindustan. They were due to arrive later that very day. Suraiya knew Mohsina would enlist her help as much as possible to prepare for the guests—cooking, cleaning, brewing tea. Even with times as bad as they were, they could not forget to honor guests.

'It will just be until they get on their feet here,' Mohsina had said to her that morning. Suraiya couldn't help but wonder how long that would be. It was hard to tell how anything would go these days. But at some point, things had to go back to some semblance of stability.

How could they not?

How long could the world shake before it finally fell apart?

Chapter Seven

Iqbal sat silently on the couch. His parents were hugging and conversing with the people whose home they were in. He had done his part by "salaaming" them both and hugging the man—Jalal, he was called—and now he sat while he waited for the pleasantries to die down. His back was knotted up from the cramped train ride. They had been surrounded by bodies, and Iqbal had been forced to stand for the entire journey. His legs were throbbing, and he was grateful for the chance to finally sit. He would need to find a place where he could stretch later, or he'd wind up sore for days.

'Iqbal! Say salaam, won't you?' his mother's voice interrupted his thoughts. Iqbal glanced up and saw that a girl who looked to be about his age had entered the room, and so had a very young boy.

'This is our daughter, Suraiya, and our son, Yusuf,' said Jalal proudly. The boy strode right up to Iqbal and shook his hand.

'Assalamu Alaikum,' said Iqbal.

'Walaikum Asalam,' said the boy.

Iqbal looked up in the direction of the girl, who smiled politely at him and nodded her head, causing her scarf to slip further down below her hairline. 'Assalamu Alaikum,' Iqbal said before lowering his gaze.

'Walaikum Asalam,' she responded.

Suraiya eyed the young man with curiosity as she went to and from the kitchen, bringing tea and snacks to the coffee table where her father and the young man's parents, Hassan Uncle and Zarmeena Auntie, were all sitting. He hadn't touched his cup of tea yet, choosing to sip on a glass of cold water instead. And he wasn't eating much, taking only two biscuits at her parents' urging in order to avoid being impolite. His hair was buzzed to an even stubble on his scalp, his eyes were lined with thick layers of dark kohl, and his nose looked mangled, like someone had been chewing on it. When he lifted his glass to take a sip of water, she noticed a scar running up along his upper lip. Where his ears should've been, there were instead two crushed globes of flesh. Suraiya recognized that ear shape. He must have been a wrestler back in Hindustan. A quiet intensity radiated from him, but it was oddly calming. Reassuring. Controlled.

'It will be good to have more men in the house!' Jalal was saying. 'The more there are, the safer a home is in these times. We must all stick together now.'

'Ah,' countered Hassan, 'but who is the "we," my friend?'

Jalal smiled at him over the rim of his teacup. 'Well, "The people of Lahore" is what I'd like to say, or "The people of Pakistan." But I can't say that.'

'So you mean Mussalmans?' asked Hassan.

'No,' said Iqbal. The attention of the room turned to him, 'Mussalmans aren't blameless in any of this either. Nobody is blameless,' he said.

'The boy is right,' said Mohsina.

'He is right,' agreed Jalal before turning back to his friend. 'So, I'll say that "we" means everyone in this room, how's that sound?'

'Hear, hear!' said Zarmeena, raising her cup in a salute.

They all laughed, and after chatting a little while longer, everyone moved to the dining room for lunch. Suraiya and Mohsina served it together, shooting down Zarmeena's offers to help with, 'You've traveled so far!' and, 'We can't let you work as our guest,' and, 'Please, sit down.'

That night, it was decided that Zarmeena would share Suraiya's room with her, and Hassan with Yusuf. Iqbal would sleep on the couch in the sitting room. Suraiya went to the kitchen while Zarmeena was changing in the bedroom. On her way back, she found the young man, Iqbal, setting up his pillow and a quilt for the night.

'Is there anything I can get you?' she asked politely.

'No, thank you. I'm okay.' He hesitated for a moment before saying, 'Please don't feel compelled to maintain the mehmaan nawaazi the whole time we're here. At least not with me. I know my parents don't expect it either, but they don't know how to say it.'

Suraiya raised her eyebrows at him. 'And you do know how to say it?'

He reached up and scratched one of his bulbous ears. 'I just said it.'

'You did just say it, but how do you know it wasn't an incredibly rude thing to say?' she asked.

Iqbal stopped scratching and stared at her. 'Was it rude?' he asked earnestly. 'I'm sorry. I didn't mean to be rude. I just don't want you going to all the extra trouble, that's all. Things are hard enough as it is for everyone.'

'Maybe spoiling a guest was the one thing we had as a way to distract ourselves from everything, and now you've told me to stop, Bhai.'

For this, Iqbal had no response. He just stared at her, then lowered his gaze, staring at the crook of her elbow. 'I'm sorry I said it,' he mumbled.

Suraiya considered dragging her joke out a little longer but took pity on him after seeing the look on his face. 'I'm only teasing you, Bhai. You weren't rude. I'm relieved. Serving tea to strangers isn't the most enjoyable thing to do. Although my parents aren't likely to accept you deeming it unnecessary, and I will have to do it anyway.'

Iqbal glanced up at her face again and smiled, the scar giving the effect of a wrinkle above his mouth when he did.

'That was a rude joke to play. I'm not very good with my words, and that leads to me being horrible at figuring out anyone else's as well.'

'What are you good at then, Iqbal Bhai?' Suraiya asked.

'Oh, I'm "Bhai"? Well, Suraiya Baji, I'm a fairly decent pehlwan.'

Suraiya nodded. 'I see. I had guessed as much looking at your ears.'

He smiled. 'Yes, well, Iqbal Pehlwan is what people usually call me.'

'Acha, so is that what I should call you?' she asked.

'Call me whatever you'd like,' he said.

Suraiya puffed up her chest and held her arms out wide at her sides as if she were showing off her musculature. 'Pehlwan Bhai, does that work?' she asked.

Iqbal smiled again. 'Whatever you'd like,' he repeated.

Suraiya relaxed and saw that he was looking down again. Those two smiles he'd given her were the most expressive she'd seen his face since he'd arrived.

'We appreciate you and your family allowing us to stay,' he said suddenly.

Suraiya blinked and saw that he was looking up once more. 'You heard my father earlier,' she said. 'It works just as well for us. Who would want to mess with a home that has a pehlwan living there?'

'If only things like that mattered anymore,' he replied.

Before Suraiya could ask what he meant, Zarmeena poked her head into the living room. 'Oh! There you are. Feel free to come into the room now, beti.' Her eyes flicked from Suraiya to her son quickly. There was curiosity in them.

'Coming, Auntie. I was just asking Iqbal Bhai if he needed anything before I turned in,' said Suraiya with a smile.

'How kind of you,' said Zarmeena.

'Amma, I was telling Suraiya Baji how thankful you and Abba are that we're allowed to stay here.'

'Your father knows how to get favors from his old friends,' Zarmeena laughed.

Iqbal nodded before turning to Suraiya again. 'Well. Goodnight,' he said.

'Goodnight,' said Suraiya, walking out of the room with Zarmeena.

Iqbal let a few seconds go by, making sure nobody was coming back into the room, before closing the door, taking his shirt off, and switching off the light.

The sounds coming from the street below kept him awake a while. He lay there in silence, trying to decipher each one.

Chapter Eight

The two families adapted to the new living situation rather quickly. Jalal and Hassan usually went out for supplies together and were sometimes gone for hours at a time, navigating through the more chaotic parts of the city. Iqbal would now sit at the door with Yusuf, playing games with the boy and teaching him about wrestling. Jalal's pistol was now tucked into a vest Iqbal wore over his muslin shirts. The city was teeming with refugee camps that had been set up to house the thousands, if not millions, of new residents of Pakistan. Every day, Jalal and Hassan would bring home news of what they had seen, which parts of the city were most dangerous now, who had been killed, what new illnesses were going around, etc.

They intentionally left out the more horrid details so as not to alarm everyone at home. The only one privy to the things they spoke of over whiskey in the evenings was Iqbal, who would stand in the corner with his arms crossed, a shadow over his face as he listened.

On their trips out of the house, Jalal and Hassan also kept a lookout for empty homes in places where things had settled a little for Hassan and his family to move into. According to Hassan and Zarmeena, all of their money was packed into one of their suitcases—a giant wad of cash to start a new life in the new Pakistan. But it took months for them to find a good spot, which left plenty of time for the two families to get to know each other.

Following that first conversation before bed, Suraiya found a reason every night to stop in the sitting room and have a conversation with Iqbal. Sometimes, the conversations were very brief. Sometimes they simply didn't know what to talk about. But Suraiya also found that Iqbal just wasn't always very talkative. This bothered her. Not because she longed to have heartfelt conversations with him specifically, but because she hadn't been around anyone her own age in months. She felt herself receding into the role she played at home, and she was afraid that if things went on the way they were going much longer, she wouldn't know how to break away from that. Another reason for her annoyance was simple curiosity. All they could ever talk about at home now was what was going on outside, the state of things, what they'd heard on the radio, who had done what to whom, who had retaliated and in what area, what the casualty rate was, etc. etc.

Iqbal did not participate.

He would listen. He muttered a response occasionally, but that was it. Suraiya was curious to know where his mind went during these discussions. She felt sure it had something to do with his occasional brooding silences.

One afternoon, Suraiya was settling down at the dining room table with a cup of tea. Zarmeena and Mohsina had already had theirs and were in their rooms for an afternoon lie-down. Jalal and Hassan were out seeing about an empty flat that was only a few blocks away. Yusuf was in his room. Iqbal was seated in front of the door, newspaper in his hands and gun stuffed into his vest, as per usual.

As Suraiya sat down at the table with her cup, she noticed that

Iqbal's head was tilted to the side and his eyes were closed. She cleared her throat. Iqbal didn't respond. She looked around and then kicked the leg of the table. Iqbal woke with a start and looked around, wiping the corner of his mouth with the back of his hand.

'Would you like a cup?' Suraiya asked him.

'Is that chai?' Iqbal asked.

She nodded.

He sighed and said, 'Yes, I guess I better have a cup. No use sitting here if I can't stay awake.'

His pehlwan's diet didn't allow for chai, but lately he'd had a cup every once in a while, when he needed to stay awake or if it was very cold. He told himself he'd get back to the old regimen once things settled. But a voice in the back of his mind always whispered, You mean if things settle again.

Iqbal pushed the thought to the back of his mind as always, got up, and stretched before sitting in a chair at the table.

'Sugar, yes?' Suraiya asked.

He nodded. 'Yes. As much as you gave yourself, please.' She poured him his cup and set it down in front of him. 'Thank you,' he said, leaning forward to blow on it lightly before taking a sip.

'Would you like a biscuit?' Suraiya asked, pushing her plate forward a little so it rested between them both.

He took one and thanked her again. 'You make very good chai,' said Iqbal.

'I'm sure you've had better,' Suraiya replied with a smile.

He shook his head and said, 'Pehlwans don't drink chai.'

'Oh, that's right; how could I forget? No chai, no paan, no daru, no smoking. No love even, correct?'

Iqbal finished chewing and swallowed the biscuit before responding. 'We do love. We love what we do, and we get married like anyone else does. Just maybe not as young as others; not while we are training and competing,' he said.

'And what about everything else?'

Iqbal smiled at her. 'You are correct about everything else.'

'So,' Suraiya leaned back in her chair and smiled back at him, 'Iqbal Pehlwan Bhai has no wife he left behind on the other side of Punjab? And no wife to be waiting for him here in Lahore?'

Iqbal shook his head. 'None.'

'Well, I hope it's worth it,' she said.

'Mm. There was a time a few years ago where I did consider it. This fellow who trained in the same akhada as me, he had a cousin who was visiting for the summer. She would come with his brother every evening to pick him up after our practice. I was seventeen at the time, and I desperately wanted to ask for her hand.'

'What happened, then? Did you ask?' Suraiya was hunched forward, invested in every word.

Iqbal laughed. 'Oh yes, I asked. I asked my coach what he thought I should do. And he smacked me on the ear, said he had been training me since I was a child so that I could be a great pehlwan, not a modern-day Majnu. And then he made me do two thousand baithaks. He said he wanted me to sweat out my desires. I couldn't walk properly for a week afterward. And the soreness was enough to kill any desire I had to marry.'

Suraiya stared at him, shocked, and he burst out laughing at the look on her face. The sound of his laughter startled her. It might've been the first time he'd laughed since he had arrived. 'That's horrible!' she said.

Iqbal shrugged. 'Maybe. Maybe not. Who knows? The instincts of a seventeen-year-old boy can't be the best thing to follow. For all I know, I was done a great favor.' Still grinning, he asked, 'How about yourself? Any close calls with marriage? Or maybe you have a husband hiding in one of the cupboards somewhere?' He glanced over at the cabinet near the stove that was visible from where they were sitting.

'Is that a joke, Iqbal Pehlwan Bhai?' Suraiya feigned shock. 'A real joke? One that can even be considered funny? Haye! What did I put in the chai?' She smirked.

He smiled and shrugged. 'I guess I'm very tired and not behaving like myself because of that.'

She grinned. 'Well, I'll have to enjoy this while it lasts. But to answer your question, no. I have no husband. A boy and his family brought a proposal along about two years ago, and I turned it down.'

'Why's that?' asked Iqbal.

'He wasn't my type.'

'What is your type, then?'

This time, Suraiya shrugged. 'I'm not sure. I'll know when I come across it. But I do know that it wasn't him.'

Iqbal chuckled at this and then fell silent again, sipping his tea quietly while looking around the room.

'Have you been having trouble sleeping?' asked Suraiya, wanting to push the conversation forward before it crawled to the same awkward, silent end that chats with Iqbal usually did.

'A bit, yes,' he said. 'Not because I'm lacking anything!' he added hurriedly, seeing the concern flash across her face. 'You and your family provide more than enough—I mean that. But it's hard with everything going on out there.'

She knew what he was referring to. 'I stay up a little every night myself, trying to listen to anything that might be going on,' said Suraiya. 'Sometimes I'll hear a noise and know exactly what it is. That never scares me. Hearing people yell, curse, scream, threaten, any of that. I know what it is. But the noises I can't recognize, those are the ones that scare me. And if it ever goes silent? Even for a second? That scares me the most.'

The openness with which she admitted this to him surprised her, but she didn't regret it. Iqbal listened closely, keeping his eyes on hers the entire time, waiting for her to finish.

'I understand what you mean,' he said. 'Did you hear the gunshots last night?'

Suraiya shook her head, wide-eyed. 'No. I didn't. Was anyone hurt?'

'I don't know. I think so. There was screaming too. I suppose it's harder for the noise to carry to the rest of the house since we fixed the window, but it's still pretty clear if you're lying on the couch. I was trying to piece together what might have happened. At one point, I even considered going out there to see.'

'Please don't ever do that, Iqbal. People have been killed in all of this for less than curiosity.'

He clicked his tongue at her words. 'Ha. Well, what danger would I be in? There aren't many non-Muslims around down there anymore. I'm on the right side of it all, aren't I?'

There was something bitter in the words, something that he hadn't noticed as it slipped out, but Suraiya had.

'What do you mean by that?' she asked.

'I don't mean anything,' mumbled Iqbal.

Suraiya sat there, not knowing what to say, staring at Iqbal's hands. They were gripping his teacup, and his thumbs were stroking the rim. Finally, Iqbal spoke again. 'We aren't right just because of what we believe in. Neither is anyone else, for that matter.'

'That's a controversial opinion to have, Iqbal.'

'You don't agree with me?' He was looking at her again.

Suraiya sighed. 'That's not what I said. I'm just saying, it's not an opinion many people share right now.'

'Yes, I know. Maybe that's the problem.'

'Kya hua?' What happened? she asked.

Iqbal lowered his gaze from her face to her elbow, and then down her arm, stopping at the wrist. A lone golden bangle studded with little emeralds sparkled under the light hanging above the table.

He took a breath and began to speak: 'One of my closest friends back home was a Sikh boy. We had known each other since we were very young. We trained at the same akhada together, we ate together, worked together, slept together. Everything we did, we did together. He wasn't as serious about wrestling as I was, but he would always help me, one hundred percent. If I had a match coming up, he would cook for me and make sure I had the right food. Every massage I received after training would be from him. If I had problems with my stomach, he would stand on it and move his feet around until everything settled back to normal. I used to think that maybe he and I were brothers, that he had been separated from me at birth and adopted by a different family. That was the only reason for our difference in faith that I could think of. Not that it mattered. He was my brother, through and through. I could not imagine a life without him in it. If I tried, it made my head spin.'

Iqbal paused here. His left hand was shaking ever so slightly. He curled and uncurled the fingers slowly to calm himself and cleared his throat before continuing. 'When they announced the creation of Pakistan, I didn't think anything that happened would affect us. He and I would remain as we were. But we didn't see each other for weeks afterward. I thought maybe he was just trying to avoid everything that was going on. The neighborhood we lived in shattered quite suddenly. There were divides that weren't there before.

'Who knows what led to what? If you asked a dozen different people, they'd point in a dozen different directions, depending on what religion they belonged to. Someone says a gurdwara was burned down first, another says a mosque, someone says a Sikh woman was attacked, others say Mussalman. I don't know. Everyone has some blame. Regardless, one day I looked outside, and it looked like there was a war being fought. A mob of people all fighting each other. Spilling blood in the name of this and that. So, I ran out. I don't know why. I don't know who I was trying to fight. But I was caught up in it all, like everyone was. I knocked someone down and another person ran at me. We struggled for a moment, and I managed to pull off the cloth that was covering his face. And there stood my friend, with no recognition of me in him. Maybe I didn't have any for him either. Maybe that's why he did what he did.'

'What did he do?' Suraiya asked quietly.

Iqbal hesitated a moment, and then reached down with one hand, grabbing the hem of his shirt, and rolled it up to his ribs. His stomach was like a cobblestone road of dark brown. The only thing out of place was the scar that went up from the bottom of his abdomen, past his navel, and stopped right below his sternum. An ugly trench, still not completely scarred over, cutting through the flat muscle. A small 'oh' escaped Suraiya's lips, so quiet it almost sounded like a sigh. Iqbal smiled at the reaction and lowered his shirt again. 'It's why we decided to leave. Once I had healed enough. Abba Jaan was afraid I would want revenge. He wasn't wrong.'

Suraiya looked at him. There was a veil of sadness over his face as he said this. 'You haven't seen him since?' she asked.

Iqbal shook his head. 'No. Sometimes I wonder if he came to his senses after that day and took it upon himself to avoid me. He knew where we lived. If he wanted to come and finish me off, he very easily could have done so.'

'Hosak ta hai…' Suraiya spoke slowly, 'k usko apna dost nahin nazar aya uss waqt, bas ek aur Mussalman nazar aya.'

Iqbal nodded. 'Perhaps. I suppose that could apply to everyone though, couldn't it? We stopped seeing each other as people and started seeing only the religion someone follows.'

'Not even two years ago we were all one country,' said Suraiya. 'And now it feels like the world has been split in two.'

'Mm. And regardless of where you are, it's all burning around you,' said Iqbal, pointing in the direction of the sitting room window. 'You can smell it if you sit there. Even indoors. It's like burnt rubber in the air, ash in the throat. How is this the freedom we were all running toward?'

She didn't have an answer to give. The question hung in the air around them. It hung in the air outside the apartment as well. It was a question hanging over both nations, but one whose looming presence few people acknowledged, and fewer still would ask out loud.

'I lost a friend as well,' said Suraiya after a moment.

Iqbal looked at her, waiting for her to go on. He was tired of talking. He hadn't shared any of that story with another person before now. 'How?'

'She was a dancer.' Suraiya saw the blank expression on Iqbal's face and cleared her throat. 'A very specific kind of dancer. One certain men only see for a certain price.'

Realization clicked in Iqbal's eyes, and his brown cheeks turned a dark maroon when he blushed.

She laughed, 'Itni sharam, Pehlwan Bhai?'

'I'm sorry. Just not used to it. You described yourself earlier, the way we live.' He smiled at her shyly. 'Please continue. Don't let me stop you.'

'Hm. Well, her stepfather kicked her out after her mother passed away. She had a little apartment she shared with another girl right near the Heera Mandi. I would visit her from time to time. At some point she began working; she never really told me how. Maybe it was the girl she was living with who showed her a way she could earn money, or maybe someone approached her. Maybe it was something she just decided to do on her own because it was close by. I'm sure she had her reasons, but we never spoke about her work much. She was my friend, regardless of what she did. Regardless of her religion.'

'What was she?' he asked

'Hindu,' said Suraiya. 'The brothel she worked in, it took girls from all backgrounds. I suppose every brothel does. All of those labels tend to fall off in a place like that. But there were a lot of girls from Hindu backgrounds where she worked. And all of the good and pious Mussalman men in the area assumed that women who didn't belong to their own faith must be women who were deserving of anything but a semblance of decency. They set themselves upon the brothels and cleared them all out. Burned down a few of them. Girls were killed in the middle of the street; the lucky ones. Others suffered much worse. Their pimps were killed too.'

Iqbal's hands clutched the teacup so hard the tendons of his knuckles were quivering. Suraiya noticed for the first time how strong the hands looked, and somehow found herself marveling at the fact that despite his grip, the teacup had not broken or even cracked.

'I don't know if she was killed or not. Maybe she got away. Some of them were able to get away, escape before the men attacked. She might have crossed the border somehow, along with everyone else. I don't know. When I pray for her, I pray that she's okay, that she's unharmed. I don't know if that means that I believe she's still alive or not. . . .'

Her voice trailed off into a contemplative silence that wrapped around them both. They were looking at each other, but also not. She was seeing him while staring at the rim of his teacup, and he was seeing her by staring at a spot on her shoulder, her voice still fresh in his ears, his own words still echoing in his head.

'How could all of this lead to a place we call home?' she asked quietly.

Iqbal didn't answer her. He didn't know how to. Suraiya's arm was on the table, her fingers bent and resting in the middle, next to the biscuits. Bright red polish shone on her nails. She curled her fingers slightly, and Iqbal's grip on his cup loosened. His hand slid onto the table, his own fingers centimeters from hers now. Suraiya lifted her pinky and placed it above his. Iqbal responded by turning his hand over and slipping it into hers.

Both hands were trembling . . .

Both owners still shaken by what they had shared.

Chapter Nine

Amidst the panic, the stress, the worry, and the uncertainty, love managed to creep into the apartment and blossom. It quietly carved out a place for itself in the spaces that hung between the two families. It occupied the words that Suraiya and Iqbal exchanged in their conversations. Once it had grown enough, it added its own sweet scent to the choked air that Iqbal had said hung around them.

After the tea they shared that day, Iqbal and Suraiya spoke every day. Iqbal no longer maintained his brooding silences. He almost always had something to say now, or else he listened intently to whatever Suraiya said. Something of a wall had fallen away. The sound of her voice calling him 'Iqbal Pehlwan Bhai,' echoed in his ears even when she wasn't around—especially when she wasn't around. And it brought a smile to his face.

The two of them soon found themselves waiting until the other inhabitants of the apartment were busy or not around to converse. There was no reason for this, but they did it anyway. Though it was subtle at first, eventually the change in Iqbal became pronounced enough that Hassan and Zarmeena recognized it. 'I think he's adjusted now,' Zarmeena said to her husband one day after breakfast.

Suraiya seemed happier to Mohsina and Jalal as well, though they could not understand why. But they didn't complain. Happiness was such a rare thing for so many in those days that its presence in their home was what mattered to them, not the reasons for it.

In the spring of 1948, Hassan finally found a home he liked. It was only a few minutes away from where Jalal and his family lived, but a little closer to the refugee camps that had been set up all throughout the city to house the immigrants from across the border. It was cheap, but big enough to house his family comfortably. Once businesses began operating regularly again, Jalal also used his connections at the bank to get Hassan a job as a secretary for one of the bank managers. 'It is only for a little while,' Jalal explained shyly to his friend, fearing that the position might rub him the wrong way. 'Let things settle down a bit more. You'll move up. Or maybe you'll even find a better job for yourself. But for now, let this pay your bills.' Hassan had no qualms. He was simply thankful for the chance to earn money and have his own home in the new nation.

On the morning of the day they were to move into their new home, Iqbal was awoken on the couch by the sound of someone whispering his name. He sat up and rubbed the sleep out of his eyes, looking around to see Suraiya seated on the couch opposite him, her scarf wrapped loosely around the back of her head. He stretched and glanced at the door. She had closed it after coming into the room.

'What's the matter?' he asked.

'You're leaving today,' she said.

'I know,' Iqbal looked down at his hands. He did not like what being around her did to him, sometimes; the nervousness. It was foreign to him.

'I thought we should have one last conversation before you go,' said Suraiya. 'Who knows when I will be able to have chai with you again?'

'We will visit often, I'm sure. Our fathers are two little boys when they're together, and our mothers seem to have gotten close as well. And I told your little brother that I would teach him wrestling. We will see plenty of each other, you and I.'

Suraiya raised an eyebrow at him. 'You seem to have a reason to visit everyone in this house except me. Or maybe you don't want to visit me?'

Iqbal raised his head to look at her and shook it. 'That is not true, Suraiya.'

'Isn't it, Iqbal Pehlwan Bhai?'

'It isn't. Of course I want to visit you. You have become a very close . . . person, since we have lived here.'

'A close person?' Suraiya repeated.

'Yes. A close person.'

'I'm not sure what you mean, Iqbal Pehlwan.' The use of his name alone, without her teasing, made him squirm.

'I don't know how to explain it, Suraiya.'

'Okay.' She stood up and cleared her throat. 'I'm going to go make some chai. Everyone will be up soon.' Before she walked out of the room, she turned around at the door and looked at him again.

'I'm going to miss you, Iqbal,' she said.

Iqbal gave her a sad smile, 'I'm going to miss you too, Suraiya.'

That night, after Iqbal and his family had left, Suraiya lay in her bed, the bedroom solely hers once again. She was staring up at the immobile ceiling fan, watching a small spider slowly build a web between two of the blades. Suddenly, she got out of bed, strode out of her room, and into the sitting room where Jalal and Mohsina were sharing a bowl of halwa, Yusuf lying nearby on the floor, reading a book.

'Yusuf, go to your room. I want to talk to Amma and Abba about something,' she said.

The boy looked up at his sister and then at his parents, to see if they would support the command. Mohsina met his gaze and gave a nod. He sighed, stood up, and left the room.

'What is it?' asked Jalal casually.

'I want to marry Iqbal Pehlwan.'

A loud cough and the sound of retching filled the room, and Mohsina thumped Jalal on the back repeatedly until it subsided. He wiped spit and flecks of halwa from the corners of his mouth with his thumb, gaping at her with a mixture of anger, confusion, and—was that a hint of joy? Mohsina's face held an incredulous expression. She was looking her daughter up and down, as if she were trying to process the fact that the statement had come from the same body.

'Uh, go to your room,' said Jalal.

'Why?' asked Suraiya, ready to argue.

Jalal sighed and said, 'We will come speak to you in a moment. Just go, Suraiya.'

She considered pressing the issue, but then turned around and went back to her room. The sound of their voices seeped through the walls. They weren't exactly arguing, but it wasn't a calm discussion either. After a little while, they fell silent. And a little while after that, Mohsina came into the bedroom, closing the door lightly behind her. Suraiya sat up.

'I have to ask you something,' said Mohsina.

'What is it?'

'First you have to promise me you won't lie to me about it. You have to tell me the truth.'

'I promise I will tell you the truth, Amma.'

'Khuda kasam?'

Suraiya reached up and pinched her own earlobes before replying, 'Khuda kasam.'

'Okay. Did anything, erm . . . did anything happen, between you and the boy while they were here?'

'No,' said Suraiya simply. 'We talked. That is all.'

'What would you talk about?' asked Mohsina.

'Politics. Things happening right now. Friends. School. Just, anything. We would talk. What does that matter? Nothing happened between us, but I like him, Amma.'

'Hmm . . .' This was not a day Mohsina had expected to come anytime soon. She had thought that maybe in a year or two, they would start looking at suitors for Suraiaya. They might've started the year before, had everything not changed. 'Does he like you too?' she finally asked.

'I think he does.'

'You think?'

'I know he does.' Suraiya's voice was firm.

'How can you know that if he hasn't said it?' asked Mohsina.

'It's obvious. The way he speaks to me; the way he looks at me. I don't know how to explain it exactly, but I just know it. He didn't say it. I don't think he knows how to say things like that.'

Mohsina sighed and looked Suraiya in the eye. 'A pehlwan? Of all things?' she finally asked.

'What's wrong with that?' countered Suraiya.

'Nothing, meri jaan, nothing at all. It's just . . . unexpected.'

Mohsina stood there for another moment, looking around the room, as if she'd be able to find the words she'd lost somewhere in the dusty corners, before finally saying, 'Okay,' and walking out.

Jalal came into the bedroom a few minutes later and sat at the foot of the bed, smoking a cigarette. Suraiya watched him blow out cloud after cloud of smoke, taking much longer than he usually did. She could see his jaw clenching and unclenching as well. Finally, he turned to her and said, 'Such much shaadi karni hai usse?' Do you really want to marry him?

'Yes. I do.'

He nodded as if he had known the answer already. 'Okay. Get dressed. We're going to their house.'

Half an hour later, the barely furnished sitting room of Hassan and Zarmeena's new home, still crammed with boxes and bags, was filled with excited squeals and congratulatory shouts. Of course, Iqbal had said yes before the words even completely left Jalal's mouth. Suraiya smiled to herself as Zarmeena embraced her, kissing her cheeks and the top of her head, saying over and over, 'I can't believe you're going to be my daughter now!' Iqbal was hugging Yusuf, grinning from ear to mangled ear. His eyes met hers. She knew she hadn't been wrong.

The ceremony took place just two months later. It was a small, private affair. Hassan and Zarmeena had nobody they knew in Pakistan whom they could invite. What few of their family, friends, and relatives had migrated to Pakistan were scattered across country, but most of them were still back in India. One of Suraiya's aunts attended, along with her three sons. The rest of the guests were neighbors, some people from the bank, and a few local wrestlers that Iqbal had become acquainted with recently.

It was a tremendously happy day for them both. As they sat next to each other during the dinner, Suraiya placed her pinky on top of Iqbal's under the table, and he responded by turning his hand over and slipping it into hers.

Suraiya cried when it came time for her to leave with Iqbal. Silently, like she knew good brides were meant to do. Until Jalal pulled her into a final hug, and she felt her father's chest trembling against her, and saw that his beard was wet with tears. He had only cried in front of her once before, when his mother had passed away. Even then, he had cleared his throat and pretended to be busy reading the newspaper. This time, he made no attempt to hide the tears. And Suraiya buried her face in his chest. Iqbal waited patiently, holding the door open for when she was ready. He hugged Jalal himself once Suraiya was in the car, his new father-in-law pecking him on the cheek. Mohsina spun an amulet over his head one more time, warding off the evil eye before pulling him down to kiss his forehead herself. Iqbal smiled at them, and his own parents, and the rest of the wedding guests, before ducking his head and getting into the car with Suraiya. The burnt smell of the city was not present that night. They could smell only the ittars, powder, and flowers on each other.

Chapter Ten

Their new life together suited both Iqbal and Suraiya well. Suraiya began the process of finishing her schooling to get a degree. She told Iqbal that she wanted to start her own school. 'You never told me you wanted to teach,' he said.

'Well, I had to have some things to surprise you with, didn't I?' she responded with a shrug. Iqbal had begun working at a local gym as a health and sports instructor. Every morning after the Fajr prayers, Suraiya brewed tea at the stove and watched from the kitchen window as Iqbal rubbed oil on his body and performed calisthenics on the terrace to warm himself up.

She loved the new life she shared with him, and he loved the new life he shared with her.

Their quiet adoration for each other could be seen, and even felt, by everyone around them. Hassan and Zarmeena were witness to it during the week, and on weekends, when the young couple went back to Suraiya's home to visit, Jalal and Mohsina were able to see it as well.

It was not a love defined by sweeping, long-winded declarations. It was defined by the smallest things and the simplest gestures. It showed in the habit they had of gripping pinkies, before Iqbal turned his hand over and slipped it into Suraiya's. In the way he would clasp two fingers around her wrist and gently squeeze it when she set his tea in front him every morning. It was in the way they glanced at each other through the shrouds of exhaustion that curtained their eyes at the end of each day, when she would meet his eyes from across the room and send a feeling of contentment into his tired body.

Iqbal took to scribbling little notes and leaving them for her to find in the drawer where she kept her jewelry. Simple things; scraps of poetry he had read in the newspaper that morning, or at a book stall on his way home the day before. At the bottom of each one, he would write, in sloppy Urdu, 'I am sorry, I am no poet. I am still simply your pehlwan.' Suraiya kept the notes in the small, handwoven drawstring bag that her wedding bangles had come in. The notes thrilled her. She did not mind the simplicity of them. She did not need long love poems, for there was enough poetry in the sound of his murmurs against her skin every night, and the quiet laughter they shared in the darkness after the candle was pinched out. She sang him no songs, for there was enough music in the sound of her pushing her bangles onto her wrists every morning as she got up before her morning prayers. It wasn't the call from the minaret of the mosque that woke Iqbal every morning; it was sound of those red and gold loops singing on her skin that opened his eyes at dawn.

In 1957, Suraiya and Iqbal moved to Karachi, which was then still the capital of Pakistan. It was something Suraiya had been wanting for a while. She had gotten her degree and had started her own tutoring course, working out of the home that she and Iqbal moved into two years after getting married. 'Let me think about it, jaan,' had been Iqbal's response when Suraiya first broached the topic of moving to Karachi. He had grown bulkier with age, his shoulders and chest bulging through the kurta-and-sweater-vest combo he usually sported, his large thighs easily noticeable through the legs of any pants or shalwars he wore. He had grown his hair out as well. It was no longer cropped close to the scalp—instead it was thick and dark, covering his whole head, but cut clean at the nape of his neck. A small mustache rested above his upper lip. He hadn't gotten any new scars on his face over the years, but he looked older now. A grown man, with impending wrinkles and a high forehead just beginning to peek out on his visage. Suraiya's hair had grown longer, the black color of it more vibrant. It hung just above her waist. She had gained a bit of weight as well, and Iqbal could never resist the temptation to wrap an arm around her waist and rest his hands on her hips. He loved how she felt in the crook of his arm. Suraiya's eyes had darkened as well, the almond color changing to a deep chocolate one, her face tightening with age, highlighting how beautiful a woman she was. Laugh lines graced the corners of her eyes and mouth, evidence of the happy life she led.

A few months after the subject was brought up, the couple moved. Suraiya had an uncle who was a cleric, and there was a home available in the colony he lived in. She and Iqbal went to see it once, via train, and fell in love with it immediately. It was a two-story house, more than enough room for the two of them. And for children, if they decided to have them. It was something they had begun discussing.

Suraiya found work at a small tutoring center not far from Model Colony. Iqbal, on the other hand, quit his job as a manager at a gym and instead dug up and started running his own akhada. The move had surprised Suraiya at first. She had advised against quitting his job until after he got the wrestling pit up and running. But the first weekend after it was finished, Iqbal brought her to the new training arena to show her. The sight of the smooth dirt ring that he had built and blessed himself put a smile on Suraiya's face, and she grabbed Iqbal to kiss him on the cheek. 'It's beautiful,' she said. He smiled at her, the surprise reaction causing his cheeks to flush.

Iqbal's akhada quickly began earning the business of boys and men from all over the city. Sports like cricket, volleyball, and hockey had yet to virtually wipe out the popularity of native sports, and so there were plenty of people who still wanted to learn how to wrestle. It was also the first akhada in Karachi, since the majority of the pehlwans in the country lived and trained in the Punjab region, where the wrestling culture was strongest. Iqbal took on other pehlwans to help with training. Anyone claiming to have credentials to help with coaching had to first step into the akhada with Iqbal and wrestle him. If, by the end, their skills had managed to convince Iqbal that they were qualified, he would hire them. If a person's skills weren't up to par, he was asked to join the akhada anyway. 'I can make a true pehlwan out of you, if you want,' is what Iqbal would tell them. The akhada closed only once. On September 4, 1959, when Suraiya and Iqbal's son, Bilal, was born. The sight of more than a dozen burly young men with flowers for ears all cramped together in the hospital waiting room was a comical one.

He trained and coached many a wrestler to national and international fame. National champions and Commonwealth Games champions alike would credit their training to his akhada. Daniyal Pehlwan, Mohammad Pehlwan, Obaidullah Pehlwan, and countless others who went on to become championship-level athletes all heralded their old coach as the reason for their successes. Iqbal himself competed occasionally in local matches. Suraiya would sit in the front row always, with Bilal in her arms, smiling proudly and grimacing every time her husband's body felt the impact of the dirt, or of another pehlwan slamming against him.

Eventually, he stopped competing. Age caught up to him. He was still healthy, but a bit stooped over, and it took longer for everything to wake up in the morning. Bilal grew older and began training with the rest of Iqbal's students. It put a smile on Iqbal's face to watch his young son going through the calisthenics in his loincloth like the other boys; to see him practicing the techniques Iqbal taught them. Iqbal's hair was now long, graying at the sides and in back, the skin on his body taut save for a bit of sagging around his face.

Suraiya, meanwhile, worked at the tutoring center steadily for about a year. Eventually she became its head and converted it into a school, with extra tutoring still available after classes were done for the day. Young girls from Model Colony, who had degrees but not jobs, and who made a steady allowance tutoring young children after school in family living rooms, were brought in as teachers. For the first few years, it was a primary school only. More and more young children attended every year, their parents encouraged by the results. In the early years, Suraiya would meet with every new student's parents herself at the time of enrollment, but as the school expanded, she simply did not have the time. Two more buildings were constructed within ten years, and students of all ages were taught after that, up to the university level. Suraiya now held assemblies in the school's main hall, speaking on a flat podium with a microphone in front of her. Bilal did not attend the school for very long—only two years, before testing into high-ranked academy thirty minutes from where they lived. Iqbal would drive him to school every morning, and he would leave his akhada at the end of the day's second practice to go pick Bilal up and bring him home.

Suraiya's face grew thinner as she got older, sharpening her cheekbones and making her eyes seem bigger. Her hair wasn't as long anymore. It only fell to her upper back these days, and during the day she wore it in a neat bun that was streaked with copper where she had dyed her gray hairs with henna. Her eyes had grown weaker, and she wore glasses now from time to time, though she never wore them at home unless she was reading something before bed. Whenever she forgot to take them off before she fell asleep, Iqbal would reach over and pull them off for her.

One night, after they had finished making love, Iqbal laid there naked with the covers pulled over his upper legs and groin. The curve of his bare hip was visible, and it was there that Suraiya was curled up, absentmindedly stroking the bare skin of the exposed hip. The sheets were drawn over the lower half of her body and her hair was splayed out on the bed, where one of Iqbal's hands was stroking it idly. Suddenly, her fingers changed their course and very gently touched the scar he had shown her the first time they'd had tea together. It was soft and almost leather-like to the touch, and Iqbal jumped in reaction. Suraiya moved up to lay beside him, her fingers still slowly making their way up the old wound. He didn't move to stop her, but his hand came up to rest beside hers, and his fingers rested lightly on her wrist as it worked its way up. 'Do you still think about him sometimes?' Suraiya whispered.

Iqbal looked at her. He lowered his fingers from her wrist and nodded slowly. 'All the time. Anytime I see it in the mirror.' He touched the scar himself. 'Every time.'

Suraiya kissed him, cupping the side of his face in her hand. When she spoke again, she said, 'Sometimes I remember those months, and I can almost taste that uncertainty again. The fear. It's like it's right outside our window.'

'Not much has changed, meri jaan,' said Iqbal.

He closed his eyes, and Suraiya rested her head on his chest, looking through the curtains out into the cloudy night.

Riots had broken out in East Pakistan that week. The people there were not content with the fact that Urdu had been declared the national language. The language did not to represent them, they said, or their culture, or anything that they knew. Once again, Home looked like it was going to tear itself apart.

Suraiya retired after the class of 1981 graduated, and Iqbal retired from his coaching a year later. Handing off his akhada to the care of one of the younger instructors, he would still show up once in a while to a local dangal as an honored guest. Sometimes his former wrestlers would pay a visit to his home, wanting their new wives and children to meet their old coach, and he and Suraiya would host them graciously, as they did with any of Suraiya's former students who remembered their old teacher. They would talk about their new jobs, reminisce on how they'd developed an interest for such-and-such under her tutelage, and marvel at how it had gotten them to where they were in life.

Bilal got married eventually, and they were both overjoyed to see their son and his wife so happy on their wedding day. The girl's name was Fatima. Bilal had met her at university, and the two were a year into their courtship before informing either of their families, but Suraiya could remember only a few occasions when she felt happier than she did showering the girl with fragrant flower petals as she walked by on the way to the car that awaited the newlyweds.

They had their home to themselves again after that. Sometimes Suraiya would wake up in the mornings and think she was forty years younger. Just her and Iqbal, the house a world for them to exist in privately.

The two of them together.

Every morning, she woke him by leaning down and letting her wet hair tickle his face, leaving streaks of water on his cheeks and eyes. The first breath he drew upon waking was filled with her scent, and that of the perfumed tulips and orange blossoms she added to her baths. She would laugh at his reaction, and he would pull her back into bed.

After bathing himself, Iqbal would walk to the corner shop to get fresh jalebis for breakfast. They soaked them in bowls of milk, and after eating them, Suraiya would use the syrup-infused milk to make chai. The syrup would rise to the top, cutting streaks of sparkling silver across the surface.

'I think I am dead already,' Iqbal whispered to her one night as they lay next to each other.

'Why do you say that?' Suraiya asked, tracing a scar on his bicep.

'What heaven could there be, aside from this?'

Suraiya smiled and clucked her tongue. 'Blasphemer,' she teased.

They carried on like this in their old age. The doors and windows were sometimes left open while they lay next to each other, her head on his chest, his hand stroking her back.

'They have no shame!' the neighbors would whisper furiously.

'Uncle-ji is a lovesick dog!' the neighborhood children teased every time they caught a glimpse of the couple out on a walk together.

Iqbal would laugh with them. 'He is! He is! And you will be too, but none of you will get a woman who compares to my beautiful bride. This star that fell to earth! This angel who heard my prayers up in heaven one day and said, "I will marry poor Iqbal!"' And Suraiya would shake her head and hit his shoulder, telling him not to talk like this in front of children. But she'd laugh with him as well.

It was the neighborhood children who first noticed Iqbal when he was walking back from the corner shop one morning. A bag of jalebis in hand, he suddenly stopped walking, swayed on the spot, and collapsed. Blood pooled under his head where it hit the ground, and the children ran to get help.

Suraiya was at home. Their granddaughter, Aasiya, was crawling on the floor while she prepared the things for breakfast. The bowls of milk had been set on the kitchen counter. They were thrown out the next afternoon, when someone finally noticed where the rancid smell was coming from.

PART THREE
SALIM THE CHAIWALLAH

Chapter Eleven

July 2, 2017

Salim was not asleep. He knew he wasn't. But he wasn't completely awake either. He was dozing off in a chair with his arms crossed over his chest. Another minute like this and he would slip into a heavy sleep, one where he might not wake until the dream ended completely and left a permanent imprint on the walls of his mind. But someone in the kitchen banged a metal something against another metal something, and the loud clang caused Salim's drooping eyes to snap open. He blinked rapidly to clear his head, looked around, smacked his lips, and stood with a low groan.

Time had been kind enough to not give Salim anything very detrimental as he aged—not yet anyway—but the one thing he found to be entirely unavoidable was pain. Everything hurt, always. Some sort of ache, some sort of strain was always present. He felt and acted like a young man most of the time, and by the grace of God he was still strong enough to take care of himself, but regardless of all that Salim had grown old. He knew it when he stood up and his knees and ankles tightened with discomfort. When he moved, he could swear his hips and lower back made sounds like a door hinge in need of oil; a long, internal creak. His arms, covered in graying hairs, were still strong and heavy, the shoulders a bit stooped but still broad, his back still straight and powerful, his chest still big enough to house a voice that boomed when it needed to, and legs still thick enough to carry it all. But fat had accumulated, mostly around his midriff. An old man's paunch had grown, unnoticed, until it was too late to stop it.

Yes, Salim was an old man now, and he was still getting used to the changes that came with that. The biggest one, even bigger than his changed body, was how tired he felt all the time. 'What kind of life is this? To work every day?' he said to himself upon waking some mornings. Most days he just wanted more time to sleep. The same zeal for his work was not always present the way it had been when he'd first opened his shop. He often caught himself fantasizing in the middle of the day about going home in the evening so he could sleep. Salim hated this new habit in himself.

But it was still the early morning. He just needed a strong cup of freshly brewed chai and he'd be good to go for a few hours at least. Stretching, he stepped out of the back room and into the kitchen, passing a stack of large jute sacks filled with sugar. One of the boys who helped him run the shop, Rizwan, was darting around the kitchen, going back and forth between brewing a large pot of chai on the stove and frying puris for the breakfast crowd that would be coming in after an hour or so.

Salim called Rizwan over and told him to pay attention to the puris. 'Leave the tea to me,' he said.

'Are you sure?' the boy asked.

Salim nodded.

'Okay. Oh, Ashfaq is here,' he added.

At these words, Salim looked up and over the counter to see the young man seated at one of the corner tables, his palm against his cheek, silently brooding while drumming his fingers on the metal tabletop.

Salim clapped Rizwan appreciatively on the shoulder, before calling, 'Subha bakhair, Ashfaq Mian!' The young man rose from his seat as Salim came around the counter and pulled him into a big hug. Ashfaq's arms were not able to completely wrap around Salim's torso, so he returned the friendly squeeze as best as he could. 'What brings you here this morning?' Salim asked after they pulled apart.

'I thought I'd have some of the best chai in the world for the last time before I leave.' Salim's face fell a bit at the reminder, but then he grinned big.

'Remind me, how long before I see your face in my shop again?'

'One year, Salim Baba,' said Ashfaq.

'Inshallah,' replied Salim. 'Now, let me see about that cup of chai for you.' Ashfaq sat down again while Salim went back behind the counter to check the pot that was simmering on the stove. A caramel-colored skin had formed on top, and the edges of the scalding hot chai had bubbled up the edges of the pot, threatening to boil over. Salim picked up a ladle and stirred the mixture slowly, breaking the skin before scooping some of the chai up and pouring it back into the pot with one fluid motion. After doing this a few times, Salim turned the heat down as low as it could go, and the bubbling slowed and finally stopped completely, the thick, light brown drink barely moving in the pot. The smell of cooked sugar and cardamom rose from the chai, and Salim smiled to himself before grabbing a cup from under the counter and ladling a generous amount through a strainer and into the cup.

He carried the cup over to Ashfaq's table and set it before him. 'Brewed fresh, first cup of the day, Ashfaq Mian.'

'Thank you, Salim Baba,' said Ashfaq. He looked up at Salim and smiled, then glanced at the entrance of the shop, and then at one of the opposite corners.

'Kya hua?' What is it? Salim asked.

'Has, erm, Aasiya been here at all this morning?' the boy asked.

'Ah.' A smile spread on Salim's face. 'No. She has not. Why? Any particular reason you're looking for our gul so early in the morning?'

Ashfaq shook his head shyly, though he was unable to stop himself from grinning at Salim calling her 'OUR gul.'

'Well, if you had plans to meet her here, I'm sure she'll be along soon enough. That girl has never let you down, Ashfaq Mian.'

'Oh, I know it,' mumbled Ashfaq. He turned his attention to the chai, taking the first sip and closing his eyes as it went down.

Salim patted him on the back before turning around and going back behind the counter. Rizwan had finished frying the puris and was now preparing a thick, bright orange halwa to serve with them. He tossed a handful of slivered almonds in as he stirred the sweet.

'I'll wrap these,' said Salim, nodding his head at the puris. 'What time does Mehmood come in again?'

'In an hour or so, saab.'

Salim grunted and began wrapping the puris in newspaper, binding them tightly with rubber bands so the heat wouldn't escape. A small, greasy pile began to form as he stacked the wrapped packets on top of each other. Right as he was finishing, the bell above the shop door rang and he looked up. A young woman stood there, looking around the shop. Her scarf was draped loosely over her head and about her shoulders. Her eyes fell on Salim, and he gave her a big smile, which she returned.

'Subha bakhair, azizam!' he called out as he came out from behind the counter again, wiping his hands on his sides as he approached her. The girl lowered her head a little so he could place his hand atop her head, though it was unnecessary since Salim was so tall.

'Asalam Walaikum, Uncle,' she said.

'Walaikum asalam!' he replied, 'You know, I was thinking of you earlier, meri gul.' Aasiya smiled at him again. 'Why were you thinking of me, Uncle?' she asked.

'Well, I had a customer early in the morning who was asking about you. You might know him?' And with his head, Salim gestured toward the corner where Ashfaq was sitting.

'I don't think I know him,' said Aasiya with a grin.

'Maybe you should go and make sure,' Salim said, smiling. 'I will bring another cup for you in a moment.'

Salim went and grabbed one of the small tin pots hanging above the stove and filled it up with chai from the big pot. He grabbed a clean cup and a tin of biscuits, which he placed in the front of his apron so his hands were free to carry the pot and cup. When he returned, the young couple was already absorbed in conversation, leaning in close to one another and speaking softly. Salim didn't like to eavesdrop on the young ones that came to his shop, so he didn't try to approach unnoticed. Instead he said, 'Here you go, children,' to announce his arrival, before he set the cup down in front of Aasiya and poured some chai into it, then pulled out the tin of biscuits and placed it on the table.

'Salim Uncle, please . . .' Ashfaq made to pull out his wallet, and Salim responded by smacking him on the shoulder.

'Put that away! You know my rule: if you're here together, you don't pay. I'll square it up with you next time you're here. You'll be a big, American-educated man by then!'

'That won't be for another year!' the boy responded.

'Well then I will wait,' said Salim. 'But I can't guarantee that others will be so patient.' He nodded at Aasiya. 'This is your gift from me.' And then Salim bowed his head slightly and placed the pot down between the two of them on the wire rack that sat in the middle of every table.

There was a soft spot in Salim for most of his regulars. He knew them by name. He knew their families. And they knew him. Salim noticed people's snide comments about the way he ran his shop. They said he didn't know how to be a good businessman. That he placed relationships with his customers on a higher pedestal than he did the desire to earn money. Some called him an idiotic refugee who had no idea how to make it in Pakistan, although not as much now as before.

'The Pathan has cow dung for brains,' a young man had once said to his friends, back when the shop had first opened. Salim had been conversing in Pashto with a boy from the neighborhood. It was well known that the shop had been opened by an Afghan man, and for whatever reason many people had assumed that because of that, he didn't understand what they were saying.

Salim's ears had perked up at the customer's insult. He had encountered such attitudes countless times before, but not in a situation like this. His shop, his hard work, something he had struggled so much for, and still there was hostility toward him. Right next to the stove, there was a dagger that he used to keep hanging off a hook. Salim had reached down, grabbed it, and then leapt over the counter. He had been in his thirties then, his physical prime, still agile and strong. A body that could support the anger coursing through him.

'Get out of my shop!' he spat at the group, in Urdu. They looked up at him, surprised and a bit fearful.

'We haven't finished our drinks yet,' said the one who had insulted him. Salim pointed at the man with the tip of the dagger.

'I'll throw them out; that's not a problem. But you get out, and don't come back. Or I'll show you just how easily this blade cuts through flesh. Understand me, you dog?'

The group eyed each other and then, very slowly, stood up and walked out of the shop. The one who had insulted him paused outside to spit into the dirt before getting into his car and driving off with his friends.

But over time, encounters like that became less frequent. People grew to respect Salim more; they grew to love his chai and the food he cooked, which was a blend of Pakistani dishes he had learned to make in his youth when he'd first come to the country, and the Afghan dishes he had learned back home from watching his wife. He stopped caring, eventually, about the snide comments of those who looked down on him. Perhaps time had calmed his anger a little bit.

But he had also become known for something else. Among the young people, his shop had become known as a place for couples to come if they wanted to spend time together and have fun without the scrutiny of the owner burning into their backs the whole time. It had begun years ago; a young man and a woman had stumbled into the shop together. They were dressed nicely, but haphazardly, as if they'd been late for something and thrown their clothes on in a rush. They asked for some food and sat down at one of the corner tables to talk. As Salim approached them with the food, his instinct to eavesdrop kicked in, and he was able to gather that the young couple had just run away from home and gotten married in secret. Or rather, they had attempted to. The cleric had changed his mind at the last second and gone to notify the girl's family, hoping for a reward. They had fled from the mosque together and stopped at the first place they saw for some food.

Salim set the food down in front of them and the groom reached into one of his pockets to grab his wallet. 'No.' Salim shook his head. 'No. You two are together; you are in trouble. You don't pay.'

The couple looked up at him in shock. 'We will leave,' said the groom. 'We are sorry to bother you.' They stood up to go, but Salim stopped them again.

'Do you have a place to go?' he asked.

'Why do you care?' snapped the groom. The bride placed a hand on his arm, and Salim smiled at her before turning his attention back to the groom.

'I mean no offense, son. I am simply trying to help. I did not mean to overhear, you see; it just happened as I was bringing your food to your table. I would like to help you.'

The groom was suspicious of everyone after the cleric.

'What's in it for you?' he asked.

Salim laughed a great big laugh. 'You're a calculating one. Good. That's smart. But there's nothing I want from you. More love is never a bad thing to add to the world. I would simply like to help you do that.'

The bride smiled at this and said, 'We don't have enough money for two train tickets. I have a friend who lives in Multan. Her father is a maulvi and willing to marry us. We just have to get there.'

'Hey!' The groom stared at her, dumbfounded, and she shrugged.

'Here.' Salim reached into his pocket and pulled out a wad of folded bills. He pressed it into the groom's hands. 'Use this.'

'This is much more than we need!' said the groom, looking up from the money to Salim to his bride.

'Are you sure?' the girl asked. Salim smiled at them both.

'I am your elder. No more questions. Keep the money, use whatever is left over to keep yourselves afloat until you find work in Multan. Now sit down and eat. Quickly. And then go. If anyone tries to take you from this shop before then, I'll deal with them.'

Salim had done something similar on two other occasions. The rest of the reputation he had was built simply on the fact that couples enjoyed coming to his shop. They had nicknamed the corner tables the 'lover's corners,' a moniker that made him chuckle and shake his head. He had no idea what compelled him to support it all, to help couples run away, to give them tea and food for free if they came in together. He believed what he had said to that young groom the first time, but he felt it was more than that as well. The only other conclusion he could draw was that he himself had married young, and his wife, Nilofar, would have approved of what he was doing. Sometimes he felt that she did, from wherever she was. 'I'm still trying to impress you after all these years,' Salim would say out loud sometimes, speaking to her, hoping his words carried over. The boys who worked for him just thought he was talking to himself, as they knew many older people to do past a certain age.

So, he let Ashfaq and Aasiya have their time together undisturbed. He didn't go over to ask if they wanted anything else and told Rizwan to do the same. Salim busied himself with running his shop. When customers began coming in for breakfast, he interacted with and served them, not letting their attention divert to the two in the corner—just in case someone recognized either of the young couple. Of course, the worst of the fallout would fall upon Aasiya. The boy would leave for America the next day, and even if that wasn't the case, he would still be afforded all the leeway that young men usually were. Once the shop filled up a little more, curious eyes stopped wandering over to the corner and instead began darting around just looking for a place to sit, or else eyeing the extensive menu painted above the counter. There was more tea to be brewed. Mehmood, his other assistant, arrived at some point and immediately took Salim's place behind the counter, serving customers and putting a fresh pot on the stove, which Salim tended to while yelling orders at Rizwan for what to get out and chop up for him so he could begin cooking the dishes for the rest of the day.

A little over an hour later, once the rush had died down a bit, Salim saw that Ashfaq and Aasiya had both stood up and were getting ready to leave. He handed the ladle off to Mehmood and went up to Ashfaq, pulled him into another big hug, and kissed him on the cheek. 'You take care of yourself in Amreeka!' he said. 'And study hard. Make us all proud!

You've plenty of people here who will always be supporting you, zergai.' He turned his attention to Aasiya and smiled. 'Young people always find ways to keep themselves busy, and young lovers find ways to make all time shrink into one moment. They make it last, or they make it pass in the blink of an eye if they need to.' The words belonged to a very old song Salim had once heard his mother singing. It had stayed with him all these years. She had sung it again on his wedding day. The next words were from a Bollywood film that had once been very popular: He will sit and say to himself, azizam, thinking he is speaking to you; Look how incomplete I am without you my love, how incomplete you must be too.

The young lovers smiled. They recognized the song, and they both bowed their heads so Salim could reach out and brush his hand over them. They said their goodbyes and then left the shop. Salim watched the door swing shut behind them and was overcome by a sudden wave of sadness. It surprised him, and for a moment he considered going home early, but he shook his head and dismissed the ridiculous notion—and the sad feeling. Instead, he went back into the kitchen.

Chapter Twelve

Salim examined the large wooden cutting board that was set on the countertop. Rizwan had chopped onions and left them in a large pile on one side of the board; on the other side he had left another pile, this one of peeled and chopped carrots, all ready for use. Off to the side in a metal pot was meat that had been cleaned and chopped, the bright red color a testament to its freshness. The boy had a knack for knowing what was freshest at the butcher's and just how to have it cut. Next to that was a tray on which he had set out all the spices Salim had said he would need. Whole black pepper, brown cardamoms, green cardamoms, cloves, a few sticks of cinnamon, bay leaves, cumin seeds, and the smallest pinch of saffron. 'Warm spices,' Nilofar had explained to him years ago. Next to the stove, he could see, there was a very large and shallow bowl that was normally used to carry large amounts of vegetables. In it was soaking enough rice to feed the whole restaurant. Everything was ready and waiting.

Salim approached the counter, pulled the rings off his fingers, pocketed them, and began to work. He reached into the cabinets under the counter, pulled out a mortar and pestle, and carefully dropped all of the spices from the tray into the bowl. Then he gripped the long pestle like an ice pick and began smashing all the spices, cracking them, breaking the hard shells, softening them up before beginning to slowly grind them in circles. The task made the muscles in his large forearm tighten and bulge, and his nose was hit by the scent of the spice mix being formed by his own hands. Finally, after about ten minutes or so, the bowl was full of fine powder, freshly ground and ready for use.

He had an electric grinder he could have used to make the task much easier, but for some reason today he wanted to grind them by hand. The sadness he had felt earlier was still there—he could feel it lingering in the back of his mind. Nilofar would have ground them by hand; it was only right that he do the same.

A pot big enough for a child to sit in had been placed on the stove already. Salim poured oil into it and let it warm up before dropping in the chopped onions. While the onions were browning, he went over to the fridge and pulled out a dish containing a paste of mashed garlic and ginger that he had prepared the night before. Once the onions had browned, Salim added the meat, stirring it into the onions slowly, and then added the paste of garlic and ginger, frying it all together, allowing the color of the meat to change on all sides. Water was added next, almost enough to fill the pot up completely, then a palmful of salt. Salim stirred slowly and turned the heat up, letting it all mix into a rich broth and cook down as well. While that was happening, he placed a frying pan on a separate burner and caramelized some sugar with a little bit of oil, and then threw in the carrots, along with an equal amount of raisins. Once the carrots softened and the raisins puffed up, he turned the heat down low and covered the pan to keep them warm until they were needed.

Once the meat stock had reduced, Salim poured it through a strainer into a smaller pot in which he had caramelized some more sugar, separating the meat from it. He then added a few spoonfuls of the ground spice mix to the stock, stirred it, and set it aside. In another pan, Salim browned a few slices of onion that he had purposely left aside earlier, and then added the cooked meat to the pan, along with teaspoon of sugar, lightly frying it in the sugar and oil for a few minutes before setting it aside. Lastly, the large pot in which the broth had been prepared was placed on the stovetop once again. This time, Salim added the soaked rice to it, along with all of its water, and poured the stock back in over the rice, along with the remainder of the ground spices, before carefully adding the meat in, layering it within the rice, and finally adding the carrots and raisins on top. The pot was covered, with a thick, clean sheet wrapped around the lid to imitate the effects of a pressure cooker, and the heat was turned to a medium low.

Nearly a half hour later, once the smell of the cooked spices was at a peak, Salim uncovered the pot and was greeted with a face full of aromatic steam. The pulao was ready. Just the way Nilofar had taught him.

He called Mehmood into the kitchen and had him taste it. The boy smacked his lips and grinned big. 'Perfect! Like always! I'll take it out and put it on a low heat so it keeps warm for the lunch crowd.'

Salim gave an approving nod and patted the side of the boy's face affectionately. He couldn't taste the pulao himself. It always tasted off to him. But everyone told him it was perfect, so he used their judgement as a gauge. His own scale was based on the taste that Nilofar's touch used to give the dish. He had learned it from her, but he couldn't give it that same flavor. And so, he could not eat the dish, at least not when he made it himself. Even if he was wracked with hunger, his own pulao could never satisfy him. One bite and his face would fall; his appetite would flee. Anything else would satisfy him, but not the dish they'd had the most fun with on the day that she had taught him.

'That's not how you cut the carrots!' she had yelled, laughing as she watched him bring a knife down the way a butcher would, slamming it into the vegetable and chopping it into big, sloppy chunks. 'It's not a piece of beef, jaan!'

Salim had shrugged. 'Won't it taste the same?'

Nilofar had responded with a shake of her head. 'You do it properly in my kitchen!' She had then smacked the back of his hand playfully and taken the knife from him. She spent the next half hour carefully showing him how to slice the carrots properly.

The memory brought a smile to Salim's face, and he blinked, forgetting for a moment where he was. In that blank moment, the sadness came rushing back. It was so overwhelming that it dizzied him, and he had to clutch the countertop to keep himself steady. What the hell is this? Salim asked himself. He thought of her often. Every time he made one of her favorite dishes, or something she had shown him how to make, he thought of her. And yes, it came with a bit of melancholy. But never like this. He hadn't felt so unbearably sad in years. He hesitated, making sure the effects had worn off and he had steadied himself enough to walk. Then Salim went back out into the shop and called Rizwan and Mehmood over. He said to them that he wasn't feeling well and was going to go home. The boys looked up at him with concern. Salim never left early. He disregarded the expressions on their faces. 'Can you boys run the shop for me, or shall I close it for today?' he asked.

'We can run it, Salim Dada; don't worry,' said Rizwan.

'Yes, yes, we know how to handle things around here. We will count up all the money and message you the total for today before we close. Don't worry,' agreed Mehmood. Salim smiled at them, partly for reassurance, because he didn't want them worrying about him, and partly because he appreciated how ready they were to help. Many of the boys from the area had gone through employment at Salim's tea shop, and eventually they all left to pursue other things. These boys would too one day. Salim knew he would be sorry to see them go, but he was sure they would visit whenever they had the chance, just as so many of the others did.

'Alright then. You two are in charge for today. I am just not feeling well. Inshallah I shall feel better tomorrow and be back to top form,' said Salim.

Rizwan replied, 'Don't worry about that, Salim Dada. You just go and rest. There is no rush. Mehmood, get him a cab.'

During the cab ride home, which wasn't very long, Salim closed his eyes and rested his head against the window. 'Very tired today, saab?' asked the driver.

'I am,' mumbled Salim.

Salim's apartment was on the second floor of a two-story building. On the way up the steps, he thought he was going to fall over again, so he clutched the railing to support himself. The downstairs neighbors' son was speeding around on his tricycle at the foot of the stairs. He looked up and waved at Salim, who smiled in return. 'Be careful,' said Salim. 'You don't want to get hurt and trouble your mother, do you?'

'I took ALL of the chocolates!' the boy cried proudly in response. 'I have them ALL!' Salim's nod conveyed that he understood, and the little boy, proud of himself for having been able to communicate such an important message, resumed riding up and down the hall.

The short interaction had provided enough rest, and Salim finally managed to enter his own home. He walked to his bedroom, where the bed had been left unmade, and fell on top of his blankets. The sadness washed over him completely. He felt he was going to be sick, and so he closed his eyes.

He squeezed them tight.

He waited . . .

And waited . . .

Chapter Thirteen

They had danced the attan together at a neighbor's wedding. Salim was in the outer circle, seventeen years old at the time, dressed in his gray tunic and black vest, a scarf with the colors of the Afghan flag in one hand and a sword held in the other. And Nilofar, also seventeen, had stood in front of him in the inner circle, her traditional dress a bright red, bejeweled with little mirrors and silver ornaments that made her shimmer with every spin as the music played faster, the dancers moving in time with it. After each pass, Salim would turn his head toward the inner circle and catch her eye, and she would hold his gaze, her eyes burning, making him feel more alive than he ever had before.

He spent the remainder of the wedding slowly moving in between the apricot trees in the neighbor's garden, trying to catch her eye again. Nilofar noticed, but she ignored him, even when her giggling friends whispered to her that Salim was staring at her. She shushed them, and they continued to circle each other around the garden.

Only after the tea leaves were nothing but dregs at the bottoms of everyone's cups, and the hookahs were being puffed on sleepily, and half the lanterns had been blown out to cast a dim light over the remaining wedding-goers lounging around the garden—only then did Nilofar approach him under the trees, with her scarf partially drawn up over her head and face.

'You're not very subtle,' she whispered, and before he could open his mouth to respond, she spoke again. 'Go to my father if you like me that much. I like you, but I'm not going to agree to anything if it's not done properly. Go see him tomorrow afternoon.' And she started walking backward, back toward the garden, and Salim took the opportunity to speak up.

'Is that a "yes" in advance then? Are you agreeing?'

Nilofar grinned at him over her scarf and stooped down to pick up one of the fallen apricots. She threw it at him and whispered, 'Go to him!' before running back across the garden, to where the women were lost in the trance of the old Dari wedding songs they were quietly singing on an old charpoy in the corner.

Salim and his parents went to Nilofar's father, Ayub Shah, the very next day with a proposal. Ayub Shah spent a week mulling over the proposal. Nilofar was his only child. He had to be sure he did this right, to ensure that she was as happy as she could possibly be once she left his home. Over the course of that week, Salim walked by the back wall of Nilofar's garden every morning on his way back home from the mosque, trying to catch her eye while she was out preparing the tandoor for breakfast. She wore her scarf drawn slightly over her head, pulled across the side of her face just a bit. He had a feeling that she noticed whenever he walked by, but she refused to look up at him. He wasn't sure why, but the thought that she was intentionally ignoring him made him smile. Finally, as he was walking by one morning, she glanced up and met his gaze. She raised her eyebrows, smiled, and blushed before hurrying back into the house where her mother was calling her from the kitchen. Salim's face split into a grin, and it took everything he had in him to avoid whooping with joy.

He had to hold it in until that evening, when Ayub Shah invited them over for dinner. When they arrived, he opened the door wearing a finely tailored navy blue shalwar kameez.

'Mobarak Bashe! Congratulations!' he said. He and his wife, Meena, had accepted the proposal.

'Nilofar agreed almost immediately,' said Meena, beaming. Salim laughed loudly and hugged his future in-laws tight.

In the weeks leading up to the wedding, Salim walked by Nilofar's garden wall every chance he got so he could drop a tiny scrap of paper into the garden. She would nonchalantly walk over once he had passed and quickly stoop down to pick it up and pocket it. She wouldn't look at it until she was locked in the bathroom. Only then would she see the number Salim had written that day—counting the days left until their wedding. When there were only two weeks left, great pains were taken to keep the future bride and groom away from each other until the auspicious day. Salim's friends and other men from the neighborhood began walking to and from the mosque with him, so he could no longer pass by the back wall whenever he wanted to.

Nilofar was likewise accompanied everywhere by her mother, or any of the hawk-eyed neighborhood women, who would loudly shoo her away or shield her from view whenever any group of young men walked by, on the off chance that Salim might be among them. 'It would be bad luck!' they explained to her. 'Besides, a man's desires will reach their peak on the wedding night if he doesn't see the girl's beauty before then.'

And finally, the day arrived. The nikkah ceremony took place in their local mosque following the Maghrib prayers. Ayub Shah and his brother sat across from Salim and his father on Nilofar's behalf. The rest of the room was filled with male relatives from both sides. Salim was glowing with happiness, dressed in a new cream-colored suit that his father had gifted him, with a bright green scarf draped over his shoulders. After

Salim agreed to the marriage three times, the mullah shuffled over to the next room where Nilofar waited with her mother and all the women from both sides of both families. She sat in the very center of the room, wearing a bright green dress covered in shimmering gold sparkles. A veil was drawn over her face, and she sat with her knees pulled up to her chest and her eyes downcast. When the mullah sat next to her and asked her if she approved of the marriage, she had to fight the urge to shriek with joy as she said, 'Qabool. Qabool. Qabool.'

At the wedding celebration, Salim and Nilofar sat next to each other as they were showered with flower petals from trays piled high with jasmine, dried tulips, lilies, and pomegranate blossoms. They sat next to each other at the end of the long row of dinner tables as platters upon platters of roasted lamb, rice, and bread were brought out. They beamed as they watched people rush at them, fighting over who got to sit closest to the newlyweds.

They walked side by side to the car at the end of the night, under a shower of yet more flowers, with a copy of the Quran held above their heads by a member of the wedding party to cast a blessed shadow over them. And finally, once they were in the back seat of the car, they turned to each other and smiled. Salim gestured at the veil, asking for permission, and Nilofar nodded. He gently pulled the veil up over her head and looked into her hazel eyes for the first time as her husband. They rode back from the wedding hall in silence, hand in hand. It was the fall of 1976. The war would begin in just a couple of years and tear their lives apart, but in that time, they lived and loved with tremendous passion.

They moved in with Salim's parents for a few months while Salim saved up enough money from his job to cover half the cost of a plot of land on the other side of town. It had yet to be developed and was being sold off for relatively cheap. Once he had half the money, Salim borrowed the other half from his father, and one Saturday afternoon, he took

Nilofar to the plot of land and purchased it right in front of her. After signing his name on all the papers presented to him by the now former owner, Salim turned to her and said, 'I am going to build our home here.'

It took him nearly eight months to do it, but with the help of two friends who owned a small construction company, Salim was able to build himself and Nilofar a beautiful little home on that plot of land. He and Nilofar moved in during the fall of 1977 and hosted big dinners for their friends and family every weekend. Salim helped Nilofar in the kitchen to the best of his ability, but the endeavors usually ended with him being chased out because he was slowing things down. During the week, he would rise each morning to go pray at the mosque, and find Nilofar awake, having finished her own prayers, with freshly brewed tea for the two of them. They would sit and have tea with naan and apricot jam. They talked quietly, and Salim would sing softly to her, old Pashto ballads or Bollywood songs. She would close her eyes and hum along, a big smile lighting up her whole face in the dim early morning light that peeked in through the windows.

When he came home from work in the evenings, Nilofar would be reading in the nook near the window. Salim would wrap an arm around her waist and kiss her cheek and neck. 'You still haven't left me yet,' he would say.

'Stay on your toes. I will soon,' she would reply with a grin. She would make dinner then, while Salim watched, and once in a while she tried to teach him how to make what she was cooking. Sometimes the results were disastrous; other times she would taste the end result of his labors, smack her lips, and say, 'I couldn't have made it better myself, janam.'

At night, before bed, he would read to her.

She would lay her head on him, her thick, dark hair splayed out beautifully across his bare chest, with her arms wrapped around his neck.

He would hold her tight as he read, his glasses balanced at the very end of his nose, sleepy eyes peering over the top of them to look down at the words on the page.

Such a blissful life together made war seem like a bad dream, something far off, to hear about on the radio or read about in the papers. A piece of hot gossip that would be gone soon enough. Until it came barreling into their lives without warning, the same way it did for countless others. It started with a neighbor being arrested in the middle of the night. The rumor was that he had been named as a supporter of the Mujahideen, but nobody could be sure. Still, the rumor became the truth.

'We won't leave,' Salim said to Nilofar one night as they listened to the radio. 'This will all pass. We don't need to go anywhere. It will be okay.'

Two weeks later, a firefight broke out at a market without warning, and a few dozen civilians were caught in the crossfire between Soviet soldiers and Afghan locals. Salim's parents just happened to be there, shopping for groceries. Salim could not recognize his father's face when he went to retrieve the bodies. Too many bullets had hit it and blown it apart. He identified him by the wedding ring on his finger and the black leather sandals on his feet.

They left two days later, after Salim's parents were buried. Ayub Shah had a friend who knew someone who smuggled people across the border into Pakistan for a small price. 'It is safe there, at least. Meena and I will leave two days after you,' Ayub Shah told them. 'We will meet in Peshawar. At least we shall all be together until this war leaves our home. Then we can come back.'

Nilofar fell ill on the first day of the long ride across the border into Pakistan. Salim hoped that once they arrived in Pakistan, she would recover. It was simply a case of nerves, he told himself, a result of the fear that hung thick over them and all the other people being transported with them in the tight space. Once they had proper food, a bath, some clean clothes—once they had a home, he was sure, she'd be alright.

But that was not the case.

She got weaker once they arrived in Peshawar. Ayub Shah and Meena never arrived in the city the way they'd planned to. Salim checked the nearby camps every day for any information he could find, describing his in-laws to anyone who was just arriving, asking if they'd seen them at all; if something had happened to them at all on the journey. He found no answers, so he and Nilofar could do nothing but wait.

The tiny, cramped flat they moved into with another family did not feel like a home. Even though it was the middle of winter, there was barely any heat to provide warmth to the people stuffed together in their building. Once a day, the building's manager would burn coal in the basement furnace for a half hour, the building's residents would go down and crowd around it, huddled close to the warmth. Salim would carry Nilofar down and sit with everyone else, wrapped in his shroud. A half hour later, water would be thrown onto the coals, and there would not be any more heat until the next day.

The noise that came from dozens of crying children did not soothe Nilofar in her condition, and the air around them was choked with the fear that the war would not end, that the Soviets wouldn't leave. And then it filled with a poisoned sweetness that rose from the blind hope that it would all end any day now, and they'd all go home soon. Tomorrow, the next day, the next week, the next month, and so on.

Salim tended to Nilofar as best he could. He went out every day to find odd jobs and used the money he earned to buy sugar pills and expired vitamins off hawkers on street corners, who guaranteed that their pills would cure all ailments. He bought necklaces carved in the name of Allah, talismans, and chipped rosaries that were sworn to purge the body of all illnesses—that anyone who touched them or wore them would find themselves in better condition than ever before the very next day. He fed her himself and helped her to the washroom five times a day, he bathed her twice a week with his own hands, using a pail of water warmed up on the old stove in the kitchen and a sponge. He prayed five times a day for her speedy recovery, and every night, he rubbed her aching body until she fell into a restless sleep.

She wasn't alone. Many of the children and elders who lived in the neighborhood contracted similar illnesses. There were whispers of typhoid and TB breaking out. A few of the elder women even whispered about this being their punishment from Allah for leaving their homeland. For abandoning Afghanistan.

Within a month, Nilofar was dead.

She was buried behind a small mosque right up the street from their building.

Salim didn't cry for an entire week. Instead, he silently choked on his grief. His nose could not smell, his tongue could not taste, and everything felt numb against the tips of his fingers. There was a ringing in his ears, an indescribable pain in his chest. It was as if losing her had caused an explosion inside of him, a blast so cataclysmic that it obliterated every sense that connected him to the living world. Finally, a week later, after he had prayed the Isha prayers, he brought his hands together to pray for her soul and began to weep. There were no choked sobs that carried in them the sound of the pain he felt inside; there were no howls, as of a wounded animal. It was silent. A cascade of tears sliding down his cheeks, moistening his beard, and he held his head in his hands and cried.

A mullah was sitting some feet away, having just finished his own prayers. He noticed Salim hunched over and could tell by his shaking shoulders that the man was crying. This is a man who truly feels the love of Allah in his heart, he thought to himself.

Decades later, Salim found that the sweetest dreams he had were the ones filled with memories of their wedding night. He could still smell the perfume of the flower petals thrown at them; could hear the laughter of the wedding guests echoing in his ears. He could still see Nilofar nodding at him in the back seat of the car from under her shimmering green veil.

Chapter Fourteen

The saltiness of his tears on that day in the mosque was a taste Salim could still remember. He opened his eyes and licked his lips. It wasn't just the memory—he had started crying in his sleep. With a groan, Salim pushed himself up into a sitting position and wiped his eyes. Nilofar crossed his mind every spare moment he had, but he hadn't felt the pain of her absence in a long time. He pulled his kurta off and threw it onto the pile of dirty clothes in the corner before going into the bathroom to splash water on his face. The cold water felt good, and Salim gripped the sink hard, the knuckles of both hands shockingly white in the low light of the bathroom. He took three deep breaths, an assurance that he was still steady, before turning around and heading back to his bedroom.

Sitting against the headboard, staring at the calendar on the wall, Salim tried hard to figure out what it was that had brought it all back to him so suddenly. Had it been seeing Aasiya and Ashfaq together? But no, Salim saw couples together almost every day, and this hadn't happened before. But how many times had he seen two young lovers before an impending separation? He couldn't think of another such occasion before today. They were usually leaving together, or sure to be together again soon.

This morning had been different.

With a heavy sigh, Salim reached over, opened the drawer of his bedside table, and fished out a box of cigarettes and a matchbook. Things became more focused once he started to smoke. A dingy ashtray was balanced on his sternum, right above the slight swell of his paunch. So many years had passed. He had heard more times than he could remember that time heals all wounds eventually. Or rather, it dulls the pain they bring. But the pain of losing Nilofar had yet to be dulled. He missed his parents as well. He even missed her parents, whom he had never been able to find. They had all become memories, distant and blurred. But she remained as vivid as ever in the forefront of his mind. Time had not helped his pain; it had cemented it and only made it grow stronger. He had gotten better at ignoring it after a while, but he was foolish to ever have believed he could leave it for good. It was nearly a year since the last time he had broken down like this when thinking about her. He had assumed that would be the end of it. It was all the more painful to be mistaken after such a long time.

Nilofar had become a fixture in his life, even in death. Salim had no idea how to get rid of the love he still felt in his heart for her. It influenced everything he did. Sometimes he wondered if a mistake had been made. That maybe he should have died with her; perhaps he too had fallen ill and taken a medicine that happened to work and forgotten about it all. Or perhaps he had been meant to go back to Afghanistan to fight and be killed in battle, only to be reunited with her in the hereafter. Aging was unpleasant, but it brought him closer to her. That was the only thought that eased him.

Since Nilofar's death, he had not been with another woman. There were plenty of places he could visit in order to tend to his desires. But he didn't. There might have even been a chance or two at remarrying, but still, he hadn't taken them. It was too late now. He was too old. Perhaps if he had money, and the desire, he could. But he had neither. Perhaps the money wouldn't even be necessary. He was well respected, kind, popular—some would describe him as handsome, even at his age. But none of that mattered. Sharing the remainder of his life with anyone else would just be passing time.

'I cannot get rid of you,' said Salim out loud.

No response.

Of course not. He hadn't expected one.

He became lost in his thoughts, snapping out of it only when a bit of ash dropped from the cigarette onto his bare chest. He had been holding it up to take a drag, and failing to do so, for who knew how long. As he blinked and looked up again after brushing the ash off his chest, Salim noticed the calendar. It was the second of July.

Perhaps that was part of the reason for his melancholy state. Tomorrow would mark ten years since the day Irfan was killed. Salim had always been fond of Irfan's family. He had been fond of Irfan too. In fact, he had just seen his younger brother, Sameer, that morning after Fajr prayer.

In the weeks following the boy's death, rumors had flown around the neighborhood that Irfan had joined with the Lal Masjid in Islamabad once the army began its raid on them in 2007. Apparently, he had been killed by a mortar strike while hiding out in a bunker, waiting for soldiers to come in so he and his cohorts could attack them.

These were rumors Salim did not believe.

He had known the boy. Irfan was one of the many boys who had worked for Salim when he was younger, running to the market to get flour, milk, eggs, and other things for Salim when he was about thirteen or so. When the boy grew up and stopped working at the teashop, Salim refused to accept his money whenever he stopped by. Or, when forced to take it, he would sneak it to Irfan's younger brother, Sameer, whenever he saw him.

It took months for Salim to hear that the boy had taken up the jihad and run off to Afghanistan to fight the Americans. That was in 2002. Sitting there now so many years later, Salim could still recall the shock and mild anger he had felt upon hearing the news. How could the parents have allowed it? They were educated people; they should've known better than to believe false propaganda and the cries of fanatics. What gave the boy, or anyone, the right to storm into his, Salim's, homeland and claim the role of its protector?

But then Salim learned that the parents hadn't allowed it. In fact, they hadn't even known about the boy's plans until after he left. He had run away without warning to do what he felt was his duty.

The boy came back years later.

Salim had felt relief, though he didn't know why. He knew what kinds of things Irfan had probably gotten up to there. But he couldn't help it. The tenderness was still there.

The last time he saw Irfan before he died, the boy had come in for chai with a friend. Salim could still recall seeing a look in the boy's eyes that he had seen only right after he came back from Afghanistan a few years prior.

It was a brokenhearted look. A look of conflict. A sense of doom threatening to swallow him whole.

A few weeks later, they were burying him.

'I'll take over a box of sweets tomorrow,' Salim spoke out loud again. 'The family deserves it after all they've been through.' He glanced over at a faded photograph that was framed on his bedside table: Nilofar smiling through her veil on their wedding day. He put out the cigarette and placed the ashtray back in its place before grabbing the picture. Salim lay there, staring at it, matching every feature of the face that could be made out with the way he saw her in his mind.

'Won't you say something to me?' he asked, touching the picture gently.

Salim clutched the photo tightly against his chest as another wave of exhaustion washed over him. He sighed and let his heavy eyelids close. Nilofar was waiting for him in the darkness. She was laughing and urging him along.

'Come on!' she said.

'Will you speak to me now?' he asked. 'I have missed you so much. Won't you speak to me now?'

Nilofar nodded.

Salim smiled before drifting off.

PART FOUR
SAMEER

Chapter Fifteen

July 2, 2017

There was a heavy stillness in the dawn air when Sameer stepped out of the mosque. He gently nudged his way through the small crowd at the door to the spot where he had left his shoes, curling his toes slightly as he pulled them on to feel the water from his ablutions pool under his feet. As he stepped through the gate onto the dirt outside, Sameer noticed a row of stray dogs standing across the street near the market, staring silently in the direction of the mosque, watching the people disperse. Once, when they were much younger, Sameer and his older brother had run home from the mosque to tell their mother about this strange phenomenon. She had told them that dogs were Allah's witnesses, and on the Day of Judgement they'd give firsthand accounts of who had come to pray as they were supposed to, and who hadn't. A smile crept across Sameer's face at the memory. He watched the dogs for a moment longer before turning the corner and beginning the walk back home.

A hint of purple light was cutting through the sky, casting an eerie glow on the dark shadows of people quietly beginning their day. Some were on their way home from prayer, and others were getting into their cars to head out early to their offices. The shapes of beggars sleeping under the shade of the almond trees that lined the street came into view, as well as the silent, sleepy watchman positioned in a chair at the end of the street by the gate to the colony. He was slumping in his chair, a weathered AK-47 slung over his thin shoulder. Sameer moved silently between the rows of houses, nodding his head and murmuring a greeting whenever he passed by someone on the street.

He slipped through another gate at the corner that led to his street. Glancing up, he noticed the woman who lived at the end of the lane was out on her rooftop performing her dawn prayers. Her white hijab caught the purple light, giving the impression that she was glowing as she bowed west toward Mecca. She would go inside and start making breakfast after she finished, he knew; preparing for the day, getting things ready for her husband before he had to go to work, her children before they left for school. This was her moment of solitude, of serenity, when everything was still; the short moment before the animals of the day woke up, and after the animals of the night had gone into their holes to sleep. In a few minutes' time, the sun would be out completely, the birds would be chirping, the world would suddenly be filled with noise. Awake.

The gate to Sameer's own home had been left unlocked, as it usually was when he left for the mosque in the mornings, and he quietly pushed it open and let it close behind him. The lock fell into place with a dull click as he kicked his shoes off and nudged them under the charpoy that took up one side of the small courtyard. There was a sink built into the wall right next to the gate, and he washed his hands and face there once more before looking at his reflection in the small mirror hanging above the basin. Dark kohl lined his eyes, and water droplets ran down his face as if following invisible pathways into his beard. He grabbed the small bottle of almond oil that rested on the ledge of the sink and squeezed some onto his hands, rubbing it in gentle circles around his eyes to wipe away the kohl. After a few more splashes of water, Sameer sighed and threw his head back to look up at the large neem tree that took up most of the small garden next to the courtyard. Slivers of early morning light were cutting through the serrated leaves that spilled over onto a corner of their terrace. During spring and summertime, the tree attracted hundreds of mosquitos, and unless one went out onto the terrace with a heated coil, a candle, or some repellant, it was to a barrage of painful bites that would blister and leak water all season. But in autumn and winter, there were no mosquitos to worry about, and even in a place as hot as Karachi, where the temperature didn't drop by much, the tree provided a cooling, sobering effect in the evenings. It gave off a dull sulfuric smell, one that Sameer often found to have an intoxicating effect whenever he was perched on the edge of the terrace after midnight.

At that moment, Sameer found himself wondering, as he often did, about when the tree had been planted here and who had planted it. When any of Pakistan's numerous illnesses and infections descended upon Karachi, his mother often used the leaves to make powerful and incredibly bitter teas and draughts. She used them to help with her arthritis as well, and Falak, Sameer's sister-in-law, had used the same draughts to combat breakouts and summer rashes, back when she had lived in their home. Sameer placed his hand on the slender trunk for a moment before yawning and heading inside through the kitchen door.

The lights in the kitchen and dining room were still turned off, but the small light above the stove was on, and his mother, Khursheed, bustled about in its dim glow. She was brewing a pot of chai while wordlessly reciting her prayers, her lips tracing the familiar patterns of the Arabic words. Sameer cleared his throat, and she spun around with a gasp, lightly clutching at her chest. When she saw him standing there with a grin on his face, she frowned and shook her head at him in admonishment before beckoning for him to come closer. Sameer stepped past the counter that separated the dining area from the kitchen, and then bowed his head slightly, his muscles reacting automatically to their regular morning routine. Khursheed closed her eyes, finished saying her prayers, and grabbed Sameer by the back of the neck before lightly blowing on the top of his head, casting her blessings onto her son to protect him from the evil eye and the suffering of the world.

Sameer straightened up with a smile on his face, and Khursheed squinted up at him in the dim light. She often spoke of how, at one point, he had been no bigger than the palm of her hand. In her eyes, Sameer knew, the little boy he had once been was still visible, despite the full beard that now lined his cheeks and jaw and the long, dark hair that fell to the nape of his neck. She reached up and touched the side of his face with her thumb, near his left eye.

'You missed a spot,' she said quietly.

'Huh?'

'The kajal, you didn't get it all off,' said Khursheed. 'He won't like that when he sees.'

Sameer reached up with his own hand and rubbed the spot she had just touched. 'Abba won't see it.' He paused before asking, 'Is he awake?'

'In the living room.' Khursheed gestured with her head toward the door on the other side of the dining room. 'Go say salaam to him. I'll bring his chai once it's ready.' She turned her attention back to the pot on the stove. Sameer sighed and turned to leave, rubbing at the spot Khursheed had touched near his eye as he crossed the dining area and pushed the door open.

Other than her bedroom, the living room was the room that Khursheed had spent the most time decorating and redecorating constantly when they had first moved into their home. When questioned by her exhausted husband and sons, who were tasked with moving everything around according to whatever new idea struck her, she would say that it was the room where all visitors would form their first impressions of the family. Therefore, it was of the utmost importance that the room be absolutely perfect. It was furnished with a large rug that went from one end of the room to the other; bright scarlet with gold patterns woven in to resemble the designs of Islamic architecture—circular patterns trapped within large arcs, divided by long shapes made to resemble the minarets of a mosque. Unlike a mosque, however, there were no passages from the Quran in these designs; no Arabic lettering at all, for it would be a sin to plant one's feet upon the letters of the holy language. Instead, the stitching was made to resemble thousands of flowers. In a dim light, one could almost imagine that one was standing in a meadow instead of a room.

The walls were lined with ceiling-high bookcases, all but one filled with row upon row of novels, anthologies, biographies, books of poetry, all well-loved and well-read. The one remaining set of shelves contained a few pictures of the family in the top rows, while the rest of it was occupied with a few different copies of the Quran, some prayer mats, and a collection of glass figurines that had been gifts from family friends and relatives. Two very large off-white plush couches sat at opposite ends of the room, and in the very center there was a glass coffee table, which held underneath it a large, copper samovar that was decorated with fine calligraphic carvings and a small ruby topping on the lid. It had been passed down in Khursheed's family for generations. She'd had a great-grandmother from Kashmir who had absolutely refused to leave the antique brewing device behind when her family had migrated to Karachi around the time of Partition. Khursheed herself used it to serve tea whenever they had guests over, or on holidays.

Behind one of the couches, a large set of maroon curtains were drawn over the wide window that looked out into the courtyard. Above the window was a clock carved into the shape of the Arabic letters that spelled "Allah," which had been purchased some years ago from a clockmaker's shop in the bustling shopping district of Tariq Road. It chimed five times a day just as the muezzin's voice was sounding through the streets, reciting the call for prayer.

Next to the coffee table, folded into the shape of a mat, was a handwoven, chestnut colored carpet cover decorated with white flowers. And lying on top of the mat, with one arm covering his eyes, was Ahmed, Sameer's father.

'Asalam Walaikum, Abba,' said Sameer quietly as he stepped into the room.

Ahmed opened one eye to peek at Sameer and grunted softly, 'Walaikum Asalam.' He closed the eye once more and asked, 'Is your mother making chai?'

'Yes, it should be ready soon.'

Ahmed grunted again, this time with approval, and Sameer stood there, staring at his father for a few seconds, expecting him to say more. When he didn't, Sameer silently crossed the room to sit on one of the couches while they waited for Khursheed.

She pushed the door open a few minutes later, balancing a tray laden with three cups and a plate of rusks in one hand. Sameer got up to take the tray and set it down on the table, while Ahmed sat up and folded the carpet cover he'd been lying on, pushing the neat square of cloth under the couch.

Khursheed slowly lowered herself onto the floor so she could sit with her son and husband. 'The one in the middle has no sugar in it,' she said to her husband as he reached over to take a cup.

'There's nothing like a strong cup of chai in the morning,' said Ahmed as he took a sip and sighed with pleasure. 'Wakes you right up.'

Sameer had to agree as he sipped from his cup as well, feeling the familiar jolt in his brain when the hot mixture of milk, sugar, black tea, and cardamom washed over his tongue. The scalded milk and cooked sugar left behind a slightly sour aftertaste that every tea drinker eventually grew accustomed to, and Sameer combated it by dipping a rusk into his cup and biting into it before taking another sip.

'How was the prayer this morning?' Khursheed asked Sameer.

'It was good,' he said. Suddenly, he remembered something. 'Amma, there was a whole row of dogs lined up outside the masjid this morning after the prayer.'

Khursheed lowered her cup thoughtfully and tilted her head with confusion. 'You had nothing else to notice but dogs?'

'He's thinking about that old tale you used to tell him and Irfan when they were kids,' Ahmed said. 'The one where the dogs keep watch on who attends their prayers and who doesn't.'

She smiled ruefully and nodded. "That's right, I remember. I guess I had forgotten about that," she said, and then glanced at Sameer. "I can't believe you remember that."

'They're always there. I usually don't notice them but today I did, and it made me remember.' Khursheed reached over and patted the back of Sameer's hand while Ahmed watched silently. Sameer could practically feel his father brooding just a few feet away.

'Did anybody ask about me?' he asked suddenly.

'No, Abba. Salim Uncle told me to give you his salaam, that was it.'

'Walaikum Asalam,' Ahmed mumbled. 'That chaiwallah has always been a decent man. I should drop by his shop sometime. It's been a while since I've been there. He makes the best chai I've ever tasted.' Ahmed glanced over at his wife, who smiled at him. 'Other than you, of course, meri jaan.' He reached over and placed a hand on the back of hers.

'Save the charm for your students,' Khursheed said with a laugh. She looked at her husband and bit her lip before continuing: 'You really should go to the masjid, to pray. People won't notice. They're there to pray, not watch people.'

'They would notice, Khursheed. People in this neighborhood would notice.' Ahmed slurped on his tea noisily as he talked. 'I pray here. There's no shame in that. My Allah knows what I've been through; he knows what I've given in the name of Islam. Am I not allowed to pray in the privacy of my home?'

Khursheed opened her mouth to respond, but Sameer tuned them both out. This was a regular argument between his mother and father—her gently trying to prod him into changing his habits, and him remaining resolute in his refusal. It never went anywhere. The two would fall silent after a little while, and their frustration with each other faded away by the time the sun had fully risen. Khursheed would silently resolve to try again soon, and Ahmed would let his guard down until the next time the subject was brought up. Sameer often thought it best to excuse himself from the room whenever this argument began, and so he stood with his teacup in hand and made to leave.

'Where are you going?'

Sameer turned back around. Both Khursheed and Ahmed were staring up at him. 'I'm going to lay down for a while before breakfast,' he said.

Khursheed nodded. 'I'll make breakfast soon. Would you like a paratha and an omelet?'

Sameer nodded and turned to leave again.

Ahmed suddenly stopped him. 'Hold on. What's that?'

'What?' Sameer turned to face his parents again.

Ahmed reached up and gestured at his own eyes. 'Right there, near your eye,' he said. Sameer didn't respond. 'Is that kajal?' Ahmed asked.

Very slowly, Sameer nodded his head.

Ahmed exhaled through his nose. 'Why?'

Khursheed placed both hands on Ahmed's knee. 'It's very hot out; that's why he put it on. Isn't that why you put it on, beta?' There was a split second in which Sameer locked eyes with his mother, and he noticed a glint of pleading there—a desperation to avoid a fight first thing in the morning.

'Yes,' he said quietly.

'It's that hot out, is it?' Ahmed asked in a low voice. Sameer nodded again. 'Okay,' said Ahmed as he set his cup down on the table. 'It must be incredibly hot lately. I seem to notice it on you a lot, or maybe my eyes are getting old. Maybe they're playing tricks on me.' A few moments of silence followed this statement, as Ahmed waited for an answer.

'Listen, dear...' Khursheed began quietly, but Ahmed put a hand up to cut her off.

'Never mind. Just remember, boy, I see everything you do. You're my son. You are in my house. I may not always say something, but I always notice.'

'Yes, Abba,' said Sameer with his eyes pointed at the ground.

'Good, then that's all I'm going to say about it.' As Sameer turned to leave the room, he heard Ahmed say in a softer voice to Khursheed, 'You spoil him. You need to stop protecting the boy from me. I'm his father. I don't want him to end up like Irfan.' Sameer didn't hear his mother's response. He closed the door behind him and went up the wide and winding marble steps that led upstairs.

Conversations like this were commonplace between Sameer and his father nowadays. They had become more frequent in the last year or so. After Irfan's passing, Ahmed's view of anyone 'too religious' had become vehement. When Sameer had first grown out his beard, Ahmed had stopped talking to him for two weeks. Whenever Sameer mentioned he was going to the mosque for his prayers, Ahmed would grunt without looking up from whatever he was doing. He blamed 'those fat, old clerics with their wild beards and their kohl-rimmed eyes' for everything that went wrong in the country. For everything that had happened to their family.

Yet, he had not always felt this way. Sameer could faintly recall the mix of alarm and mild amusement with which his parents had reacted when Irfan had first begun keeping a beard and darkening his eyes the way one of the teachers at the mosque had advised the young men in the neighborhood to do. 'Our son is a Haji Saab!' Ahmed had joked to Khursheed before clapping Irfan on the back; Khursheed had been quietly pleased with her eldest son's new appearance, remarking on how pious he looked. 'A respectable man,' she'd said.

Sameer did not know why he now chose to follow suit. He didn't hold the same abhorrence for religion that his father did, although he did understand the resentment. Sometimes Sameer felt incredibly wary of it all himself, and in these moments, he considered abandoning it all. But there was something about it that he couldn't leave behind. In a way, it brought him closer to the memory of Irfan. That was not something that Sameer could fully let go of. He feared that if he made himself forget how to pray, he would forget Irfan as well. Already he wasn't sure if he could properly remember his brother's face anymore. Khursheed said often that Sameer resembled him, but whenever Sameer looked in the mirror, he wasn't sure if it was his own face he was staring at, or some hazy memory of Irfan's.

At the top of the stairs to his right was a sliding glass door, framed by a set of olive-green curtains that one of Khursheed's cousins had sewn herself. The door led out onto a spacious terrace, which had a large, woven plastic mat spread across it. In one corner of the terrace, a bamboo ladder was propped against the roof. On the nights when sleep eluded him, Sameer liked to climb up to the roof and stretch out on the charpoy that Ahmed had put up there years ago. Even on the hottest summer nights, there was guaranteed to be a cool breeze carrying over from Clifton Beach to wash over him, gently lulling him to sleep. The best sleep was to be had on the roof. Even if it came only an hour before the call for dawn prayers, it was sure to leave Sameer feeling more rested than he ever felt after a full night's sleep in his own bed.

To the left of the stairs sat a large metal chest, pushed to one corner of the landing. It was filled with clothing, blankets, and extra bedding for whenever guests stayed over. The chest was flanked to either side by doors. The door on one side led to the guest bedroom, which was fully equipped with an A/C unit and a bathroom. On the other side were two more doors: one leading to Sameer's bedroom, and the other leading to his parents'. Both bedrooms had their own bathrooms, but only Khursheed and Ahmed's had an A/C unit. Sameer didn't mind this, as he found the ceiling fan and the extra fan set up in the corner of his bedroom to be enough for him. There was also the fact that the A/C was never a consistent source of relief, as it operated based on the whims of Karachi's load-shedding measures.

One might think that the measures would not be as stringent in the summer, but one would be mistaken. Once the power went out at noon, it stayed off until just before the Maghrib prayers in the evening, around seven p.m. They owned a generator, but not one strong enough to power both the air conditioning and the refrigerator, so they had to decide what they wanted to turn on when the generator was running. Everyone had agreed that keeping the food in the fridge cold was more important than basking in the air conditioning. Besides, the ceiling fans worked with the generator, and that was enough.

Sameer went into his bedroom and closed the door behind him before making his way over to the window to open the curtains. The sun had almost completely risen now, and the bright golden rays lit up the bedroom and Sameer himself, standing in the window. He closed his eyes against the light, feeling the warmth of the sun wash over his face and the top of his chest.

After stepping away from the window, Sameer glanced around the room. It was an incredibly large room for just one person. Half of one wall was taken up entirely by a large wardrobe, and right next to that was the door that led to the full bathroom. Between the window and the bathroom door stood a modestly sized desk which held a neat stack of books in one corner. The rest was taken up by various notebooks and loose sheets of paper. Sameer's queen-sized bed stood in the upper left corner of the bedroom, right across from the door, hardly taking up any space at all, and the ceiling fan spun slowly overhead. The remainder of the room was practically all open space, save for a few dumbbells, books, and clothes scattered near the wardrobe.

Once, this room had been both his and Irfan's. In those days, there had been two beds and plenty more boxes and bookshelves taking up space in the bedroom. The room had looked and felt lived in. Now, it almost felt like it belonged to someone on the verge of leaving, as if the person occupying the room was not yet sure of whether they'd be staying much longer. There was too much empty space, and unless they had visitors or Khursheed came up to speak to Sameer about something, there was too much silence. As Sameer sat down on his bed, the only sound in the bedroom was that of the birds singing outside, and under that, the sound of the milkman's bike going up and down the lane, knocking on people's gates to deliver plastic bags of milk tied off with rubber bands.

Sameer took a glance up at the calendar that hung above his headboard and looked at the date: Friday, July 2, 2017. Sameer sighed and thought about how things would go tomorrow, the third, and for the week that followed. He would spend the days tiptoeing around the tense bubbles created by his parents. Ahmed would be quiet one moment and explode with anger or frustration about the smallest thing the next.

Khursheed would be somber and shaky. She would spend the bulk of her days alternating between praying and reading the Quran, pausing only to brew some chai or cook a meal—doing so only to stick to her familiar routine, as nobody would be eating or drinking much anyway. In the moments when she could be sure that nobody would walk in on her, she might pull out a photo album or two and sneak glances at the old pictures of Irfan and Sameer as kids. Sameer knew this, because after doing so she would call Sameer into her room, and she'd give him extra blessings, close her eyes and run her hands over her son's head more times than she usually did. It was as if she was trying to will all of the energy in her heart into a shield that would cast away all manner of curses, misfortune, and the evil eye that might befall him and, as a result, take away her remaining son.

Sameer himself would spend the day in a haze. He would go to the mosque when the azaan rang through the streets. He would walk back home without really thinking about where he was placing his feet, and then he would go up to his bedroom, where he'd stay until night fell and it was cool enough to go out on the terrace. This was how it went every year, on the week that marked the anniversary of Irfan's death. Each member of the family would fold into him- or herself, and once the week passed, they'd recover. As if nothing had happened. As if there'd been no pause at all in the regular routine.

Chapter Sixteen

Sameer walked over to his desk and crouched down to open the bottom drawer. Reaching into it, he pulled out an old gunny sack he had stuffed inside under a pile of folders and old papers. He tugged on the drawstring to open it up, and then he overturned the contents onto his bed. A thick envelope spilled out, along with a few faded Afghani notes, a maroon amulet, and an old bullet casing. When he picked up the envelope, Sameer felt the roughness that had settled into the paper over time, and he imagined that he could feel the grains of dirt trapped between the fibers of the envelope underneath his fingers. He opened the envelope and took out the letter that was inside, setting it down on his bed.

The letter had been written in a notebook, and the edges of the pages that had been torn out and bound back together were starting to fray with age. The color of the paper had turned a yellowish brown with time, and some of the ink had faded a bit, as if the writing had somehow been pressed even further into the paper fibers. The script was bolder in some places, where Irfan had resumed writing after he had left off with a different pen, or in the places where he'd scribbled something out, or written with such fervor that his words had nearly bled through to the next page. Sameer ran his finger over the worn pages and held the notebook up to his face. He felt as though he could still smell Irfan in the letter. He felt that he could remember the mountains, deserts, fields, small towns, and cities in Afghanistan. Places he'd never been to, or been close to, but that seemed as familiar as his own home because Irfan had been there, had written about them in this letter. He'd put a bit of everywhere he had been into the letter and given it all back to Sameer.

As hard as he tried, Sameer couldn't remember the exact moment Irfan had decided to go and fight the jihad against the invading Americans in Afghanistan, although he had been quiet and withdrawn for weeks before he left. Sameer had been very young at the time, only seven or eight years old. Irfan was barely sixteen.

On the evening of September 11, 2001, the two boys had come home after playing cricket with the rest of the neighborhood boys all day and found their parents in front of the television in their bedroom. Ahmed was sitting at the end of the bed, his brow furrowed with worry. Khursheed stood next to him, her hands over her mouth. On the screen there was an image of a building with dark smoke billowing from it, and out of the side of the screen a plane flew in and crashed into the side of the building. There was a burst of flame, and the building crumbled. Sameer had been too young to know what was going on. In fact, he thought that his parents were watching some sort of action movie. But he could tell something was wrong. When the plane hit the building, Irfan gasped next to him, Khursheed started muttering prayers, and Ahmed groaned loudly. They showed the same clip over and over. Reporters on the television screen chattered about the first real wound ever dealt on American soil. They were talking about Afghanistan. They were talking about a man called Osama bin Laden.

Ahmed switched off the television and turned to look at his family. 'It's only going to get worse from here,' he said quietly.

'What happened, Abba?' Irfan asked.

With a heavy sigh, Abba began to explain that the man mentioned on the TV, Osama bin Laden, was the leader of a group of people called 'Al-Qaeda,' and that they had stolen four planes and crashed three of them into American buildings and killed many people.

'They're going to come here now,' Khursheed said with panic in her voice. 'They're going to attack all of us. They'll use this,' she pointed at the blank television screen, 'as an excuse!'

'We don't know that,' Ahmed said calmly, but they could all could hear the doubt in his voice.

'Are they really going to attack us?' Irfan asked.

'No. They wouldn't come here. Besides, Osama bin Laden is from Saudi Arabia. Not Pakistan. They've no reason to come here, beta.'

Khursheed opened her mouth to say something but stopped when Ahmed shot her a quick glance. Instead, she began to shoo the boys upstairs to their room.

'Go to bed! Don't worry about this, it's not yours to worry about! You've still got school in the morning!'

Once they were upstairs in their room and in bed, Sameer turned onto his side and whispered his brother's name. "Irfan Bhai, are you awake?" He heard Irfan roll onto his side as well, and in the sliver of moonlight poking through the gap in their curtains, Sameer could make out Irfan's face peering at him in the darkness.

'What's wrong?'

'Was Amma joking when she said America would attack us?'

'I don't think she was joking. I think she was just worrying. I think Abba is right.'

Sameer was quiet for a moment, and then he asked, 'Is Osama bin Laden a Muslim?'

'Yes.'

'But the news people were saying he killed lots of people. A Muslim wouldn't do that. He wouldn't kill lots of people for no reason, not if they weren't bad. If they weren't Shaitan.' When Irfan didn't say anything, Sameer prodded: 'Would he?'

'Some might, Sameer. If he was a bad person, he might. There's bad people everywhere.' Irfan's voice was thoughtful, as if we were mulling the words over as he said them; wondering, as Sameer was, what could make anyone so desperate to hurt someone else.

Sameer spoke again: 'America is so far away. Have you ever been there?'

Irfan laughed. 'No, why would I have been there?'

'Not even before I was born?' Sameer asked shrewdly.

'No. Not even before you were born. The farthest I've ever been is to Tando Jam with you and Amma and Abba. And once when I was a baby, Abba took Amma and I to Multan, but I don't count that because I don't remember it.' Silence followed this statement. Irfan rolled over so he was facing the wall again and closed his eyes.

'What happens if they do come?' Sameer asked.

Irfan groaned. 'What happens if who comes?'

'Americans.'

Irfan hesitated before answering. 'I don't know. It has to happen first. Go to sleep now, Sameer. Say your prayers and go to sleep. We've got school in the morning. No more questions, okay?'

'Okay.'

Chapter Seventeen

Sameer lay on his bed, staring at the immobile ceiling fan. The power had just gone out, and Ahmed was out back trying to start the generator. It stalled once, twice, then there was a click and it roared to life. The fan whirred back into motion, and Sameer's eyes followed its blades as he felt himself sliding back into the space of his memories. He could see the day when Irfan left in quick bursts in his mind: being awoken early that Sunday morning while visiting relatives; his aunt and uncle piling him and all of his cousins into a car and driving him home. He remembered Khursheed clutching him to her chest and the feeling of her pressing her lips to the top of his head as soon as he walked through the door.

She whispered prayers only he could hear, and since he didn't know what else to do, he wrapped his arms around her neck and laid there. His Aunt Rubina told her children in a hushed whisper to sit quietly in the living room, and the children, able to perceive that something was very wrong, did just that, speaking to each other in voices that barely registered as whispers. Rubina bustled about, cleaning up the kitchen and preparing a meal. She held her rosary wrapped around her wrist, and she murmured prayers while she worked, coming over every few seconds to blow on the top of Khursheed's head and kiss it. Her husband, Musa, sat next to Ahmed, who was sitting silently on the stairs, his face ashen and drawn, his eyes expressionless.

A thought occurred to Sameer, and he raised his head from Khursheed's chest. 'Amma,' he said quietly. Khursheed looked at her son's face, into his eyes, and Sameer wondered if she could tell by looking at him just how curious and afraid he was. 'Amma,' he said again.

'Yes?' Khursheed's voice was a hoarse whisper.

'Where is Irfan Bhai?' he asked.

Ahmed glanced up at this; so did Musa. The whispers of the children from the other room stopped as well, as they listened closely for the response. Even Rubina listened as she worked. Khursheed had simply called in the morning and told her that something had happened with Irfan, but she hadn't given any details.

'Where is he?' Sameer asked again.

'He went away for a little while, beta,' she said.

'When will he be back?' Sameer stared at her while she tried her best to think of an answer to give to him.

She finally shook her head and said, 'I don't know. But pray for him, okay? Your brother needs your prayers. You're young—you're innocent. Your prayers echo louder than others. They're stronger. He will be back soon, inshallah.'

Ahmed stood up suddenly. 'I'm going to go lie down. My head hurts,' he murmured.

'I can go to the store and get you some medicine, Bhaiyya,' said Musa, but Ahmed waved him off.

'No. I just need to lie down.' And he went into the bedroom and shut the door behind him. A small click sounded as he locked it.

A couple months passed without Irfan before Sameer finally learned that his brother had gone to Afghanistan. Khursheed told him one night after Ahmed had gone to bed. They'd just finished dinner in front of the TV in the bedroom. Ahmed had shut it off in the middle of the news, cursing loudly. They had been talking about how militants were now operating largely from the tribal areas near the border in Afghanistan. American and British troops were not used to the terrain, and this was an advantage for the Taliban and others fighting against the western forces. But the American and British forces had the advantage of airstrikes, and they had just shown the aftermath of a strike near Khost province, very close to the Kurram region in Pakistan. Burnt bodies of young men dressed in black and brown shalwar kameez were being dragged from the rubble, bent and broken weapons clutched to their chests and their beards gray with dust. They were young, all younger than thirty. Civilians had been killed in the strike as well, though there wasn't much footage of them being dragged out of the rubble.

Ahmed had fumed for a half hour. 'Stupid, insolent children! Who are they to fight a war? What good does it do anyone for them to run across the border and get themselves blown to smithereens for a bunch of fat clerics? For a country whose government would kill them as soon as their foreign masters tell them to?!'

Khursheed listened silently, and once Ahmed had exhausted himself of his rage, she took Sameer's hand and led him from the room.

'I'm going to put him to bed,' she said. Ahmed grunted as she closed the door behind her.

'Why is Abba so angry?' Sameer asked after Khursheed had tucked him in and said his prayers with him.

'He's worried about your brother,' said Khursheed quietly.

'Irfan Bhai? Why?'

Khursheed sighed.

'You must promise to not tell anyone outside of our family. Do you understand?'

Sameer nodded.

'Irfan is in Afghanistan,' she said.

A moment of silence followed, and then: 'Is he fighting over there?'

Khursheed nodded. 'He thinks he is doing the right thing, and so he is fighting people who want to harm our brothers and sisters in Afghanistan.'

Sameer considered this response. 'Do you know when he'll come back?' he asked.

Khursheed shook her head.

'I hope it's soon,' said Sameer. 'I hope the war ends tomorrow. I miss him.'

Khursheed's eyes followed his gaze to Irfan's empty bed, and then she leaned over and kissed his forehead. 'He's with you, meri jaan. Your brother is always with you.' She put a hand on his chest. 'He's here.' And then she tickled him a little, to draw out a smile, and she said a final prayer and blew on the top of his head before switching off the light and leaving the room.

಄಄಄಄

As he recalled all of this, Sameer sat up and reached over to grab the letter he'd neatly laid out on the bed. He had found the letter in Irfan's old desk a few months after he was killed. It had been neatly tucked away among a few folders and notebooks. Sameer had no idea when Irfan had intended to give him the letter, or if he had ever truly intended to at all, but it was addressed to him and it was obvious just by looking at the letter that Irfan had spent a long time writing it. Weeks, maybe even months. Some parts were hastily scribbled, as though Irfan had taken a moment to quickly write down something he had just remembered, and other parts were neatly written for pages upon pages. As though Irfan had taken a few hours out of his day or his night to sit down and meticulously record his memories.

The letter contained Irfan's most honest thoughts and feelings, and they were written down for Sameer. He had wanted to say all of this to his younger brother—perhaps the letter was simply meant as an outline for a real conversation that Irfan had hoped to broach with Sameer once he was a bit older. Regardless, it did not happen that way. Irfan had been killed, and the words written in this letter were the most powerful account of his brother that Sameer had left. More than photographs, more than videos, even more than his own memories of Irfan.

Sameer smoothed out the sheets of paper that had been stapled, folded, and refolded countless times and, just as he had done so many times before, began reading.

It took him nearly an hour to get through it. Though he knew the letter word for word by now, Sameer still lingered often on the faded spots, trying to remember what they'd looked like the first time he'd read the letter. He wanted nothing more than to preserve Irfan's handwriting somehow, to keep him alive in the pages.

The first time he had ever read the letter all the way through, Sameer fell ill for a few days afterward. For days, weeks, he couldn't shake the sense that Irfan was still alive—that there was no way he could have been killed when he had survived everything he described. It felt, somehow, like he was just somewhere else, recovering from injuries or on his way home, writing another letter for Sameer. Khursheed and Ahmed knew nothing about the letter; they simply thought Sameer had been hit with a new wave of grief.

It took a long time for him to be able to read it again; the second read-through was easier to stomach, though still difficult. Every subsequent reading over the years was easier than the last. Now, Sameer could finally read the letter without letting his mind wander to the thought that his brother was still out there somewhere. But even so, every time Sameer unfolded and smoothed out the old pages, he still felt that, somehow, a part of Irfan was nearby.

Sameer lay back when he was finished, setting down Irfan's letter on the bed beside him, and watched the fan whirring lazily above him. He could remember clearly, Irfan's body arriving three days after the siege in Islamabad, wrapped in a clean white shroud. He remembered how Khursheed had fainted upon seeing it, and how Ahmed had broken down in tears at the gate, the howls of a wounded animal escaping his throat as he beat his chest and tugged on his own hair like a madman. Falak Baji, Sameer's sister-in-law, had helped him to his feet and shooed Sameer inside as black tears of smeared kohl slid down her face. For some reason, no matter how hard he tried, he could not remember how he himself had felt in those days. It was almost as if the ensuing months had been blocked out of his memory. He remembered the cloud of mourning that descended on their home, after the customary visits from guests giving their condolences passed. It didn't seem like anyone in the family was human anymore. They were robots, trapped in a routine—instinctively engaging in the actions they knew and suffering the pain of loss whenever they had time to spare.

Not even a month after Irfan was buried, Falak's family arrived at their home to whisk her away. She was not carrying a child and was still fairly young. She could be remarried. The brief marriage to the boy who had been killed amongst the rabble at the Lal Masjid could be left behind. Khursheed and Ahmed had not put up much resistance, but Sameer could remember Falak locking herself in the room she had shared with Irfan the night before her father came to pick her up. He could remember hearing her sobs reaching his room across the hall. She had come in to say goodbye to him before leaving, hugging him tight and leaving tearful kisses on the top of his head. Whispering in his ear, 'He loved you, Sameer. He loved you. He wanted so much for his little brother.' Before walking out of the room, she turned to him and said, 'You can always come to me for anything, Sameer. No matter who I am with, or where I am. Irfan will always be my husband, and you will always be my little brother.' Sameer could recall that night after she left being the first time he had cried since Irfan's body was brought to Karachi.

The changes came after Falak left. First, Ahmed stopped going to the mosque for prayers. In fact, for a few years, he stopped praying altogether. He would glare at men who walked by with skull caps on in the street, who had beards on their faces. In every single one, he saw a reason for Irfan's death. But after a while, the anger faded. The aging man couldn't hold onto it for very long. It exhausted him, and combined with the pain of his loss, it only served to burn him out twice as much. Khursheed, on the other hand, began praying to an almost obsessive level. Every morning, she would cast her blessings upon Sameer, and on Ahmed, who would grunt as she did it, and she would spend most of the day with her rosary in hand. Unless she was in the bathroom, or doing some sort of hard physical task, she had her rosary wrapped around her wrist, and she'd be muttering prayers under her breath.

At first, she and Ahmed argued about this almost daily. Neither of them was able to understand how the other was coping with their pain. But eventually, they came to an uneasy and unspoken truce. They learned to gather the hurt and store it within themselves, choosing to not try and dictate how the other chose to handle it, but also agreeing to not discuss it at all. Although they were still married and still loved each other, Irfan's death had created a gulf between them, and they had become islands unto themselves. They were so wrapped up in their grief, they couldn't notice how their remaining son was affected by it all, how very lonely he had suddenly become.

Sameer sat up in bed as the reel of memories playing in his mind's eye came to its end. He went to the door, opened it, and went back downstairs. Two hours had gone by, and he hadn't even realized it. Ahmed and Khursheed were not in the sitting room anymore, so he went to their bedroom door and knocked before pushing it open. Khursheed was sitting on the edge of the bed, praying silently, her scarf wrapped tightly around her head, her fingers counting her rosary with an instinctive rhythm.

'Amma,' he said quietly. Her eyes snapped open and she turned to look at him standing in the doorway. 'I'm going to go to Salim's for a little while,' he said. Khursheed stood up and walked over to him, and he bowed his head slightly, letting her cast her blessings over him again. This time, she kissed the top of his head after finishing. She walked him to the gate and held it open after him, watching as he walked up the street.

When they had been younger, on family trips to Tando Jam, Irfan and Sameer would walk along the train tracks in the evenings, once it was certain that no more trains would be coming for a little while. Sameer would stumble and giggle, his little feet hurrying to keep up with his older brother. And Irfan would urge him along, telling Sameer to keep his balance, to do as Irfan was doing. As she watched him walk away, Khursheed smiled as she noticed that Sameer's gait had not changed much since then. He had the balance of an adult, but she could still see the small child walking along the tracks. She blinked, and a ten-year-old Irfan was walking alongside him, his young, unblemished face laughing.

Urging his little brother along.

Guiding him as they walked the tracks together.

PART FIVE
THE LETTER

In the name of Allah,
the most beneficent,
the most merciful.

Asalam Walaikum, Sameer.

I hope that when you read this letter, you are safe and sound. I don't know where I should begin. There is so much I want to say to you, because you're my little brother, and you need to understand. But I'll admit I have selfish reasons for writing to you as well. I have no one I can talk to other than you. You and Falak. But even her, I cannot talk to like this. I have so much I want to say, and that is making it harder to figure out exactly how to say it all. I want to tell you about my time in Afghanistan, but the few years I spent there have blended into one big blur. I can't recall where I've been sometimes. Some of the places I remember might not even be real. I could've dreamt them up one night, and they could have joined the sea of memories without me noticing. Who knows?

I can say I've been to another country now. Although, I have to admit, Afghanistan still felt like home sometimes; like I'd simply gone to a different part of Pakistan. And other times, it felt like I was in a completely different place altogether. Perhaps at times when you miss home the most, you find a way to see home wherever you are. Or maybe there just weren't that many differences between here and there. I don't know. Such big questions are not for my consideration. But anyway, I'm going off topic.

Some boys I made friends with at our mosque introduced me to their teacher, and he taught us the meaning of jihad. He had put in our heads that we were destined to be true martyrs, and we believed him. He was the one who arranged our passage to Afghanistan. It was easy to sneak away, we were told that we would not need to bring much with us. A plastic bag with a change of clothes was easy enough to leave the house with. I went to the mosque for prayer like I always did, and after we prayed, we left. We were received at an old mosque near the border, and the mullah gave us dinner and breakfast. It was nothing more than stale chapatis and a watery daal, but we all ate our fill. There were two other groups as well. One of them was mostly made up of older men around Abba's age. Some were even older, in their late forties and fifties. They spent the night talking to us younger boys, telling us of how they'd gone over to Afghanistan during the war against the Soviets as well. One of the men, Salman, talked about how he and his older brother had gone to fight. His brother was killed after stepping on a landmine. Salman's face was still as he talked about it, but there were tears running down his cheeks. 'He was a shaheed, and we were all proud of him back home. In our entire village, everyone knows his name. They renamed the pharmacy after him,' he said proudly.

After praying Fajr in the morning, we were all divided into two groups. One would leave in the morning, and the other would leave after Maghrib prayers in the evening. It would be too risky for all of us to go together—a large group would draw too much attention. I was with the group leaving in the morning. Salman was with me. The mullah had us wait in the back room after we performed our Fajr prayers, and he walked in a little while later with a young man, no older than twenty-five or so, by his side. 'This is my son, Abbas,' he said. 'He will be going with you. There is a contact waiting for you near the entrance to the Khyber Pass; he will lead you through Afghanistan.' We all salaamed Abbas and before we left through the back door, the mullah stopped him and muttered a quick prayer: 'O Allah, watch over my son, my only family, and watch over all of these sons of Islam. Bring them back safe and whole. Make them fortuitous in their fight against those who wish to destroy us. And if they are to die fighting for you, O Lord, I beg you, grant them the highest place in Heaven.' And with those words blanketing us, we all left for the Khyber Pass.

We piled into a jeep that was waiting behind the mosque, two people in front and the rest of us covered by a thick blanket in the back. The contact, a man called Mumtaz Shah, was waiting for us at the entrance to the pass next to a large truck. It was seafoam green and decorated almost entirely with large paintings of bright marigolds and jasmine flowers. Mumtaz Shah was a tall, heavyset man with a thick but tidy dark brown beard and a long black shawl wrapped around his head. He had a bit of a gut that was lined slightly by his shalwar kameez, but he was still solid. His shoulders were broad and strong looking; his hands were tough and thick. Despite his size, he moved like a predator: agile, smooth, and powerful. He crushed our fingers as he shook our hands one by one. I still remember the hard leather feeling of his giant calluses against my palm.

'All of you, in the bed of the truck, under the tarp and blankets,' he said after he'd finished greeting us. 'Except you, chacha.' He placed a hand on Salman's shoulder. 'You can sit in front with me.'

As the remaining seven of us clambered up the ladder fixed on the back of the truck, Salman protested a bit: 'I'm strong enough to be back there with them.'

Mumtaz Shah responded quite calmly: 'It would be disrespectful of me to not insist that my elder sit comfortably with me. It is a long drive. They are the jawaans, the youth. Our time is past. Let them rough it out a little.' At this, Salman laughed and then agreed to ride up front with Mumtaz Shah.

Under the tarp and blankets with us was a bundle of water bottles, a box of stale crackers, and two silver bowls to drink from. Once the truck started moving, one boy whispered, 'How long do you think it'll take us to get there?'

'Probably not long,' responded another. 'We'll be at the Americans before sundown!'

'No, we won't, you idiot,' chimed a third boy. 'They've got to train us a little first. We're probably going to a camp. Somewhere away from the fighting, where we can't be found.' The second boy scowled at the one who'd called him an idiot, but he remained silent. All of us were wondering the same thing: what would our training consist of? And when would we finally have to use it?

It was dark by the time the truck finally stopped. We'd all fallen asleep at some point under the thick layers of tarp and blankets. Once the sun started to go down, it was pitch black under there. I couldn't tell how much time passed before I nodded off, and I didn't know how much time passed after I fell asleep. It must've been a while, because my legs had gone numb. I stretched them out in front of me in the darkness as a knock sounded on the side of the truck. The blanket and tarp were yanked off, and we all blinked groggily up at the blurry silhouette of Mumtaz Shah, outlined by the moonlight.

'Get out,' he said. We all slowly clambered down from the roof of the truck, stretching and groaning. The truck had stopped behind a large formation of rocks at the base of a cliff. There was a wide crevice in the middle of the formation, and Mumtaz Shah had carefully nestled the truck inside of the crevice, making it difficult to find unless you knew where to look for it. 'Start climbing.' Mumtaz Shah pointed up behind the rock formation at the jagged and weathered face of the cliff.

'How far up?' one of the boys asked.

'You'll see caves once you're high enough. That's where you stop. Go into the second cave to the right and take the tunnels winding right.

I'll be behind you the whole time.' Mumtaz Shah looked at Salman and added, 'You go last, chacha. I'll be right under you to help you along if you need it.' He glanced back at all of us. 'What are you waiting for? Go!' he barked. We all jumped and immediately ran to the base of the cliff and began scrambling up.

It was the first time I'd ever done something so strenuous, Sameer. I hadn't even gone up a few feet when I felt my forearms and fingers burning. More than once, I lost my footing, or I placed a hand or a foot on a weak point only to have it crumble under my weight and leave me with the feeling of having my stomach drop. Although Mumtaz Shah didn't say it, I'm certain that if one of us had fallen, we'd have been left behind. I wasn't the only one struggling; I heard the other boys muttering a mix of prayers and curses as they climbed. One of the boys let out a loud, 'O Allah!' as he lost his footing, and from under us we heard Mumtaz Shah shout, 'Quiet!'

I didn't look down at all—I would've fallen if I had. There was no noise except the howling of the occasional gust of wind passing by, and our grunts, prayers, and curses. After what seemed like forever, I reached a very wide ledge protruding from the cliff. It seemed to wrap itself around the whole formation, or at least as far as our eyes could see. I pulled myself up. Two of the other boys had gotten there before me, and they were leaning against the first cave, panting, trying to catch their breath. One of them was the one who had called one of the other boys an idiot in the truck. I stood near him, hunched over, feeling the sweat run down my back while I tried to catch my own breath. Finally, I straightened up and looked at him.

'Second cave to the right?' I said. He nodded, and we began to walk along the ledge together. 'What's your name?' I asked as we walked.

'Bashir. Yours?'

'Irfan.' We shook hands and continued in silence. After a few moments, we reached the entrance to the cave.

'Want to go first?' he asked. I shrugged and stepped into the cave. I could barely make out the two tunnels ahead of us. 'To the right,' mumbled Bashir from behind me. I nodded and began walking. The light coming in from the mouth of the cave was soon behind us, and we walked in darkness. My eyes adjusted a little, and I could make out the faintest shadows of stalagmites coming up from the cave floor, but navigating was still difficult. We felt our way through the darkness by leaning against the cave wall and groping out our path. The sound of voices echoed faintly behind us—the others had caught up by now. I could hear Bashir's breathing mixing with my own. I've never experienced silence like that, the kind where breath vibrates like a deafening echo. I don't know how long we walked, but after some time, the path suddenly became more visible. There was a light growing in the cave with each step. And voices as well—not the whispers behind us, but low voices coming from up ahead. After a few more paces, the path rounded out. We found ourselves in a wide space that was lit up by a fire crackling in the corner, as well as by the moonlight streaming in from an opening that led out onto the other side of the cliff.

There were nearly a dozen men seated around in this cave, some near the fire and a few near the opening, peering out into the desert with their guns slung over their shoulders. They stared at us, the light throwing menacing shadows over faces that were already hard and weathered.

'Asalam Walaikum,' Bashir and I greeted meekly.

'Walaikum Asalam. Where are the rest of you?' asked one of the men. He was sitting in front of the fire, unarmed. A wispy black beard hung from his face, and a scar was embedded deep into his right cheek. The light from the fire made his face look half caved in, and the effect made Bashir and I hesitate before responding. The man stood up. 'Where are the rest of you?' he asked again.

'They're coming,' I said.

The man smiled. 'Good. Come here. Sit down.' He beckoned us over. When Bashir and I stepped forward, he came over and embraced us both, shaking our hands as he pulled away. 'Two young boys to head our cause. Allah has blessed us indeed. Sit down; warm up. Someone get them some shawls!' he said as he readjusted his own black shawl over his shoulders. Someone draped a shawl over my back, and I wrapped it around myself, suddenly very aware of how cold I was. One of the men sitting near me leaned forward and offered me a cup of chai, and I accepted it gratefully.

While we sipped on our tea, the man who had greeted us introduced himself. 'My name is Nadir Malik,' he said with a slight bow and a smile. 'I'll introduce everyone else once the rest get here.'

A few moments passed. Bashir and I sat in silence while the rest of the men resumed their conversations. Nadir paced with his hands clasped behind his back. At last, the rest of the boys stumbled into the cave, and Mumtaz Shah came behind them, Salman leaning against him as they walked.

'Sorry for the delay; I had to help chacha here," Mumtaz Shah said as he let go of Salman, who slid down the cave wall to rest in the corner.

'No matter, no matter. Asalam Walaikum to you all,' said Nadir. He went through his men, introducing them one by one, and we introduced ourselves in turn, exchanging 'salaams' and embracing one another until finally, everyone was seated. Nadir was the only one left standing, pacing slowly still. Cups of tea and bowls of leftover rice were passed around to the newcomers, and everyone silently waited to see what Nadir would say next. Even the men guarding the opening in the cave wall had their heads cocked in our direction so they could listen in. There was no doubt who the leader of this group was.

'Welcome to you all, my brothers. The other half should be here by dawn. If I've calculated correctly, they are going through the Khyber Pass as we speak.' Nadir spoke slowly, with a smile on his face. His eyes seemed to twinkle with every word. 'I cannot tell you how much it pleases me to see so many of our young' —he nodded in my direction— 'and our old' —he glanced at Salman in the corner— 'are willing to fight for a holy cause. Indeed, Allah himself has blessed this land with loyal sons. Those who are willing to do anything to protect it; to protect the blessing of Islam that has been granted to us.' There were murmurs of agreement at this, and I too nodded my head with pride. Nadir stopped pacing and stared at the entrance to the cave, as if he were sizing up a jinn visible only to him. 'But,' he said, his voice now low, 'what are we protecting it from?' He paused, not expecting an answer, only giving the question time to linger in the air before continuing. 'Islam has been under attack for years. And finally, they've come for us in our homes. They are out there." He pointed toward the desert outside. 'They are killing brave and honorable soldiers of Islam. Killing men and women and children. They are staining our land with our own blood. Why? Is it because they blame us instead of the Jews for knocking down their buildings? No. It is because if they wipe us out, then they are one step closer to seizing this world. The Americans will succeed where the British failed. They want this unconquerable land of Islam to fall, and they are here to make sure it happens.' His words hung in the air like thick smoke, wrapping themselves around us. A palpable sense of fear and rage radiated from every single one of us. Nadir nodded, indicating that he knew what we felt. 'You will see the state of our faith today when we are out there. You will see how our own brothers and sisters have been brainwashed by them—how they flock to those kafirs who give them empty promises of a "better life" if they betray their land and their faith. You will see a land filled with Shias and Ahmadis, and others who believe in false idols; blasphemers who have deviated from the truth and gone unpunished for far too long. It is our duty to change all that. It is our duty to strike these invaders and these parasites from our land. They have poisoned us for too long!' Nadir pumped his fist in the air, and we all gave a yell and pumped our fists with him. 'Are you ready to lay down your life for our Allah, for our beloved Islam?' he asked.

'We are! We are!' went up the cry.

'Are you ready to obliterate those who would challenge Him? Who would destroy His holy land?' he asked.

'We are! We are!' went up the cry again. The air was electric now, and the sparks from the fire seemed to shoot up higher. The wind itself seemed to be shouting with us outside, howling with increased force. Nadir leaned forward, his face glowing in the light, the flames reflecting in the depths of his eyes, his scar twisting the smile on his face into an insane leer. 'We will set out after Fajr, my brothers, my fellow Sons of Islam,' he said. 'Get some rest. You will need it.'

And then he sat down, quite suddenly, as if nothing had happened. He wrapped his shawl around himself and engaged in conversation with one of the guys sitting near him. The rest of us suddenly became aware of the fact that he had stopped addressing us. Everyone snapped out of their haze and started getting ready for bed. Someone murmured something to one of the guards about it being his turn to keep watch. Everyone else spread out, some propping themselves up near the fire to quietly carry on conversation until they fell asleep, others moving to curl up in the dark corners. I got up and, after assuring the guards that I'd be within their sights, walked out of the cave. I sat down near the ledge outside and stared out at the land around us.

The moon cast an odd glow on the desert. The sand seemed to sparkle under its light, like millions of stars had fallen from the sky and settled on the ground. It almost seemed as if it was moving, like water. A shimmering ocean of stars stretching out as far as the eye could see.

'There must've been water here once,' said a voice from behind me.

I turned to see Bashir standing there. 'Why do you say that?' I asked.

'How else would all these caves could have formed in the cliff? There must've been a great sea here years ago. Centuries ago. Maybe before there were even people here.'

I pondered this for a moment. 'Well, where did it go, then?' I asked.

Bashir shrugged. 'I don't know. Maybe there were too many sinners and it was dried up as a punishment.'

I didn't say anything to this. Bashir seemed to think he had said something quite profound, because he laughed and added, 'It's okay. Maybe we can bring that back too. If we right the wrongs . . . Anyway, I'm going to bed. You should too, Irfan.'

I nodded and mumbled a 'goodnight' to him as he went back inside the cave.

'Maybe we can bring that back too,' he had said, and suddenly Nadir's words echoed in my mind again. I pictured the American soldiers who were killing our people. There was a roar in my ears again, but it wasn't from my own breathing this time. It wasn't even from the wind blowing around me.

It came from inside somehow, inside of me. I could feel it vibrating through my body, and only I could hear it. Only I could feel the pounding in my ears, only I could feel my heart thudding hard and loud enough to shake the Earth. . . .

I would like to tell you briefly about Nadir Malik, to give you an idea of the kind of man I was following. He had spent nearly a decade fighting for independence in Kashmir. According to the stories the older men would tell us when he was out of earshot, his whole family was killed during a raid by the Indian military one night. They threw grenades into all the houses in his neighborhood and opened fire as people ran out. He was only nineteen then. They shot his father and brothers as they ran out, and he was caught trying to escape through the back of their home with his mother and sister. He was held down with his arms tied behind his back and made to watch his mother and sister being raped by the soldiers.

'The mother tried to escape; she tried to fight off the man who was on top of her and shield her daughter,' whispered one of our brothers one night as we sat around a fire. 'But the soldier who was on top of her shot her in the head, and then he cut off the hand she had scratched him with.' Once they'd finished with her, his sister was shot too, and the soldiers hung her body from a tree before loading up the survivors, including Nadir, into their trucks and taking them to prison.

Nadir spent a year in prison, undergoing torture by the police the entire time, along with other prisoners from Kashmir. It's how he got the scar on his cheek—they'd carved into his face one day after he urinated on a guard's shoes. They tried to make him denounce Islam, to make him embrace any other religion—but being a proud Muslim, he refused. Finally, one night, the guards decided to brand him with the 'Om' symbol on his chest. Two guards held him while a third approached him with the branding iron. Suddenly, the Arabic word for 'Allah' appeared on his chest, burning bright, startling all three of the guards. Nadir felt the strength of a dozen men coursing through him, and he was able to overpower the men who held him. He murdered the guards, making sure to brand their faces with the iron, and escaped with three other prisoners. They fled back to Kashmir and crossed the border into Pakistan, where they trained to fight against those who were occupying their home. After two years, the name Nadir Malik was spreading across the region. He had led dozens of raids on Indian military convoys, stealing weapons and supplies. He carried out bombing missions on patrol stations and prisons, and those he freed were led across the border into Pakistan, as well, so they could train and join the fight. The brand that had appeared on his chest was seen as a sign—it was a mark of his faith, his devotion to Allah. He had been marked by the Almighty Himself. Who could touch him? Missions that seemed impossible were handed to him. Men and women who were uneasy or uncertain about a task would have their fears quelled once they learned he'd be leading them.

And then one day, quite suddenly, he vanished. Some feared he had been killed; others said he had been called from the heavens for a much greater mission—the holy warrior had a bigger fight to carry out. A few even whispered rumors that he had fallen in love with an Indian agent on one of his excursions across the border and he'd secretly married her and left his old life behind. Nearly three years went by without anybody seeing or hearing a word of Nadir Malik, and then he resurfaced in Peshawar not long after the September 11 attacks in America. He was older and, according to him, he had seen things. 'There is a greater enemy coming,' he would say. 'I have felt it; I have seen it in my dreams. They will come for us, and I must be here to help fight them.' And so, men and boys of all ages began to follow him instantly. He had a new title now. He was known as the Ghost of Islam; the man who wasn't entirely human, the one who had been marked to defend Islam. Why else would He brand this man with His own name? If Mullah Omar was the Amir al-Muminin, The Commander of the Faithful, blessed with the wisdom and powers of the last Prophet, then Nadir Malik was the man that Allah had hand-picked as his secret weapon. There could be no other explanation for how a man could have accomplished all that he had so far. None of us ever saw the mark, but some were convinced that it gave off a dull glow underneath his clothes while he slept.

That was our leader; the man we discussed in whispers anytime he wasn't around.

Those first few months were exhausting. We were constantly moving, never in any location for more than two or three days at a time. We'd pile into the truck—Nadir and Mumtaz up front always, along with one or two other people, and the rest of us would hide in the back under the tarp. Once the second group arrived, the day after we did, there were twenty-six of us in total, all crammed together. Sometimes only for an hour or so, sometimes longer. We'd stop and stay in caves; we'd stay in the sparse woods or rough valleys of the mountains we climbed. Nadir Malik explained our constant movement by saying, 'The Americans don't know this land like we do. They could search for centuries and never come across us. But there are traitors from Pakistan and Afghanistan helping them. They've been bought to spill the blood of their brothers and sisters, and they help them navigate this land. They don't know it as well as we do, so we must keep moving.'

No matter where we were, we all rose at dawn every day to pray Fajr. If we stayed close enough to a town, we'd hear the call to prayer being called from the minarets of a mosque, but even if we didn't have that, none of us could stay asleep when the time for prayer came. We took pride in this. We were convinced that this was proof we were meant to fight off the invaders. We truly were holy warriors. Why else would our eyes snap open automatically at the auspicious hour? After prayer, we ate breakfast, which usually consisted of nothing more than cooked onions, some naan, and chai. And then we'd begin our exercises, which consisted of push-ups, sit-ups, squats, and hand-to-hand combat training that Nadir Malik, Mumtaz Shah, and two of the other older men presided over. They taught us how to handle guns: hand pistols, Kalashnikovs, and AK-47s. We would disassemble them and then reassemble them, unload, reload, over and over. We would practice holding them in certain posi-tions; we were made to run up and down the sides of mountains with them we were made to sleep with them.

'You have to be ready at all times. You must not rest easy,' Nadir would bark at us. 'We are warriors, and a warrior does not sleep soundly.'

We worked on our shooting skills as well, whenever we could afford to. Sometimes we had to be wary of nearby towns or villages we hadn't scouted yet. Maybe American or British soldiers were stationed there without our knowledge, and if they heard the gunshots, they could bomb us. The only time I had fired a gun before that was on a hunting trip with Abba and his friends. You probably don't remember, Sameer, since you were very young. I must have been ten years old at most, and Abba let me aim his rifle and fire at a duck. I remember thinking the world had split open—that's how loud the gunshot sounded to me. I missed the duck, of course. Abba and his friends laughed and tousled my hair.

Things weren't so lighthearted for us Sons of Islam. Mumtaz Shah would watch over us holding a stick, and every time someone missed their target, he would bring the stick down hard across the backs of both hands. 'Steady your aim!' he would yell. 'Your hands tremble like a woman on her wedding night! Do you think you'll get a second chance to aim at an American soldier when he's charging at you? They who make a show of killing us? They who would kill us and then maim our corpses to put on a show for their generals and their president?' Bashir and I both had deep welts on our hands for weeks, although I admit, he honed his skills much quicker than I did.

Despite the constant movement, we didn't engage in any great battles like we all thought we would. Not until we were about a year into our 'holy mission.' We vented our aggression at the locals we encountered, once we were allowed to start scouting the towns and villages. Beating up anyone who dared to speak out against our cause, who tried to convince us that what we were doing wasn't the right way to go. Or, once in a while, getting the chance to fight with a local brave enough to refuse when we asked for food, water, or any other supplies. For the most part, though, people were compliant, since we didn't show any immediate aggression. Plus, Nadir was convincing. He would speak in the most beautiful Dari and Pashto, easily convincing people to supply us, gently suggesting to anyone who showed a hint of support for the Americans that perhaps they had been misled. That he or she would be forgiven for falling for their propaganda.

'They are not to be trusted, Aunt,' he explained to an old woman we encountered once. Most of her body was covered with a burqa, but her hands were visible, and in them she carried two plastic American flags. 'They bomb our mosques and our hospitals. They aim to bring an end to our Islam,' he explained to her.

'But that can't be true! They dug a new well in this town, two young soldiers together! They were no older than my own grandsons, and they even gave me medicine for the ache in my bones! You must be mistaken.'

Nadir patted her hand gently. 'Shaytan lives in disguises, Aunt. Even the first of us, the creations closest to Allah himself, were fooled by him when he came to them in the guise of a serpent. But they were forgiven, were they not? Allah forgives those of His sons and daughters who ask for it, those who recognize the Devil for what he is.'

The old woman sounded like she was weeping under her burqa. She threw down the flags and kicked dirt onto them. She clasped her hand in front of Nadir and said, 'I had no idea they were doing this! I swear it!' Nadir convinced her that Allah understood she had been deceived, and He, in His unending compassion for His creations, would forgive her if she asked for it. And if she helped devout Muslims who sought to bring an end to the Western crusade against Islam. The old woman did her part by giving us a sack of potatoes, some onions, and even an old box full of gold jewelry that she had managed to hide from the Taliban during raids. 'I thought I might sell it and give the money to a mosque,' she explained sheepishly when giving us the jewelry. There was a smirk on Mumtaz Shah's face as he took the box from her.

That same little town was where I received my first taste of blood, my first fight in this holy war I had elected to join. Mumtaz Shah and I went to the baker's shop to ask for a bag of flour.

'Two hundred Afghani,' the baker said without looking up from his tandoor. I glanced up at Mumtaz Shah, and he gave me a glance that said to try again, and this time, to demand it.

I cleared my throat and raised my voice a bit: 'I don't think you understand. We are not customers; we are soldiers of Islam.'

The baker looked up at me and said, 'I don't give a damn who you are; a sack of flour will cost you three hundred Afghani.'

'You said two hundred before!' I countered.

'Did I?' the baker scratched a scab on his nose and shrugged. 'Well, now I'm saying three hundred.'

I stared at the man, unsure of what to do next. I could feel Mumtaz Shah's eyes on me. He could've easily just threatened the man and taken the flour, or even roughed him up a little bit. Nadir might've even been able to talk the man into giving us what we wanted. But I quickly realized that this was a test and, no doubt, word of my performance would get back to Nadir. And maybe if I was deemed too meek or unassertive, they'd send me back to Pakistan, or worse, kill me.

With this thought in mind, I stared hard at the man, doing my best to remain stone-faced, and said, 'Give us a bag of flour, you dog. Or I'll have to take it from you.' I expected him to be intimidated, but instead the man stood up, enraged. He drew a dagger from his waistband.

'You bearded little shit!' he roared. I took a step back and drew my pistol, pointing it at him as he took a step toward Mumtaz Shah and me.

The baker stopped in his tracks and glared at me. 'You sons of whores! You come here and you think you can steal from us? You're not soldiers, you're thugs! You, the Taliban, all of you! You gutter mullahs! All your talk of your great Holy War, and when the Americans arrive and drop their bombs you shave your beards and go into hiding! Look at you now, boy, pissing yourself pointing that gun at me. I'd kill you with my bare hands if you didn't have that on you!' He spat at my feet. I didn't know what to do. I looked over at Mumtaz Shah for help, and to my surprise he was still watching me. The man's words had affected him. I could see the fury in his eyes, but he was waiting to see what I'd do. I looked back at the baker, who was still unmoving, his eyes darting back and forth from Mumtaz Shah and I. 'Go on then!' he yelled. 'Kill me already! Or don't you have it in you?'

A moment passed, then another, and finally: 'Drop the dagger then, and see if you can kill me with your bare hands,' I said.

I heard the words as I said them, but I couldn't recognize the voice as my own. The baker obviously hadn't been expecting this either, but he quickly disguised his shock with a sneer. 'I'll drop this if you put that gun away. Your friend can't get involved either.' Again, he glanced at Mumtaz Shah. I nodded slowly, and the man dropped the dagger just as I lowered my pistol. He charged quickly, surprising me with how fast he moved. In a second, he had knocked the gun out of my hands completely and wrapped one hand around my throat. I tried to break his grip and trip him, but he lowered his hips and wouldn't budge, one hand still clasped around my throat while the other one controlled my wrist. I brought a knee up to try and create space. It worked for a moment, then suddenly the man rammed his head up under my chin. I fell back, stunned, and he followed me down, pinning me in place while he strangled me. Black spots erupted in front of my eyes; I was going to die, I was sure of it. His hot, stale breath tickled my ear as he snarled and cursed me. I was going to die and Mumtaz Shah would let it happen. The man straightened up above me, looking into my eyes while he choked me. He wanted to see the life fade out of them. I let go of the hand on my throat and started scratching his arm and his chest, trying to do anything to get away. The man leaned in close, his face right above mine, the scab on his nose glistening among the black dots that were now spreading as a curtain across my eyes. I felt my hand move like a ghost's, entirely on its own, going from his arm up to his face. My thumb dug into his right eye, piercing the thin, watery layer of his eyeball, pushing into his skull. The man screamed in pain and the hand on my throat shot up to his eye; the grip on my wrist loosened, and I broke it to reach up and jam my other thumb into his left eye.

Warm blood poured out over my hands, making my palms stick to his face as I rolled us over, winding up on top of him. His screams rang in my ears as he clawed at my hands, trying to pull them away from his eyes.

Finally, I pulled my thumbs out of his skull and stood up, panting hard as the baker writhed on the ground, his blood staining the dirt around him as his body bucked and shook. My gun was still on the ground, and I leaned down to pick it up. I became vaguely aware that I was pointing it at the man, who was now sobbing blood into the ground, curled up in a ball.

Someone yanked on my collar to pull me back, and I turned around. Mumtaz Shah was staring at me. 'That's enough,' he said quietly. He held a sack of flour in the crook of one arm. 'Let's go.' He led me away from the scene as the townspeople slowly approached the baker, eyeing us with a mixture of fear and hatred. As we finished loading everything onto the truck, I became aware of a searing pain in my throat. It hurt to breathe, and I could taste blood, no doubt as a result of the man headbutting me. My hands and clothes were sticky with a combination of cold sweat and warm blood. My thumbs were completely covered in dark red and smeared over that was a film of milky white fluid. 'You did well,' said Mumtaz Shah in a low voice as we drove back to camp.

I didn't talk much once we got back to camp, aside from answering some questions to explain my appearance. Most of the talking was done by Mumtaz Shah, who detailed my fight with the baker like a scene from an epic novel. There were nods and cheers of approval from everyone, and Nadir himself said only a true man of Allah could've shown such resourcefulness and viciousness in a fight against a grown man.

'But you see how He instills compassion in our hearts as well?' Nadir asked everyone. 'The baker was trying to kill Irfan, but Irfan didn't attempt to do the same. He let him live. The man will suffer for going against those who work under His will, but he will live. And maybe in time, he shall be forgiven.' Everyone murmured in awe and in agreement. I sat there thinking about how I'd pointed my gun at the man after gouging his eyes out. Was that the compassion Nadir was referring to?

I finally threw up once everyone else was asleep, Sameer. I had held it in while cleaning myself up, I had held it in during prayer, and during dinner, while everyone was talking about what happened. But once they were asleep, I walked into the trees near our campsite and I vomited in the darkness. All day since we had gotten back that afternoon, and for weeks afterward, the only sound I could hear was the sound of that man screaming as he writhed on the ground. And I couldn't sleep either, because every single time I closed my eyes, the only thing I could see was blood pouring out of the two punctures where his eyes had been. I still find myself waking up in the middle of the night sometimes with the memory of that man's blood slowly pooling out and staining the ground around him.

That incident seemed, to me, the spark that set us all on the path we had so enthusiastically sought when we left home. At last, blood had been spilt, and we knew that we were capable of spilling it. We set up camp for longer periods of time now. Nadir was confident that we were now true soldiers who could stand and fight against anyone who tried to come up against us. We'd overtake any small militias established by locals with the help of American soldiers. Afghan locals could rarely stand against us for long. The bulk of their forces were made up of young boys or old men, and decades of war had exhausted them. The American and Afghan militaries couldn't tend to these small areas for very long. The Taliban's ranks had swelled once again in the east and south, as more and more men from our Pakistan crossed into Afghanistan to fight the jihad.

It really felt like a war now. We'd pick up what we could from newspaper stands to try and keep up with everything that was going on. The Pakistani military was now helping the Americans in its own tribal areas, trying to help them navigate the treacherous terrain. 'But even they don't know it the way the locals do!' laughed Mumtaz Shah one evening. 'It may as well be the blind leading the blind!' The Pakistani government was also attempting a crackdown on Islamic leaders who had connections to the Taliban and Al-Qaeda in the big cities like Karachi and Islamabad.

We all responded with outrage when we read a headline stating that four Talibs had been arrested in Karachi in connection to kidnappings of political officials. 'I knew this man,' said Nadir, pointing at the blurry photo of a man in his mid-thirties who had a shaved head and a long, dark beard. 'He was with me in Kashmir for a year. You see how depraved the so-called patriots of our country have become? They call him "terrorist." A man who fought for the wellbeing of Muslims in Kashmir who sought to liberate them. Their souls have truly been bought by those devils from the west!' Nadir spat on the ground. 'Inshallah, one day I will get my hands on all of these traitors and cut their throats myself!' And we all agreed. How could our own people help those who were here to kill us? The west didn't care about us; they only paid attention when they experienced a little damage, when someone finally had the audacity to lash out against them. That's when they took notice of our little corner of the world. Of our people. It was this mentality, Sameer, that fueled me endlessly in those days. I was sickened with myself for what I had done to that baker, but the hate I felt for the Americans knew no limit. I wanted to meet them already; I wanted the next town we advanced on to have some of them stationed there. They had to know that they couldn't beat us, that their leaders had sent them here to die, as had thousands before them; the Russians, the British, even Alexander the Great. I wanted to see an American soldier realize in his last moments that his hatred of us was no match for the love my Allah felt for me.

It all seems so clear now, Sameer, so clear that sometimes, I admit, I loathe myself for not realizing it back then. For not seeing the simple ways in which we were all manipulated. Nadir's intricate weaving of what was going on in the world around us, turning what we believed into a thick web in which we ourselves were the ones who were trapped. The way that he, Mumtaz Shah, and so many others gently poked and prodded at the volatile combination of our strong faith and the temperaments we had as young men. We made for the perfect pack of mad dogs that way, all of us frightened into a crazed fury. The airstrike was the perfect chance to do that, and it led to my wish being granted.

I remember very clearly the first time I saw the aftermath of an airstrike, Sameer. You might remember Jahangir from across the street, the poor boy who became shaheed during his time in Afghanistan. He wasn't even a soldier—he'd gone over as a doctor. He wanted to help people. It didn't matter to him who it was; he simply wanted to play whatever part he could in the healing of Afghanistan and its people. The boy fell victim to an American airstrike intended for members of the Taliban; that's how he was killed. The sight of his burnt, ruined body when it was returned to his home is an image that I carried with me for many years. It's what I went back to many times to keep myself going. But I hadn't experienced an airstrike yet myself, and nothing could have prepared me for when I did.

We were camped out deep in the hills surrounding a town on the outskirts of Kabul. There was a rumor that several large groups of Talibs were moving east from Kunduz to retake the capital while the American and Afghan forces were busy dealing with the influx of new Talibs in the south. It was the perfect opportunity to try and re-establish control over the country. The Americans had pushed back the Taliban and Al-Qaeda forces when they first arrived in 2001, but everyone, including them, was quickly realizing that this war would not to be an easy victory for them. Our morale was high, and there was a hum in the air, bolstered by the potential for an impending battle. We would swoop into Kabul and retake it, make it Islamic once again. And this time it would be stronger, it would last longer, because we'd have taken it from our biggest and our most dangerous enemy.

Nadir sent a group of eight over to a spot on the other side of the hills, about eight kilometers away from our camp. He had received word that there was a small group of Al-Qaeda and Taliban soldiers who were waiting to move in on the nearby town, recruit who they could, set up a post, and from there move into Kabul. The group he sent was meant to meet up with them and bring them back to our camp so we could all make the move to the city together. Mumtaz Shah told us that there was a chance we would be part of a much larger group now, part of the Taliban who had been in Afghanistan for much longer than we had. 'Inshallah, all will go well, and you will receive your education from the best holy warriors He himself has put on this earth. Aside from our Nadir Bhai, of course.'

The American bombs dropped right after the Zuhr prayer. Most of us were lying around, about to start making lunch, when suddenly the scream of planes cut through the air. And those screams were immediately drowned out by the deep rumbling sound of the earth being splintered. Everyone fell over and scrambled to their feet, shouting prayers, running around, swearing, yelling, 'Ya Allah!' Nadir was standing with his hands pressed over his ears, trying to yell over the din of the explosions. Bashir picked up his rifle and pointed it up at the sky. I ran over and yanked it toward the ground, knocking him off his feet. Mumtaz Shah was doing the same thing with everyone who had gathered themselves enough to point their guns up wildly at the sky, his shouts barely audible over the roar coming up from the ground beneath our feet. 'Don't shoot! Don't shoot, imbeciles! They'll know where we are!'

Everyone stayed close to the ground, unmoving. My arm was still pinning Bashir to the ground, but he didn't seem to notice. His eyes were trying to see through the dirt, dust, and smoke that hung in the air, waiting. A moment passed, and when we didn't hear the jets making another pass, we all slowly got back to our feet.

'Is everyone okay?' Nadir asked. We all muttered that we were while dusting ourselves off and picking up the supplies and weapons that had fallen over.

'They weren't aiming for us,' said Bashir, pointing toward the crest of hills on the other side of the woods. Thick, dark smoke rose above the trees. I could tell, even from so far away, that the area had been ripped apart by the force of the bombs.

'We have to move,' said Nadir. 'Everyone get ready. Once the sun goes down, we'll go into town.'

'What about the others?' asked Ibrahim, one of the younger boys in our group.

Nadir stared at him coldly for a moment. 'Who do you think they hit with that strike, boy?' he said. Ibrahim looked around at everyone else for support. We all looked away.

'But . . . we can't just leave them. What if they survived?'

Nadir shook his head. 'If they survived, they'll find their way back here and we'll leave together, or they'll head to the town to meet us there.' Ibrahim opened his mouth to speak again, and suddenly Nadir rushed at him, grabbing him by the back of the neck and roughly turning him so he was facing the plumes of smoke rising from the trees. 'LOOK! Look at that. Do you think anyone could have survived that? They knew what they were getting into, what they might have to sacrifice! I'd expect someone with your name to understand!' He threw Ibrahim to the ground and looked at him with disgust. 'Do you want to go home now, boy? Is that it? You've seen a bit of real action, and all of a sudden this isn't for you anymore?'

There were tears running down the boy's face. He shook his head. 'N-n-no, Bhai, I'm just—'

'Just what?' Nadir roared. He looked around at us all standing there. 'Are you all as shocked as him? Do you all want to go home now? This isn't the fight you thought it'd be anymore? Do you know how many airstrikes I've seen? Dozens! If our military didn't align itself with kafirs, we'd be able to have them too!' Mumtaz Shah came up and put a hand on Nadir's shoulder, but he shrugged it off and continued shouting. 'This is WAR, boys! More of you will be killed before it's over; maybe all of you! But that's what it takes to win! They can't kill us all!' He looked down at Ibrahim again, who was still on the ground at his feet. 'The next time you show weakness like that, I will cut your throat myself, boy. Do you understand? I will not have weak links amongst my men.' Ibrahim nodded slowly, and Nadir looked around at us all again. 'That goes for everyone, understood?' A collective yes went up from all of us, and then we slowly spread out, gathering our supplies and packing up.

Since there were eighteen of us, we went down to the town in groups of three. Nadir went with the first group. Bashir, a young man named Amar, and I were all in the sixth and final group. Mumtaz Shah would accompany us. We were to make our way down after sunset, post Maghrib prayers. We waited until the sky was that shade of bright indigo, right before it turns to the black of night sprinkled with the white of stars, before we began to move. We had agreed that our prayers could wait until we reached the town. Allah would understand that it wasn't safe to linger here any longer than necessary. We'd been walking for about ten minutes when there were sounds of whispers and stumbling footsteps through the woods to our left. Mumtaz Shah held up a hand to stop us, and we all tensed up, waiting. He slowly moved toward the sounds and crouched low, aiming his gun into the darkness. The whispers were close enough now that we could make out what they were saying: 'Help . . . please . . . help, Nadir Sahib . . . Mumtaz Bhai . . .'

Mumtaz Shah lowered his gun, and we all rushed forward to push past the thick branches and foliage. Two people moved slowly through the darkness, headed in the direction we had just come from. 'Over here!' Bashir whispered loudly. They turned, and we rushed forward to grab them, pulling them back with us to where we'd been walking. Salman, the old man, was limping along. He smelled of smoke and scorched hair and earth. In the moonlight peeking through the darkened branches, we could see that he was covered in blood, though it was impossible to tell where it was coming from. Half of his body looked like an exposed wound. He was carrying someone else along with him. Whoever it was, they seemed to be unconscious, or dead. Their feet were dragging over the forest floor, and they weren't moving.

We eased the body off Salman's shoulders, and he sank to rest against the base of a tree. Bashir and I lowered the other man to the ground. He still wasn't moving. Mumtaz Shah gave Salman his canteen to drink from while the rest of us examined the other man. He was barely breathing, and we couldn't make out his face. It was completely blackened. The blood on his body had caked over his skin completely, and it was beginning to smell. The stench of smoke and charred meat rose from where he lay. Mumtaz Shah was speaking in low tones to Salman. Bashir went over and asked very quietly, 'Who is that brother, Salman-ji?'

Salman glanced up at Bashir, almost as though he were trying to recognize who he was. He is one of the Talibs we met with. We were all about to begin moving back toward the base in groups when the air-strike hit.' He turned his attention to Mumtaz Shah again, and his voice cracked. 'We didn't even know what was happening. One minute we're all talking to each other, and the next it felt like the whole world had been blown apart.'

'How many people survived?' Mumtaz Shah's voice was curt.

'I'm not sure. The boy there was trying to crawl away when I arrived. I grabbed him, and we were able to escape from there before anyone came looking.' Mumtaz Shah's eyes darted from one spot to the other now, quickly surveying the spaces between the trees around us.

'Were you followed?'

Salman shook his head. 'We had to keep stopping along the way so I could rest and check how he was doing. Anyone following us surely would've caught up.'

'Unless they wanted to see where you were going,' muttered Mumtaz Shah.

Salman didn't notice. 'It wasn't until the sun started to go down that the boy stopped walking on his own altogether. I had to carry him myself the rest of the way. We have to get the boy help! Where's Nadir Sahib?'

'He went down to the town. We were on our way there too when we bumped into you. We can't be sure there won't be soldiers searching in these hills for more of us,' explained Amar. I was watching Mumtaz Shah, who was pacing back and forth slowly, no longer paying attention to Salman. Instead, he kept looking up and scanning the trees around us. He seemed to be trying to figure something out. After a few moments, he stopped.

'All of you, you have to go and meet up with the others in town. Now.' When nobody moved, he added with a hint of annoyance in his voice, 'I'll tend to the old man. I'm changing the plan. Are you afraid you'll get lost without me? Start moving!'

We all glanced back hesitantly at first as we made our way to the path that would lead to the slope of the hills and into town. Through the branches, I could just make out Mumtaz Shah leaning down and scooping Salman up into his arms as if he were a small child and heading back toward our campsite. When we were far enough along to be certain that they wouldn't be coming behind us, we all stopped glancing back and focused on making our way into the town.

The name 'Penhaan Khana' was painted on an old wooden signpost propped up on the side of the road. We moved in swiftly and carefully. People had, for the most part, turned in for the night, but there were a few townsfolk milling about by a tea shop. Their laughter and chatter died when they saw us walking up the road, and one of the men tried his best to discreetly run inside. I nodded my head in the direction of a heavyset old man, but he didn't seem to notice. They were all staring apprehensively at our shrouds and the outlines of the rifles we hid underneath them. One of the men hocked and spit on the ground. I felt Bashir tense up next to me, and I placed a hand on his forearm to calm him.

Nadir had told us to meet up at the town's mosque, which was doubtless the only place we'd be welcomed, as no mullah could turn away Muslims seeking shelter in a house of Allah. Isha prayers were over by then, as evidenced by the crowded tea shop, and so we wouldn't have to worry about anyone trying to spy on us under the guise of coming for prayer. The mosque was a rather small building, made of thick blocks of stone, carved to the same size and shape and painted a bright yellow color that made the building glow, even in the darkness. A short minaret rose from every corner of the roof, they flanked a large dome with sat right in the middle. Someone had also painted the Arabic words of the Kalima on both front walls, and Bismillah above the entrance.

Pulling our shrouds tighter around ourselves, we all took off our boots, placing them on either side of the stone steps outside, before pushing open the wooden door. The walls inside were painted the same shade of yellow as those outside. You could turn the whole building inside out and nobody would notice. A few long, low, polished wood tables were stacked up in one corner, intended for the Quran classes given to children who were just beginning to learn how to read and memorize the holy book. There was a short podium at the very front of the mosque, set inside the beautifully carved alcove from which the imam would lead prayers. And over to the right of the podium was a door that led upstairs to the minaret, from whence the townsfolk were called to prayer five times a day.

It was in front of this door that the rest of our brothers huddled, shrouds drawn over their shoulders in an attempt to dim the glow of several lanterns that the mullah of the mosque had provided for them. Nadir immediately strode over to us and ushered us in, pushing the door closed behind us. We quickly explained the situation to him; what had happened and where Mumtaz was. His smile faltered a bit as he listened, but his eyes remained cold and unflinching. If he was concerned, he didn't show it. 'I'm sure they'll be here soon,' he said once he'd gotten the whole story. 'Mumtaz is a strong soldier. He'll know how to handle it. You come and eat a little, and rest.'

We shed our bags in the corner but kept our rifles slung over our shoulders while we ate by the lanterns. Nobody would disturb us in the night. We could rest easy until dawn, when the call for Fajr would sound and the townsfolk would come in to say their prayers. Even then, we could join them without fear of something going wrong. Muslims could not attack other Muslims during prayer, especially not in the house of Allah. Knowing this, we all relaxed and talked amongst ourselves about the day's events. Nadir did not join us. He paced on the other side of the room, his shuffling footsteps seeming to echo in the shadows near the entrance.

A little after midnight, I was dozing off near some prayer mats stacked neatly against one wall when I heard a soft knock on the door. The only other people awake were the few men keeping watch while the rest of us slept. Nadir quickly moved toward the door, gesturing with one hand at the guards to relax their rifles. He mumbled something, I assume checking who it was, and a moment later he opened the door. A figure quickly slid inside. It was Mumtaz Shah, and he was alone. He whispered something to Nadir, who looked mildly concerned, then angry, and then calm. I waited for them to open the door again so Salman could come in. But once Mumtaz Shah and Nadir moved over to the corner where we had all eaten our dinner, it became apparent that Salman had not come with him.

Mumtaz Shah had left him up there.

৩৩৩৩

The Americans arrived the next day.

It was right before Zuhr, and we had decided we would start approaching the townsfolk after the prayer. The afternoon would be spent gathering supplies and finding as many youths to join us as we could. Once it was dark, we would leave for Kabul. Mumtaz Shah had hidden the truck in an alcove at the base of the hills, and he left to go back and get it after we'd had breakfast. 'If they'd found it, they'd be here by now,' he said. 'All the same, it's best that we leave as soon as we can.'

He'd been gone an hour or so when the door to the mosque flew open and Nadir ran inside, slamming it shut behind him. 'Americans!'

But we heard the sound of the jeeps driving into town ourselves, mingled with the shouts of English words. We rushed to the windows to look out. There were two jeeps, five soldiers on each, ten in all. Ten that we could see, anyway. How could we know they didn't have more coming? My hands immediately felt cold and wet. I thought I'd lose grip on my rifle. We watched as they jumped down from their transports and spread out, approaching the townsfolk who were sitting outside, eyeing the foreign soldiers with apprehension and a bit of curiosity.

Meanwhile, Nadir was trying to snap us back to reality, giving orders and telling us to move. He sent two people up to the minarets with sniper rifles and grenades. Five others went through a door in the opposite corner that had been blocked from view the previous night by the long tables—it led to the washing stations behind the mosque. Everyone else was tasked with collecting the Qurans off the shelves and hiding them, to protect them from damage in case fighting broke out. Bashir and I lowered the carved wood alcove onto its back and started stacking the book inside. Meanwhile, Nadir was grabbing the long tables and standing them up against the door to block it.

'What're they doing now?' he asked two boys, Suleiman and Arif, who were still standing by the windows clutching their rifles.

'They're going into the teahouse,' said Suleiman.

We all hurried back over to the windows to peek out. There were a few soldiers standing outside the teahouse. One of them was talking to some of the men from town. One of the men stood a few inches taller than the rest of them. He wore a dusty old vest on top of a faded blue shalwar kameez, and a cream colored pakol atop his head. There was a neatly cropped, copper-colored beard on his chin. His arms were crossed tightly across his chest, and he seemed to be talking the most. The soldier listened intently and then glanced up in the direction of the mosque.

A split second hung in the air for what seemed like hours when the American soldiers followed his gaze to the mosque. In that moment, we all took a step back from the windows so we'd be out of sight. Suddenly, a shot cut through the air like a firecracker, and then the world was filled with noise—the shouts of the Americans outside, from Nadir in the mosque cursing and barking orders at us, to our own voices tossing together a song of curses and prayers. I moved, but I don't remember how. Bashir might've yanked me away from the window. It was lucky that he did, because a second later the front of the mosque was ripped apart with gunshots. Automatic gunfire sounded outside, but not from any rifle. The Americans had opened fire with the guns mounted on their jeeps. There were shouts from every direction, and I moved with the others toward the door leading out the back of the mosque. The air was hot and filled with dust. There was no thinking or seeing before I moved. I was acting on instinct.

We spilled out into the clearing behind the mosque and took cover near the side walls. One of the boys Nadir had sent out earlier lay dead or dying on the ground, bleeding freely from his neck. I pointed my rifle around the corner without aiming and pulled the trigger. A quick burst of shots sounded, and the weapon jumped in my hands. I was afraid, Sameer. It wasn't like training. It was a battle, and I was terrified. The guns on the jeeps suddenly stopped firing, and it occurred to me that maybe they had run out of ammo, or maybe the soldiers who had been manning them had been shot by our snipers or someone else within our ranks. Whatever the case, we all charged forward, coming out from the mosque, firing in every direction, not caring who we hit—whether Americans or the townsfolk who hated our cause so much that they saw fit to help our enemies. In the wild fury of action, I saw a few of our own gunned down by the soldiers who had taken cover behind their jeeps and the buildings facing the mosque. I dove to the ground before I could suffer the same fate and pointed my rifle wildly in every direction, moving from point to point without bothering to see if my shots made contact with anyone.

An American hung dead over the back of the jeep with part of his face shot off. I wanted to glance up at the minarets to see if our snipers were still there, but I feared that taking my eyes off the scene in front of me would result in me getting hit. Bashir was a few feet away, crouched low and moving steadily toward a soldier who was taking cover behind one of the jeeps. He didn't see the other American sneaking up behind him to his right. I leapt to my feet and ran forward, not thinking about getting shot. I took aim and fired. Missed. Aimed, fired again. Missed again. The soldier turned toward me, more shots rang out in the air, and then I heard a voice shout something, but I couldn't hear what.

Suddenly, some feet away, an explosion tore the air to pieces. The whole left side of my body was blasted with heat. I flew off my feet, collided with something hard, and hit the ground. It felt like I'd fallen into a deep sleep. When I regained consciousness, everything was spinning, and there was something in my eyes. I couldn't see clearly, and my ears were ringing. I curled my fingers and felt them move, so I knew I was still alive.

Suddenly, the pain hit me all at once. I brought my knees up, trying to push myself up to my feet, to get away, to move. But my balance was off, and I fell to my side instead. There was a noise from a few feet away, and I glanced up. The American soldier I had been trying to shoot was lying on his back. We had both been blasted into a small alleyway between two buildings. He was shaking as black blood pooled around him. The side of his face that I could see had been partially burned by the explosion. I crawled closer and saw that the blood was coming out of a wound in his chest, right above the heart, and another on the side of his neck.

When I was close enough to see the beads of sweat mixing with the blood on his face, he turned to face me, a mixture of panic and shock clear on his face. I hadn't noticed from afar how young he was. He looked about my age, Sameer; maybe a little older, maybe a little younger. He took advantage of my distraction and swung his right arm up toward me. I caught his arm before the knife in his hand could make contact with my face. His left hand was grabbing wildly at my face and throat, but I pinned it under my knees and pressed my free hand to the wound on his neck. He thought I was trying to strangle him, and for a moment I thought the same thing, but my hand pressed down hard, slowing the flow of blood just a bit.

The boy's eyes went wide with surprise, and he seemed to be struggling to say something. I looked around, making sure nobody had seen us yet. There were still the sounds of shouting and gunfire cutting through the air, though for how much longer, I couldn't be sure. He was dying. I had the strange urge to help him somehow, to drag him away from the fighting and see if there was a way to make sure he got out of there alive. But I knew there was nothing I could do.

Maybe he was still expecting me to kill him, or maybe he thought there was a chance he could survive, because there was a look of desperation in his eyes. Of pleading. It remained there until there were only a few seconds left, as his blood seeped out from in between my fingers and his hand moved absentmindedly, lightly clutching my wrist. The twinkle in his eyes stilled, almost as if a sense of calm had settled in, and then it faded away entirely.

His dead eyes seemed to still hold traces of the warmth that had, up until a few seconds ago, existed as a result of the life in them. But he was gone. The blood still flowed from his wounds, yet there was no point in my trying to slow it down anymore. I removed my hand and stared at the shocking red stain that had covered it; the blood from his wounds mingling with my own, wrapping around my fingers like the warmest glove. I suddenly became aware of how much my own body hurt.

I tried to push myself to my feet again, managing to stay upright for a moment this time before swaying on the spot and falling back onto the ground. I pushed myself up against the side of one of the buildings and sat there, feeling my breath catch in my chest every time I tried to inhale. Glancing down to my left side, I finally saw that my clothes were drenched in blood. A massive burning sensation and a stabbing pain went from right above my hip up to my left armpit. I coughed and spat. My mouth filled with the overwhelming moisture that comes right before one vomits.

How long I sat there, I don't know. I can never remember how much time passed. I stared at the American's body lying just a couple of feet away, unsure of whether or not I was slowly dying myself. If I wasn't, there was a chance that the rest of the Americans could run into the alleyway at any second, having killed Nadir and the others. They'd come searching for their brother in arms, and instead they'd find me sitting there, still alive with him lying dead just inches away. And they'd kill me. Or maybe they'd torture me first, and then kill me.

Eventually, I heard the sound of footsteps pounding in my direction, and I glanced up. It was Nadir. His clothes were slightly torn and a streak of blood went down the side of his face where his scar was. He had wrapped a piece of his shroud around a wound on his head and part of his beard had been singed away, but he was alive. His eyes went from the dead soldier to me and a smile crept onto his face. Crouching down, he looked at me with concern.

'Are you okay?'

I wasn't sure if I'd be able to speak without vomiting, so I shook my head, gesturing at my wounds. He nodded quickly and grabbed my left arm, ignoring my pained groans. He wrapped it around his shoulders while gripping his own arm around my back. Very slowly, he stood up, pulling me to my feet with him before reaching under my legs, squatting, and lifting me up off the ground into his arms as though I were a child.

He carried me back out into the main street and toward the mosque, setting me down underneath the Kalima on one of the front walls. I could see the carnage in front of me. One of the American jeeps was burning, and broken glass and blood were everywhere. Bodies had been stacked in two piles a few yards away from the mosque, and I could see our men running around, dragging more and more out, surveying the wreckage. The townspeople were peeking out from behind cracked and broken windows, and the doors and buildings they'd used for shelter from the firing.

'They killed nine of us,' said Nadir in a hollow voice. 'Had Mumtaz not driven up behind them and rammed their jeeps with the truck, they might've gotten us all.'

Until then I hadn't noticed the truck, but when I looked up again, I saw it parked off at an angle behind one of the jeeps. The front was partially smashed, but other than that it looked fine.

'Bashir! Come here!' Nadir beckoned Bashir over as he came out from inside the tea shop, dragging someone along with him. Bashir handed the man off to Qasim, an elder member of our group, and walked over. He was covered in dirt and sweat, and there were a few bruises on his face and a cut on his lip. Other than that, he seemed fine.

'Irfan is hurt. Tend to his wounds. I'll go and help finish up,' said Nadir.

Bashir nodded and dropped down next to me, pulling his belt off and opening one of the pouches attached to it. He pulled out a wrap and some disinfectant cloths. 'Thought you'd died,' he said quietly as he reached over and tore open my kameez.

'I'm sorry to disappoint.' I couldn't muster up the energy to say much more than that.

'I got the one that threw the grenade after it went off. I thought he'd killed you. I was able to sneak around one of the buildings and come at him from the side.'

I closed my eyes and leaned my head back as he lifted my left arm. Bashir kept talking while he cleaned and wrapped my wounds. The bruises on his face were courtesy of the American soldier who had thrown the grenade. He told me how he had managed to knock the soldier's rifle out of his hands and how they resorted to using their fists. 'He was strong. He kept going for his pistol every time he hit me, but I would tackle him or grab him to make sure he couldn't. I managed to grab my knife and stab him in the belly. Wasn't much to do after that.' He spoke calmly, but I could tell he was shaken, even if he would never admit to it.

Once Bashir had finished wrapping my torso, Nadir called him over to where he, Mumtaz Shah, and the rest of our brothers were gathered. They had finished laying out the bodies of our shaheed a few feet away from the mosque on one side and the bodies of the Americans on the other. The townspeople were made to come out of their hiding spots so they could watch what was about to happen.

'You put your faith in western invaders,' said Nadir as he pulled a machete out from a sack that Mumtaz Shah held out for him, 'instead of holy warriors who sought refuge in your mosque as they fight a holy war. Perhaps you were misguided, or afraid. Maybe they tricked you. I don't know. Whatever your reasons, forgiveness is something we deserve the moment we ask for it! And I hope that all of you will pray for forgiveness after what you have seen here today. But before then, I'd like for you to see what these demons you put your faith in are worth!'

He walked over to the pile of bodies and pulled one off onto the ground with his free hand, laying the dead soldier down on his stomach. Hoisting the machete up with both hands, Nadir closed his eyes and muttered a prayer to himself before bringing the blade down hard across the back of the neck. The swing was strong enough to cut through tissue, bone, and muscle as if it were all butter, and the head came off the corpse cleanly. A spurt of blood and screams from the crowd followed, and I couldn't turn away. One by one, Mumtaz Shah pulled bodies off the pile and laid them in front of Nadir, who swung his blade and removed the heads. Nobody screamed anymore; they all watched in silent horror.

Finally, once the last corpse had been beheaded, Nadir turned to the other brothers, some of whom had been watching with horror on their faces, and some with sick joy. Bashir had been watching with an almost expressionless look. Qasim stepped forward, pulling someone along with him, and I realized suddenly who it was that Bashir had handed off to him earlier. It was the man from the teahouse who had given away our position to the Americans. There was a nasty gash on the side of his face, and his clothes were stained with blood.

Yousuf pushed the man to his knees in front of Nadir. A swell of noise rose up from the crowd of townspeople. Mumtaz Shah fired a shot into the air. 'Quiet!' he barked.

'I shouldn't offer you this,' said Nadir to the man. 'But I am merciful. And it would be a sin for me to not give you the chance to ask Him for forgiveness before you die.'

The man stared at Nadir for a moment and then lowered his head. From where I was sitting, I couldn't tell if he said a prayer or not, but he must've because Nadir let a moment pass before lifting up the machete one more time. He held it in the air for what seemed like longer than he had for the bodies, and for a split second I thought maybe he'd let the man go. But then he brought the blade down and cut the man's head off, killing him in an instant. Screams and cries rose from the crowd again. Some people even fainted. Mumtaz Shah fired more shots into the air, threatening them into silence.

'Burn the bodies,' Nadir instructed. 'Then bag the heads and hang them from the sign above the tea shop.' I was already lightheaded from blood loss, and my head was still throbbing from when the blast had knocked me out earlier. But it wasn't until the stench of the burning bodies made its way over to where I was sitting that I could stay awake no longer. I coughed a couple times, retched, and then lost consciousness right there against the wall of the mosque. The last thing I remember seeing was the thick clouds of black smoke billowing up from the burning pile of flesh and blood.

I awoke hours later in near darkness to a seething pain in my side. When I reached down to touch the source of the ache, my hand made contact with another person's. It took a moment for my eyes to adjust in the dim light. When they finally did, I saw that it was Bashir leaning over me, redressing my wounds. 'You took long enough to wake up,' he said in a calm and hushed voice. I became aware of a loud hum coming from under my head, and it wasn't until I glanced around and saw the shadowy figures of the rest of my brothers sleeping that I realized we were in the truck. Looking back at Bashir, I saw that he was using his flashlight to examine my side closely, pressing his fingers as gently as he could all along the length of the wound. 'We'll have to see if we can get you to a doctor in Kabul. It doesn't seem too serious, but it'll be a long and painful healing process if we don't get you to someone who has more supplies than we do,' he said before rewrapping the bandages. With a groan, I pushed myself up into a sitting position. He pointed the light at me. 'Take it slow; you're still very fragile. It's a miracle that blast didn't kill you.'

Leaning my head back against the side of the truck bed, I said in a cracked whisper, 'By the grace of Allah, I survived.'

Handing me his canteen, Bashir said, 'That's true, brother.'

I gratefully accepted the canteen and drew a long swig of the warm water. It felt like a thousand hammers colliding with my ribs on the way down to my belly, and I almost choked. We're headed to Kabul?' I asked as I handed the canteen back.

Bashir nodded.

'How long have we been driving?'

'Only a little over an hour, I think. Everyone fell asleep almost immediately, including me. It wasn't till I woke up that I thought to check on you. We tried to clean you up as best we could before we left, but Nadir was in a hurry. We had to finish and get out of there fast in case more Americans showed up. We didn't have the numbers to take on that many again.'

I felt a lurch in my stomach as I remembered exactly what Nadir had made everyone 'finish' before we left. 'Bashir, the people in that town . . . are they alright?'

Even though the shadows from the beam of light cast an odd mask over Bashir's features, I could still tell that there was an expression of discomfort on his face as he took a breath before responding: 'We didn't kill them, if that's what you're asking. Aside from that traitor from the teahouse. We had to rough up a few of the men who tried to put out the fire burning the Americans' bodies, but nobody was seriously hurt or anything. They'll have a few nasty bruises for a while. That's all.'

'Why did he do that?'

'Why did who do what? Why'd the man from the teahouse tell the soldiers where we were? Who knows?'

'No, not that!' I stared at him for a moment, and he stared back. 'Why did Nadir do that? That wasn't necessary. To do that to their bodies . . . they were already dead. We could've just buried them or burned them. He didn't have to do that to them. Or to the man. That was a Muslim man. An Afghan. Isn't he who we're fighting for in the first place?'

'He's no Muslim! He was a kafir! Why else would he let the Americans know where we were? And don't forget, they didn't just attack us. They opened fire on a mosque, Irfan. They completely tore it apart. You didn't see what it looked like inside afterward. It was like someone had let a bomb off inside. The maulvi sahib was sobbing. If we hadn't taken the copies of the Quran off the walls like Nadir told us to, they all would've been blasted to bits!'

I was frustrated. He wasn't wrong. I knew that. But I couldn't bring myself to accept that he was totally right either. 'What if they tricked him, then? What if they somehow got an answer out of him with a trick question? Or what if he just didn't know what they'd do if they found us? It's not like we bothered telling them who we were, did we?'

'Nadir Bhai must have,' said Bashir.

'But you don't know that. The maulvi sahib was the only one who knew who we were and why we were there. It doesn't mean everyone did!'

'What's bothering you, Irfan? Why are you talking like this all of a sudden? You've never questioned anything we've done before. The man had to be killed. What if more Americans came and he told them more about us? What if we'd let him live and he followed us to Kabul and attacked us himself?'

'Did he look like a soldier to you? Don't talk nonsense, Bashir!'

He seemed taken aback by my response and a little hurt as well. A few moments passed by in silence until I cleared my throat and spoke again. 'I didn't kill the soldier.' He looked confused, so I continued: 'The American. The one that got blasted into the alley with me. I landed right near him, and he was there, bleeding. I could've finished him off, but I didn't. Even when he tried to pull his knife on me, I just blocked it and pinned his hand down. But I didn't do anything. I tried to help him. I don't know why; there was nothing to help. But I tried to stop his bleeding. I held my hand over his wound until he was dead.'

A thick silence hung in the air and for a minute or two. There was nothing but the hum of the truck as it moved through the night. Bashir removed his cap and ran his hands through his hair. He sighed and asked very slowly, 'Did Nadir Bhai see?'

I shook my head. 'He was dead by the time Nadir found us. I was sitting against the wall half conscious.' Bashir stared at me. The expression on his face wasn't clear, but I couldn't feel that he wasn't entirely angry with me, so I kept talking, wanting him to understand what I was saying. 'He was young, Bashir. Very young. Maybe our age. He didn't look like an invader to me.'

'And you know what an invader looks like do you? All the great battles you've fought?' There was an edge in his voice.

'No, that's not what I'm saying. I'm just saying, he didn't look like what I imagined an American soldier would look like up close. That's all.'

'What does that matter? You said he tried to stab you! Even while he was dying!'

'I would've killed him too if I hadn't seen that he was already dying,' I countered.

'Of course you would have! We're at war!' Bashir was nearly shouting now, and someone turned in their sleep over in the corner.

I hesitated, glancing over to make sure everyone was still asleep before responding. 'I know we are at war,' I said calmly. 'I'm just saying that maybe there's more to it all. . . .'

'I don't understand you, Irfan. Nadir Bhai cuts the head off one traitorous Afghan and all of a sudden you question everything we're doing. But those Americans come in and kill hundreds of them, thousands of them, innocent ones! How is that okay?'

'It isn't okay! I hate that they're here, Bashir. They don't belong here, and I do not want them here. If they were to come as guests or visitors, that'd be another story. But they're coming as soldiers in a land that isn't theirs to fight a war their leaders made up! I ran away from home to come here. Your parents sent you to fight with pride; I left mine with a note when they least expected it! But if we kill our own, the people we came to defend, then how are we any better than them?'

'We have to punish those who betray us!'

'What about forgiveness? For those who make mistakes? How long have those people been bleeding? How long has war torn their country apart? What if they just think they're getting help? What if they just don't know who to trust? We have to forgive too, don't we?'

'You're talking like a fool! Forgiveness isn't our job. Forgiveness is up to Allah. Ours is to defend our land. To defend our people from kafir invaders!'

'How can we call ourselves His warriors then? If we can't forgive like him, how can we say we're soldiers fighting for His cause?'

At this, Bashir fell silent. He was looking at me with a peculiar expression on his face. 'What exactly do you think we should be doing, then?' he asked me quietly after some time had passed.

'I'm not sure, Bashir. I just know that I'm not certain if this is the right way to do things anymore.' When he didn't say anything, I added, 'Maybe I'll talk to Nadir about doing things differently.'

Immediately, his hand went up and he placed it on my leg, squeezing gently. 'He'd kill you,' he said.

'Well, then the only thing I can do is ask to leave.' I smiled at Bashir in the near darkness, 'How do you think that'll go?'

There was no response. We both knew, I think, what Nadir's reaction would be to something like that. We sat in silence for a few moments, and then Bashir sighed and turned off his flashlight. I could hear his thoughts tumbling over each other in the darkness, and right as I was drifting off to sleep again, I heard his voice from what seemed like miles away. 'The way you're thinking is dangerous, Irfan.'

When I awoke, we were in Kabul. Mumtaz Shah had parked the truck at the end of a neighborhood lane, behind some other abandoned cars and smaller trucks. My side throbbed with pain as I stretched upward, trying my best to not groan too loudly. Gingerly, I hopped down from the bed of the truck and looked around. Bashir was seated on a large slab of cement that had been part of one of the surrounding buildings. His shroud was wrapped tightly around him, and his eyes were bloodshot.

'What's going on?' I asked.

'There are Americans here,' said Mumtaz Shah from behind me. Before I could turn around, I felt his large hand clap me on the shoulder. 'You took quite a blow yesterday,' he said with a smile. I nodded my head and glanced back at Bashir again. He was still sitting there staring hard at the ground.

'Where is everyone?' I asked, turning my attention back to Mumtaz Shah.

'Bashir and I stayed here to watch over you. Everyone else went to go scout and see if there's a place we could take up while the Americans pass through.' He said all of this with a smile, but something felt off. 'That's a good friend,' he gestured at Bashir, 'someone to keep an eye out for you. To patch you up.' He placed his hand on my shoulder again and squeezed it hard. 'Young men need good friends to keep an eye on them. To help each other when it's needed. Or to talk them out of silly, stupid ideas.' The smile was still on his face, but there was something in his eyes that seemed menacing, like a cold flame flickering behind them. I was uncomfortable, and acutely aware of the fact that I didn't know where my rifle was. Who had picked it up after I was found in the alleyway? Had it even been there with me after the grenade exploded? I could feel my dagger tucked into the sheath on my boot, but other than that, I was unarmed. Wriggling free from his grip, I took half a step back. Mumtaz Shah chuckled at me. 'You seem nervous, boy. Relax. We already know we can handle the Americans. You spilled their blood for the first time yesterday; you're all broken in. No need to be nervous.' I glanced at Bashir again. He was glancing upward now, as if he were suddenly fascinated by the shade of blue the sky had taken that day.

'Bashir.'

He ignored me.

'The boy's tired. He tended to you half the night, didn't he?' said Mumtaz Shah. I ignored him and made to walk toward Bashir when suddenly, Nadir came walking around the corner. His shroud was drawn up, but his face was uncovered. He had an old, gray pakol on his head and a cup of chai in his hands.

'I see our lion is awake!' he called as he approached. I watched and waited to see the others come walking behind him, but they didn't. He was alone.

'The boy just woke up a few minutes ago. He's been asking where everyone is,' said Mumtaz Shah.

'Ah,' Nadir shrugged the shroud off his shoulders and tossed it onto the bed of the truck. 'Well, a group of American soldiers is stationed at the university right now, and there's a group of British soldiers about an hour and a half north of there. My source tells me the Americans will head this way around sundown, by which time, we will be gone. As fate would have it, it turns out our intel was wrong. It appears not all the British and American forces have gone south. Apparently, they inter- cepted the plans to meet here, which is why they were able to carry out their airstrikes two days ago. Some of our brothers who decided to stay behind and blend in with the locals after the Americans first came to Kabul have been spying on their movements ever since. But they had no knowledge of the airstrike.' Nadir shook his head as he said this, and finally Bashir spoke up from where he was sitting.

'Is that who your contact was? One of those old Talibs?' he asked.

'Yes. There's a good number of them scattered all over Kabul. Biding their time. Every once in a while, a treacherous kafir will tip off the Americans to one of them and they'll be arrested. Vanish in the middle of the night. Put under the kind of suffering we can only imagine. Those traitors will face worse fates than our enemies, for a far more painful eternity awaits those Muslims who betray their own. But before that, I'd like to kill as many of them as I can myself.' Nadir stared hard at me as he said these words, and I nodded, doing my best to keep a straight face. 'Do you disagree?' he asked.

'No,' I said. And the moment the word left my lips, he swung at me hard, slamming his fist into my chin.

I flew backward off my feet. I threw my arm back instinctively to break my fall but succeeded only in spraining my wrist as it bent and crumpled under the weight of my body. All the air flew out my lungs and a searing pain tore through my body. It felt as if there was a hot knife cutting deep into my side—I became distinctly aware of the fact that I was bleeding under my bandages. A groan escaped my lips, and I tried hard to push myself up into a sitting position. My head was spinning, and it felt as if though the sky, the trees, and the ruined buildings around us were all coming down on me.

'I don't like liars, boy,' said Nadir from a few feet away. Mumtaz Shah's hand grabbed me by the hair and pulled me up to my knees. His other hand grabbed me by my collar and pulled up hard, tearing my kameez as he yanked me to my feet. Nadir aimed another hard shot into my wounded torso, this time slamming the butt of his rifle into my body, and I screamed as it made contact. My knees buckled under me. Mumtaz Shah's grip on me was the only thing holding me up. Through the pain, I could see Bashir standing behind Nadir, watching. He looked horrified.

'Tell me, boy, did you kill that American yesterday?' asked Nadir, grabbing me by the throat and leaning in close. His breath was hot on my face, and his eyes shone bright with a manic glint. I was convinced I was going to die. Whether I'd be beaten to death or beheaded was still unclear. 'I thought you had committed to our cause,' said Nadir. 'I was glad to see someone so young wanting to fight for our cause. I should've known you didn't have the heart of a true Muslim in you.

You took it upon yourself to try and save a kafir? One who was here to spill the blood of your Muslim brothers and sisters?' I was staring at the ground, trying not to lose consciousness as his words rang in my ears. 'You deserve a dog's death, Irfan. You're going to be an example of what happens when we stray from His true path.' I didn't see the knife being pulled out. I didn't see it at all until the glint of silver flashed in front of my eyes as Nadir sunk the blade into my stomach.

Pain tore through what seemed like every part of my body, and I cried out. It erupted in the form of bright spots of color that flashed before my eyes as I bucked and pushed back against Mumtaz Shah, who released me and let me crumple to the ground. For a split second, I thought that I'd lost control of my bladder, then realized in a haze that the warm wetness I felt was blood running down my legs and slowly pooling around me. My hands were soaked as I held them to my side. They must've still been stained with the American boy's blood, and now they would be stained by my own as well. It felt like hours, but in reality, only a few moments passed before Mumtaz Shah grabbed me and pulled me upright onto my knees, my body throbbing dully.

Nadir had the machete in his hands, and he was pacing in front of me. 'You will not get the honor of being a shaheed. Your body will be left here in this city to rot, to be eaten by starving dogs.' He stopped speaking and turned to look at Bashir, then held out the machete. 'You pointed him out to me. You are a loyal brother of mine, Bashir. I want you to do it.'

Bashir stared at the blade for a moment before he tentatively took it from Nadir and walked over to me. His face stood out against the bleariness of everything else. His brown eyes did not shine with the same glint as Nadir's. In fact, he seemed afraid. Like he was going to cry or be sick. He closed his eyes and lifted the blade above his head, clasping it tight with both hands, but he didn't bring it down. I locked eyes with him, and he held my gaze. Finally, Mumtaz Shah lifted one hand from my shoulders.

'Give it here!' He made a grab for the machete, but Bashir pulled away.

'I can do it!' Bashir looked at me and lifted the blade up again. I lowered my head. He was going to swing this time.

What happened next, I didn't see. But I heard a strangled yell from behind me, and Mumtaz Shah's hands let go of my shoulders. I looked up. Nadir had rushed at Bashir right when the blade struck Mumtaz, and each man was struggling to pull the machete into his own grasp. Nadir was cursing loudly, and Bashir had a panicked expression on his face, but he planted his feet and pulled back hard, trying to throw the taller man to the ground.

Nadir lowered his hips and drove his head forward, slamming it between Bashir's eyes. The force of the blow stunned Bashir, and he stumbled back. His grip on the machete loosened, and Nadir wrenched it away. He took a step forward, lifting the blade up to strike, but Bashir charged forward and tackled him to the ground. He landed on top of Nadir and planted a knee into his chest, using one hand to pin down the wrist of the hand that held the machete, and groping around on the ground with his other hand. His fingers found what he was looking for a split second later, and he hoisted a stone up high before bringing it down with a dull smack across Nadir's face. From where I was lying, I could see the glazed look in Nadir's eyes, a trickle of blood flowing down the side of his face from where the stone had struck. The stone came down again. This time, a wet crack cut through the air as the stone connected with Nadir's skull. More blood flowed down his face, seeping into the crease of his scar. Bashir stood up slowly, breathing hard. He dropped the stone and wiped the sweat off his brow. It must have taken a moment to grasp what had just happened, because suddenly, Bashir looked around quickly in every direction. Nobody was approaching—not yet. He ran over and crouched down beside me.

'Irfan.' His face seemed to sway in front of me. I was aware of the fact that I couldn't feel anything anymore. My whole body had gone numb, but I knew that there was still blood flowing from where Nadir had stabbed me. 'I'm sorry, Irfan. I didn't think they'd . . .' His voice trailed off as he reached up to wipe away a tear before looking around again. 'We have to get out of here. We have to get you help,' he said. 'Quickly. Before someone comes and sees. They'll kill us both.'

Bashir hooked his arms under my arms and hoisted me up to my feet. He helped me over to the truck and, after some effort, got me into the passenger's seat. He quickly tore my blood-drenched kameez down the middle and pressed his scarf to the wound. In my head, I was screaming, but my body was too tired to force the sound out. Instead I let out a groan. Bashir glanced up at me and slowly wrapped the scarf around my waist, covering the wound completely. 'I'm going to get you to a hospital, Irfan. Hang on. Just hang on. We have to get out of here.' He ran around the truck, and in the rearview mirror I watched him crouch down next to Mumtaz Shah's body and reach into his vest to get the keys. Once he was in the driver's seat, he started the engine with a shaky hand, mumbling all the while, 'Just hold on. Going to get us out of Kabul, just please hold on. . . .'

As the truck began to pull away, I looked in my rearview mirror and watched as the shapes of Nadir and Mumtaz on the ground shrank away. My vision dimmed as well, the blackness at the corners of my eyes slowly closing in around everything else. I thought I must be dying, and right before I let myself slip away, I said a silent prayer.

You know the rest, I'm sure. I woke up from my coma in a Peshawar hospital a few weeks later. The doctors at the hospital told me Bashir had brought me in very close to death. My wounds had been kept clean and covered, so they hadn't gotten infected. But I'd lost a lot of blood, and my body had gone into shock.

After I healed, the doctors arranged transportation for me and all the other wounded to be taken home, along with the bodies of the shaheed. I must admit to you, Sameer, that I cannot recall ever feeling more fear than I did before coming back home. What if someone in the hospital recognized me? What if the remaining Sons of Islam had been able to track me down or gotten word to their sympathizers about what happened? Every waking moment was spent eyeing the door, waiting for someone to come in looking for me. I'd be killed. Or worse. When I was first told that I'd be sent back home once I was strong enough to leave, I had a panic attack and had to be sedated. Some voice in the back of my mind told me that it was a trick, that the doctors were sending me to Nadir, to the rest of the Sons of Islam, to Mullah Omar even. Anyone who would punish me the way I deserved for my betrayal. The way my nerves clanged on the ride home made it feel like I was riding on a train instead of a bus, smashing its way over the tracks.

I didn't sleep much on the way home. I had slept enough as it was. Instead, I thought hard about what I had seen when I was in that darkness I had slipped into. I felt cold, and alone. There was no warmth— none of the warmth and light that some people describe seeing or feeling as they near death. I felt afraid and regretful. Perhaps doing what I had done did not make me so fond in the eyes of Allah. But I can't be sure. Who is to say that what I felt wasn't just a symptom of my coma? Or that it wasn't my mind reacting to the medicines? I do not know. I don't think there are any people alive who can answer questions like that. But I do know that I decided right then on that ride home to completely abandon the methods I had adopted in the years since leaving, and the ideologies I had adopted before then. The ease with which I accepted that idea confused me at first. Maybe I began to realize it after I blinded the baker, or maybe it was something I had known in the back of my mind when I pressed my hand to the American boy's wounds. Or maybe it was when Nadir's knife plunged into my belly, or perhaps some part of me had decided it while we were traipsing from one town to the next at some point over the years. I do not know. But as I felt the sense of clarity wash over me, the ache in my body seemed to dull a little bit. I felt more clear-headed and less worried.

Once I got home, it became easier to start putting it all behind me. Marrying Falak made it even easier. I think she could tell, when we were first married, that some part of me was incredibly withdrawn, and despite that, she never forced me to talk about it if I didn't want to. And if I did talk about it, she listened. She would lock those hazel eyes of hers onto mine, and she would take in every single word like what I was saying was the most important thing in the world. There was no judgement there, no fear. When I cried, she comforted me. Even now, if I wake in the middle of the night from dreaming about Afghanistan and happen to wake her up as well, she'll sit upright and listen. She holds me in her arms on those nights, or she'll intertwine her arm with mine and hold my hand until we fall back asleep.

'I was told stories about who I was marrying,' she said to me one day. 'My friends warned me. They said I'd be marrying a hard man. A man who had taken the path of a holy warrior, but I could tell your appearance didn't reflect how you might really be. I was right, jaan-e-man. You have a good heart.'

I think a lot about forgiveness. Maybe my actions have been forgiven by the Almighty, but I cannot forgive myself yet. I need constant noise, because in silence I still hear Nadir's voice barking his orders in my ear. I hear the ringing of blank space building to a deafening surge before erupting into the sound of him shouting at us all over the crackle of fire. Telling us that the Americans are evil and anyone who stands complacent while they crawl into Islamic nations is a kafir who will burn for all eternity while serpents consume him from the inside out. Sometimes in my nightmares I see the deep crimson flowing out from the neck of that American boy, and he sobs loudly. I try to comfort him, to stop the bleeding, to shush his cries, and he bursts into flames in front of me. Perhaps that is why I am writing this to you. To tell somebody all of the little details that I seem unable to find the words for most of the time. Even Falak, as wonderful as she is—when she looks at me with her eyes full of a searching concern, it breaks my heart. And I feel as though I am not doing my best as a husband. Does she feel she can come to me as much as I come to her? Or does she bury her own thoughts and feelings to help me deal with mine? I don't want her to be burdened with my guilt.

A few weeks ago, I began praying on my own. I'll go to the mosque, but I won't stand with the rest of the jammat. Instead, I wait for everyone to line up, and then I position myself away from them all. I'll follow along while they do their prayers, but then I stay for longer afterward and perform my own. And in the early morning, before the sun creeps up over the horizon and the call for Fajr sounds through the streets, I wrap my shroud around myself and go up to the roof to read the Quran. Sometimes I cry. The words I whisper seem to narrate the memories that flash before my eyes, and it helps. It soothes me, and I feel a bit lighter afterward. Every ounce of pain lifted from my heart feels like an entire ton removed from somewhere deep within me. Perhaps this is the slow road to forgiving myself. Maybe it'll take another lifetime for me to truly get there. One day, when I'm old, I'll be able to look back at myself kindly. And I will understand myself better then, more than I do right now. But for right now, all I have in me is anger and regret, and I am slowly breaking the two away.

However, as I wrote at the beginning, Sameer, I have two reasons for writing you this long letter. The selfish reason, I have given you. But the other reason, the one that isn't about me, is centered around you. The affairs that compelled me to make the decisions I made have only gotten worse as time has gone on. I cannot see what or where the end of all of that will be for our country, and more importantly, our people. But I can see that you are getting older, and with each day, you understand more. You react a little more, you feel a little more. It's hypocritical of me to say that I'm prepared somewhere in my mind to stop you should you one day, Allah forbid, make the same mistakes that I did. Maybe that would be some form of perverse justice for my putting our parents through the same thing. But before we arrive at that point, I desperately want you to understand why that course of action isn't necessarily the right one.

I know that not every man going across the border or into the tribal areas to fight is like Nadir or Mumtaz Shah. Some have the best of intentions. They do not want to fight, but they are willing to give their lives in hopes of stopping the bloodshed. But I want you to understand that taking up arms and running to the border is not the only way to fight. I want there to be peace as much as anyone else does. I very much would like for all life to go back to normal, and for all the damage to be undone. I want homes to be rebuilt and families to be reunited. I would like for land that's been torn apart by bombs to be given a chance to heal so it can provide life again. I want trees to be replanted and light to be restored in the bleakest corners. I want bloodstains to be wiped off the streets and buildings, and I want all the innocents who have died to be laid to rest so they may finally find peace. And there are other ways of achieving that besides fighting. If in the future you feel that same anger coursing through you, Sameer, and the calls for jihad echo in your ears day and night the way they did for me, I want you to remember that. You can provide far more to the world by helping to rebuild a home than you can by shooting at someone because you were told to. There is more healing in the act of providing food, clothing, or shelter than there is in the act of throwing a grenade. Blood will always be spilled in wars, but there must be people to rebuild as well.

I had a dream two nights ago. It was one of the rare good ones. We were older and still living in this house. It was the middle of spring. The garden was blooming outside with fruit and different types of flowers. There hadn't been fighting in years. Falak and I had a few children, and they were playing in your lap while Amma cut vegetables in the court-yard. Abba was still a professor at the university, and we were all waiting for him to come home. There was no dread about what we would see on the news or who would call with bad news about so-and-so being killed. We were planning to go to Tando Jam, and I remembered, as a child, walking with you along the tracks at the railway station as the sun went down. That's when I woke up. In my prayers, I beg that one day, inshallah, we shall all feel that peace in the waking world.

The call for Fajr is sounding now. I will end this letter here. I hope you understand everything, including me, a little more after you've read it. Maybe when you're old enough, I will be able to say all of this to you face to face.

Love,
Irfan.

PART SIX
AHMED & KHURSHEED

Chapter Eighteen

On September 12, 2001, the only thing anyone was talking about was the attack on America. 'It'll all blow back on us now, you mark my words,' whispered the elders and the mystics. 'This will be the fall of Islam. As it is written. We are headed toward Judgement Day. There won't be any of us left. You watch.' Some people raged on to anyone who would listen about all of it being a big Jewish conspiracy. An attack carried out by Jews in America, disguised as Muslims to spark a war of faith. A few spoke out against Osama Bin-Laden and the Al-Qaeda, stating that their actions went against those prescribed in the Quran. 'How many women and children were killed?' they asked. 'We are not to harm women or children. We are not to harm animals or even cut down trees, even in times of a holy war. This isn't Islam. This is madness, and we will all be condemned for it!' Everyone had an opinion, and everyone waited to see what would happen next.

The world tuned in with rapt attention when Mullah Omar stated that he would not hand over Bin-Laden, who had sought refuge in Afghanistan, as he was a Muslim guest in an Islamic country, and the faith dictated that they could not hand him over to an enemy. Moreover, he had helped Afghanistan greatly during the jihad against the Soviet

Union, and Afghan tradition dictated that shelter had to be given to whomever asked for it.

Afghan refugees in Pakistan spat as they heard these words—a perversion of their customs, an act of defiance set to doom their homeland. Salim the chaiwallah almost drew his knife on a few patrons who cheered as they heard these words on the radio in his shop. But still, no one thought America would attack. People poured out into the streets of Pakistan, rallying. They chanted, 'America! America! Now if you come, Afghanistan will become your grave!'

In those days, Irfan tried multiple times to sneak out and attend one of these rallies. He was always caught, and Ahmed would give him a good cuff round the ear and secure the gate of their home, fastening all the bolts every time a rally started, even if it was on the other side of the city. The family would huddle together in Khursheed and Ahmed's bedroom and watch the news, waiting. And finally, in October, the Americans began their invasion of Afghanistan. Khursheed wept silently as they watched the headlines roll in on the evening news. Ahmed rubbed his temples with his fingertips. And Irfan stood near the door, transfixed. He didn't seem worried. In fact, there was almost an appraising look in his eyes. As if he were trying to figure out right then and there what he had to do next. Sameer quietly observed the rest of his family, trying to understand why they were all behaving the way they were.

The call to jihad went out the next day. 'We must defend our brothers and sisters in Afghanistan once again! As we did when the Soviets tried to invade!' cried the imam at the end of every prayer the following day. Ahmed was one of the few who didn't cheer at his words. 'We must defend Islam! This is not retribution, my brothers; this is an invasion!' And afterward, while they were praying, every Muslim in Pakistan focused on trying, through sheer faith, to will God into bringing a swift end to the impending war.

'This isn't going to turn out well for any of us,' Ahmed said at dinner that night, following the Maghrib prayers.

'You don't think Islam should be defended, Abba?' asked Irfan.

'I don't think turning this into a holy war is going to help us in the long run,' replied Ahmed. 'The way some of the men in the mosque were acting, you'd think they've been waiting for this moment their whole lives. It was the same with my students. I thought I'd have to wrestle them into their seats. They were ready to drop out and join the jihad right there in my classroom!'

'And what's wrong with that?' asked Khursheed. 'Young men wanting to fight for their land, for their faith. What's wrong with that? Your own father fought against the Soviets; you yourself have said you would have joined him had you not had to look after your mother.'

'I'm not saying there's anything wrong with that, begum of mine. I'm saying that it won't end well for anyone involved. The Americans are invading Afghanistan because they're afraid and angry, and now we're afraid and angry as well. So, what happens now? More war in Afghanistan? As if it weren't bad enough over there already.'

'The Taliban will handle the Americans,' said Irfan with a bit of pride in his voice. 'They'll drive them out!'

Ahmed stared at his son. 'The Taliban getting driven out of Afghanistan might be the only good to come of all this,' he said quietly.

Khursheed and Irfan gaped at him. Sameer stared from his brother, to his mother, to his father. Young as he was, even he could tell that the conversation had taken a serious turn at these words.

'Bite your tongue, my love!' cried Khursheed. 'How could you condemn those who fight in the name of Allah?'

'You don't see what I see, Khursheed. You don't hear what I hear. If you knew what those boys did in the name of Allah, you'd abandon your niqab and convert. Burning universities, banning girls from school, destroying libraries, people being beaten and executed in public with hardly any evidence for the crimes they're accused of. Are these not sins? Does the Quran not condemn all this as well?'

'That's all propaganda! It's American propaganda!' said Irfan.

'American propaganda that's been whispered here for nearly five years now? You're not so naïve, beta. America didn't care about what anyone was up to in Afghanistan until a few American buildings were toppled for a change. Maybe the Taliban went to Afghanistan with good intentions, but would you say you know more about what they get up to than the people who've come here from Afghanistan? Than the ones who live there now? Someone isn't good just because they say they're doing something in the name of Islam, or any religion. If someone is harmed by it, it can't be good.'

Irfan glowered at his father but did not meet his gaze. His eyes remained pointed respectfully at Ahmed's chin, and he did his best to keep from raising his voice when he spoke: 'But what about the people going over now? You don't agree with them either. All the people from Pakistan who are going to help now. To fight. You don't think they should be going either?'

'That is not what I am saying. You're not listening to me, either of you.' Ahmed glanced from his son to his wife. 'I don't want the Americans here either. I love my people as much as you do. And I'm as afraid as you are. In fact, I would say I am more afraid than you—than either of you,' he looked at Khursheed again, 'because I remember very clearly what it was like the last time someone tried to invade our neighbors. I remember the fear that came when we heard about giant tanks and planes that dropped fire from the sky, about helicopters that laid waste to entire villages in a matter of seconds. When we heard of the women being raped by the Soviet soldiers, and the babies who were cut from their wombs and tossed into fires so no future Afghans could fight. I was in Peshawar;

I saw the matted bodies, both dead and alive, of thousands of people crossing over to start a new life, and I know I wasn't the only one who was worried that maybe those demons on the other side would follow them here. Maybe our Pakistan would be next. My own father was there in that fight; I wanted to be in that fight. Not even you remember all that, meri jaan; you were only a girl then. And you,' he acknowledged Irfan, 'weren't even a thought in either of our heads. You think I don't understand this fire you have in you? You think I'm nothing more than some impish, bookworm professor. But I know all too well how you feel. I recognize that jazbah, that spirit, that burns in your eyes every time you hear on the radio about a rally starting up. And I wish I could let you go. I'm afraid of it, but I would feel hypocritical if I denied you that without a good reason.'

'Well, what is the reason then?' blurted Irfan. "If you wanted to fight, if Dada would've taken you with him, why can't I go? Forget Afghanistan—I can't even go beyond our gate to attend a rally because you won't let me!' Ifran was panting, and he was acutely aware of both Sameer and Khursheed staring at him with a mixture of shock and fear. Irfan had never raised his voice before. And despite the pride he felt at finally voicing what he felt, a small part in the back of Irfan's mind was afraid that Ahmed would get up and slap him.

So, it was genuine surprise that flickered onto his face when Ahmed put his fingertips together and smiled at Irfan over top of them. 'Let me finish,' he said. There was an awkward silence. Irfan didn't know how to respond, so Ahmed asked, 'May I finish?' Irfan nodded. 'No interruptions?' Irfan shook his head. 'Good. As I was saying, I wouldn't feel right telling you no without a reason. And the reason is not limited to you being my son; my firstborn. It is more important than even that. My reason is that when Abba-jaan, Allah grant him peace, went to fight the jihad, it was clear what the cause was. It was undeniable who the enemy was. This is not like that.' Irfan opened his mouth to say something, but Ahmed held up a finger. 'You said you'd let me finish.' Irfan gulped, and Ahmed continued: 'Anyone from our country who goes to fight is in my prayers. The people of Afghanistan are in my prayers. But things aren't so simple this time around. All this talk I heard all day of it being our duty to banish the evil that is America, of Judgement Day being on our doorsteps, all of that. It scares me, do you understand? It fills me with a great amount of fear. Not for now, but for the future. I have no doubt that there are many who are joining the fight solely to defend holy land, to defend our brothers and sisters in faith and in tribe when they are about to be punished for something they did not do. But there are also many who are fighting for other causes. They're fighting with the intent of destroying an empire that is hundreds of miles away. They're fighting because they've been told it's their duty to impose their will and spread it all over the globe. Nobody's united behind one cause; there are dozens of agendas this time around, beta. And you are too young to know the difference. You are what they look for—those who will commit unspeakable evils in the name of our faith. You, who are so full of spirit and so young. A heart willing to bleed to no end for those who are suffering. Someone, in short, they can mold. I am afraid of losing you to a cause that will lead to the downfall of our people. And while I am alive, I will do everything I can to prevent that from happening.'

Things were a little less tense after that night. Like all Pakistanis, their family kept up with the news on a day-to-day basis. Ahmed or Irfan would bring home a newspaper, and the family watched the news in the evenings on any of the dozen news channels that kept up with what was now being called 'The War on Terror.' When President Musharraf announced that Pakistan's military would help the U.S. and British forces in Afghanistan, Ahmed shut off the TV. Khursheed was shaking her head and cursing Musharraf under her breath. Ahmed rubbed his temples and suddenly stood up. Khursheed, Irfan, and Sameer stared at him. He shook his head with disgust.

'Double dealer!' he spat. 'The people of this country are running across the border in droves to fight against the Americans, and he sends the military to help them? The man's going to start a civil war! All so he can fill his pockets!'

Irfan listened, but didn't say anything. He had become very quiet about politics since Ahmed had vowed to keep him from the jihad. Aside from bringing in the newspaper every day, a few comments exchanged with his mother about what was going on, and quietly answering Sameer's questions so the little boy could understand what was happening, Irfan said nothing. Instead, he started spending more time at mosques, despite his already praying five times a day. He would hang back after prayers, telling Sameer to go home without him, and he'd be home later. If Khursheed or Ahmed ever caught him walking in through the kitchen door and asked him where he'd been, he'd calmly respond that he'd been at the mosque. Ahmed was concerned at first, worrying that his son was trying to use the guise of prayer to sneak away to rallies, but when the imam at their mosque came up to him to commend him on raising such a pious son, he put the worry in the back of his mind, convinced that Irfan was telling the truth.

In fact, Irfan didn't try to sneak out to rallies any longer, even though many of his friends did. He didn't react when many of his classmates left suddenly to go fight in Afghanistan. His teachers had the students pray for the safe return of their classmates, and a swift end to the American invasion. Many of the older neighborhood boys were gone too. Some had made their intentions to fight clear weeks before they left. They talked about it to anyone who would listen, with somber expressions on their faces. They grew their beards out, they responded thoughtfully to questions that didn't need consideration, and exchanged their jeans and t-shirts for weathered shalwar kameez. Khursheed and Ahmed both worried that this would spark another argument with their son, but to their surprise, Irfan still seemed unfazed.

Even Ahmed's students couldn't be held back any longer. Some, after convincing their fathers and mothers and aunts and uncles that this was their Islamic duty, were withdrawn from the university by their families. Their relatives would then ride with them on the near three-day train ride to Peshawar to see them off, showering them with prayers, giving them copies of the Quran to ensure that they'd be under Allah's protection, and pulling them into final hugs before they left to find a group that was going through the Khyber Pass. Others simply snuck out in the middle of the night and hopped the train alone. Then, they would cross through one of the many unregulated tribal areas and into Afghanistan, taking the first steps toward the so-called holy war that awaited them.

In December of that year, the Taliban were ousted from the city of Kabul by the American military. They fled back to the mountains, losing more ground on the way as American bombs dropped on Taliban strongholds, clearing the ground for American troops to move in. Some shaved off the beards they'd grown when they realized they couldn't escape in time, to blend in among the common folk. But Pakistanis and Afghans alike were killed by American forces or their air strikes, whether they were Taliban or not. Those who realized the wave was about to overrun them escaped to Pakistan, sneaking into Peshawar with worn expressions on their faces. 'We couldn't fight them,' they would say.

'We can fight soldiers. We can't fight bombs from the sky,' cried some in Pakistan when they heard. Sermons were given at prayer times, announcing that a great Islamic country, a holy land, had been conquered by foreign invaders, by gorre.

'The Americans have finished what the British started,' wept one imam in the capital city of Islamabad. Others, particularly Afghans who had escaped to Pakistan when the Soviets invaded, silently cheered the fact that the Taliban had been driven out. But they too feared what would happen now, in an Afghanistan occupied by American forces.

'Maybe things will finally get better. Maybe blood will stop staining the ground in Afghanistan now,' said the optimists.

'What if they move into Pakistan next?' whispered others fearfully.

'Oh, that would never happen,' they'd be reassured. 'Musharraf has licked their President's boots too much!'

Some of Ahmed's students returned, but not to the university. They came home on cots, wrapped in shrouds, with white sheets draped over them. They were delivered to their homes by truck drivers who were being paid to carry nothing but the bodies of the dead to their families. The ones who couldn't be identified were buried in mass gravesites, away from areas where fighting was taking place and bombs were being dropped.

Early one evening the following spring, right after the Asr prayers, Ahmed was walking home from the mosque when he noticed a small crowd gathered at the house across the street from his own. As he neared, he saw a truck with its tarp pulled up over the back and at least a dozen cots inside. He became aware of the sound of wracked sobs going up from the middle of the crowd, and when he pushed his way to the front, he saw the woman from across the street, Mrs. Abbasi, on her knees next to a cot. Her scarf hung around her neck, and her henna-dyed hair was exposed. The white sheet had been pulled away, the shroud had been unwrapped, and her son's burnt corpse lay underneath it all. Her fingers trembled against his raw, exposed flesh where the skin had been entirely burnt away, and she held her face against the part of his face that was still recognizable. Black, congealed blood was clumped up over the charred skin and clothing that remained on his torso and face. The men who had unloaded the cot stared awkwardly at each other as the woman sobbed over her son's body, unsure of whether they should leave. The men in the crowd watched the spectacle, shaking their heads, muttering prayers under their breath. Some called out, asking if anyone knew where the father was. A few others broke away to rush home and get their wives to come help.

Ahmed stared at the woman as she cried, 'My son! My son!' over and over, kissing his burnt and bloodied face. He noticed a movement out of the corner of his eye and glanced up. Irfan stood a few feet away, staring at the corpse, tears sliding down his face.

Ahmed pushed his way over to where Irfan stood and gently grabbed his elbow. Leaning in close, he whispered, 'Let's go, beta.'

Irfan let his father lead him away from the crowd, but the sound of the woman's sobs still rang in both their ears as they went across the street to their house. Khursheed stood in the courtyard, nervously staring at the gate as she listened to the commotion outside. 'What's happened?' she asked Ahmed when they walked in.

Ahmed glanced at her and shook his head wordlessly as he led Irfan inside.

A few neighborhood women who came out with their scarves tightly wrapped around their heads were able to lead Mrs. Abbasi inside. They consoled her and resigned themselves to handling chores around the house until her husband came home from work. Some of the men lingered outside the gate in case the women needed anything. The men who had delivered the body rewrapped it and moved it into the courtyard. It would be taken to the mosque that evening, and they would bury it the next day. Since the boy, Jahangir Abbasi, had been a shaheed, a martyr, the dried blood and dirt would not be washed off the body. He was nineteen years old.

Soon, the full story was all over the neighborhood. Jahangir had gone across the border into Afghanistan back in November, not to fight, but to work with an aid group to help children displaced by unending war. They went from camp to camp, providing medicine, clothes, water, and whatever else they could. One day, the American forces launched an airstrike on an abandoned school building near one of the camps. They suspected that a Taliban splinter cell was operating out of the basement of the building. What they didn't know was that the school building was being used by the aid group to temporarily store water, medicines, and other supplies. Jahangir and two other volunteers had gone that day to get more water tanks. The air strike hit as they were leaving. Jahangir's body was found the next day underneath some rubble by American soldiers. One of the other volunteers had been knocked underneath the jeep they had drove in on, and the other one had been blown to pieces.

They found no members of the Taliban. The splinter cell had abandoned the school two months earlier.

Irfan left for Peshawar the next day.

Chapter Nineteen

It was a Saturday, so Ahmed and Khursheed weren't too concerned when Irfan didn't come home immediately after the Zuhr prayers. They figured he was still at the mosque, staying longer to read the Quran or listen in on theological discussions like he usually did. Sameer was with Khursheed's sister that day, spending the weekend with his cousins. It wasn't until she got up to make chai before dusk that Khursheed noticed Irfan still wasn't home. 'I'll go check the mosque,' said Ahmed when Khursheed told him. She went back to the kitchen to finish making the chai, but a pit of unease had begun to form in her stomach. At the time, she had no idea why. Don't be silly, she scolded herself. He's fine. He's at the mosque.

Ahmed returned twenty minutes later. Khursheed unlocked the gate when he knocked, and her anxious face fell when she saw that he'd come back alone. 'I checked everywhere. The mosque, the stores. I even went to Salim Bhai's shop to see if he'd seen Irfan. He said he hadn't seen him since this morning, when he came in for a cup of chai after the Fajr prayers. Nobody else has seen him since Fajr either.' There was a nervous edge to Ahmed's tone. He was trying to keep his voice steady, but Khursheed could tell.

'There weren't any rallies today, were there?' she asked quietly.

'No. None planned anyway. But we would've heard about it if one had started up.' They both stood in the courtyard silently as dusk began to settle and the call for Maghrib prayer rang out in the air. Once the call ended, Ahmed spoke again. 'Call his friends' homes,' he said.

Khursheed hurried to the telephone in their bedroom and sat down on the edge of the bed. She picked up a little notepad containing the phone numbers of everyone they knew, flipped it open, and began to punch in numbers. It took her fifteen minutes to get through the names of friends whose homes Irfan could have been at. They all reassured her, saying he'd turn up eventually. 'Oh, you know how these boys are at this age! Woh aajaye ga na!' He'll come home soon enough!

Next, she called her sister to see if maybe Irfan had gone over to be with his cousins as well. Her sister, Rubina, sounded surprised when she asked. 'No, Khursheed. He hasn't been here at all. You've called his friends?'

'Yes! Yes! I've called them all!' Khursheed cried.

'Hush! Don't panic. I'm sure he'll be along.'

'Something is wrong, Rubina. I can feel it. Something's happened.' Rubina tried reassuring her, but Khursheed could hear the sliver of concern that had slipped in under her sister's voice.

While his wife was on the phone, Ahmed paced in the drawing room and finally ran up the stairs to the boys' room. He threw the door open and stood in the middle of the room, his eyes darting to each corner, unsure of what exactly it was he was looking for. Something, anything that was out of place. Anything that might help . . .

He hurried over to the wardrobe and opened every door, peering inside. There were some clothes missing. 'But those might be in the wash...' he muttered to himself. The drawers on the bottom were next. He pulled them out all the way and looked inside. There were definitely clothes missing—two of the drawers had been entirely emptied out. A third, the one in which Khursheed stored the boys' underwear and socks, was half empty. Ahmed stood up quickly and rushed over to the desk by the window. He lifted up notebooks, dictionaries, and textbooks in his search, and finally, he found a piece of printer paper covered in dark blue ink. It had been placed in between two class folders in the corner. Ahmed knew before he read it what it would say. The boy had planned this carefully. He had known his parents would check the room first. They'd need to prove their suspicions to themselves. He hadn't made the note hard to find.

Ahmed's hands shook as he read the words:

> *Dear Amma and Abba,*
>
> *I am sorry. I couldn't stand by anymore. This is my duty. I have gone to Peshawar with a group of boys from the mosque. When this war is over, I will return to you, inshallah.*
>
> *I hope you have forgiven me by then.*
>
> *Your son,*
>
> *Irfan*

Ahmed felt as if the ground had crumbled beneath his feet, and he had to grip the back of the desk chair to keep himself steady. He read the words three more times, hoping to undo what they said with each reading. A small part of him hoped something had gone wrong; maybe the boy had turned back, or maybe he hadn't even left yet. Perhaps he would come through the gate in a few moments, with his shoulders slumped and a greasy bag of pakoras from Salim's chai shop in his hand. But Ahmed knew Irfan was gone. He would be almost halfway to Peshawar by then.

Once he trusted himself enough to stand and walk without feeling sick, Ahmed quietly went downstairs to where Khursheed was sitting in the darkened drawing room. Her clean, white, cotton scarf, which she wore only for prayer, was wrapped tightly around her head. She held her rosary in one hand, pushing the beads one by one while whispering prayers under her breath. These were not the same as the five daily prayers she performed throughout the day. These were the special prayers she made as a mother, along with her regular ones, five times a day, without fail. Prayers to protect her children from harm, prayers to cast off the evil eye, prayers to ensure that her boys would return home safe every single time they left home. These were the prayers whispered by every mother in the country; by every mother in the world; in every faith and in every language. These were the prayers that transcended the boundaries of religion, and they belonged to every woman who had a child.

Ahmed stood in the doorway, watching her, wondering the best way to tell her. Where he had been in such a rush moments ago, he was now dazed and slow in his thoughts and movements. A few seconds passed before Khursheed's eyes snapped open. She saw him silhouetted against the doorway by the kitchen light. She got up and went over to him.

'We just have to w—' she started to say, but Ahmed held up his hand to cut her off.

'Come here,' he said, gently gripping her hand and leading her to a seat at the dining room table.

'What's wrong?'

Ahmed simply shook his head and handed her the note, then held his head in his hands. Khursheed's eyes scanned the note quickly, and her face grew paler with each line. By the end, her face matched the shade of the paper. 'Ahmed . . .' Her voice trailed off. Ahmed reached over and took her by the hand again, pulling himself closer to her. 'This is a trick,' she said. 'That boy is pulling a trick on us, and Allah help him when he gets home, I'm going to thrash him so hard he'll never think of doing anything like this again!'

Ahmed watched her silently as she shouted these words, and he waited until she quieted again before speaking. 'Someone at the mosque said something about a group of boys leaving together this morning,' he said slowly. 'I didn't think Irfan could be with them.'

'You have to go get him!' Khursheed shouted.

'He'll be in and out of Peshawar before I can even get to the city. I won't be able to find him, and it might be worse if I do. Who knows who he's with? How they'll react if they see him leave? Who's to say they won't kill him themselves?' said Ahmed.

Khursheed let out an anguished sob and beat her fists against Ahmed's chest and shoulders, crying, 'They wouldn't! They wouldn't!' But she knew he was right. She knew that once in Peshawar, Irfan would take his last rites, as all holy warriors did before going to war. There was no turning back after that. Not until the fighting ended, or he was hurt, or killed. And at this thought, she buried her face in her husband's chest and cried harder, soaking the muslin cloth of his shirt with her tears. Ahmed held her tightly against him, with his face buried in her hair, and he too began to cry. His tears ran down into her hair, and he breathed in the salty sweet perfume they made as they mixed with her henna dye, as they both cried over their son.

They sat like that until their eyes ran dry, and then they sat a little while longer. The call for the Isha prayers sounded, the clock in the living room chimed, and still they sat. Finally, when the power went out around midnight, Khursheed stood up and announced in a hoarse voice that she was going to bed. Ahmed followed her soon after. They lay there with their backs to each other, so lost were they in thoughts of Irfan that neither one noticed the other lying awake beside them. At dawn, when the call to Fajr rang through the streets, Khursheed got out of bed and Ahmed closed his eyes, pretending he'd been asleep the entire time.

Chapter Twenty

Three years of anxiety came to an end when Irfan returned home one afternoon in November of 2004. Khursheed was out in the courtyard hanging clothes on the clothesline when there was a knock at the gate. Sameer was at school, and Ahmed had just come home for lunch. Khursheed called out to ask who it was and received no response, so Ahmed came out and unlocked the gate, pushing the door open a little to look. Khursheed was standing behind him, her view of the doorway blocked by his shoulder. She heard a low, quiet voice say, 'Salaam.'

Ahmed stood still and silent. After a moment he took a few steps back, and Khursheed wondered why he wasn't saying anything. That was when she saw the young man step in through the gate. His face was a bit sunken, as if he had been starved for a while, and his eyes were tired. His dark brown beard hung off his chin, trimmed down slightly on the sides. Wrapped around him was a thick maroon shawl. Only his dirt-covered boots were visible under it, and a black pakol rested on his head, tilted slightly to the side.

'Asalam Walaikum,' said the young man again, and this time he bowed his head slightly in front of Ahmed, who instinctively reached out with a trembling hand and placed it on top of the boy's head, before grabbing him by the shoulder and shaking him. Tears streaming down his face, he pulled the boy into a hug.

Recognition at last set in, and Khursheed grabbed the young man's face, looking into the deep-set brown eyes, searching for the little boy she always managed to find inside them. When she found him, she clutched him to her body and sobbed into his neck, pulling both her son and her husband down into her embrace. Irfan wrapped his arms around both of his parents as best he could, feeling their warm tears pressing down on his body as they held him close. The prayers they muttered and the questions they asked all blended into one sound. There was a breeze blowing in from the open gate, and the scent of the neem leaves of the tree in the courtyard wrapped itself around the family.

At some point, the three of them went inside the house, Khursheed swaying a little as she sank into the couch and stared at her firstborn. She cried silently as she watched him remove his pakol. His hair was still long and dark, but it had thinned a little. The hairline was beginning to recede, not noticeable to anyone except her. He looked gaunt, but as he shifted his weight and rearranged his shawl, she noticed his tunic wrapping itself snugly around the muscles that lay underneath.

'You've lost weight,' she said quietly. Irfan smiled at her and pinched his own stomach.

'Not necessarily a bad thing. But I haven't had your cooking in a while. My body decided to stop hoping for it, and that helped me lose some weight.'

Khursheed laughed and stood up again. 'I'll be back with lunch, and some chai,' she said as she hurried out of the room to the kitchen. Ahmed was sitting next to Irfan, watching him just like Khursheed had been.

'How've you been?' Irfan asked quietly, turning his head slightly to look at Ahmed.

Immediately, he felt a pang in his chest and regretted the question.

Ahmed's face was still sticky with tears, and his eyes were still brimming, but he cleared his throat and said, 'We've been decent. We've been worried about you.' His hair had grayed in the front and on the sides, and it was beginning to thin out on top. His face had begun to sag just a little bit, the skin around his eyes turned to heavy bags, and his jowls seemed looser as well. The two sat in complete silence, until at last Ahmed said, 'I cannot believe you're here in front of me.'

'I can't believe it myself,' Irfan replied.

Khursheed came back in after a while, carrying a tray loaded with cups of steaming chai and plates full of sandwiches and biscuits. She set it down on the table and placed the largest cup and a plate with two sandwiches and a handful of biscuits in front of Irfan.

'Eat!' she urged.

While the tea was sipped and the food consumed, Irfan began to talk. He very slowly and very calmly told his parents about what had happened during almost three years he had been gone. Careful to leave out any specific details, he described going across the border into Afghanistan. He described the man who took him as 'big, strong, and serious,' and he described the man he had been following as 'charismatic and inspiring.' Irfan talked about the parts of Afghanistan he had seen; the deserts, the mountains, the giant cliffs, the small towns and villages, and Kabul.

'What was the city like?' asked Ahmed.

Irfan described the capital city as best he could, leaving out the fact that he hadn't had the chance to see much of it before nearly being killed there. He painted a picture of the grandeur it still retained, and the state of it after years of war. It's like a wound that nobody's allowing to heal completely before they open it again,' he said.

Most of all, he talked about a boy called Bashir, describing him as 'My best friend. Brave, much braver than I could be. And strong, tough. He saved my life.' At these last words, Khursheed and Ahmed both stared.

'I was hurt. I got hurt over there; that's why I came home. Bashir got me out of Kabul; he got me back to a hospital in Peshawar, and they sent me back home once I was healed enough.' He didn't feel the need to mention that he had been in a coma. It would only serve to cause more worry.

'Where was the injury?' asked Ahmed.

Irfan stood up slowly, sliding the shawl off his shoulders and very carefully pulling up the hem of his tunic. He winced a little as the cool air hit the clean, white bandages wrapped around his torso. Ignoring the horror on their faces, Irfan continued speaking: 'A battle broke out, and someone threw a grenade. It went off near me and an American. The American died, but I was only hurt. I was punctured by some shrapnel and . . . pieces of broken glass.'

Khursheed reached out and gently touched the wrappings. 'Are you supposed to be taking anything for it?' she asked quietly.

'I've got some medicines in my bag that the doctors gave me. Once I finish taking them, I should be fine. I just need to change the wrappings every time I bathe until the swelling and redness are completely gone.'

Khursheed nodded. She would spend the bulk of the next month chasing him around the house, reminding him to take his medicine and frantically checking his bandages every chance she got to make sure they were clean.

Irfan felt another hand touch his side, and he looked down to see Ahmed very lightly rubbing over the white cloth with the tips of his fingers. As if he could speed up the healing process with a gentle massage. There were tears sliding down his face again, and he shook his head. 'We could have lost you.' He glanced up to look Irfan in the eye. 'We thought for so long that we had. But there was a feeling, deep down somewhere. Your mother and I both felt it. And we knew you were still alive somehow. We knew you weren't dead, but we didn't know if you would ever make it back home.'

At these words, Irfan felt a pang in his heart. It dawned on him suddenly, what he must have put his parents through. What they must have imagined a thousand times over, all the scenarios that would've played in their heads every time they turned on the news or read the paper.

Indeed, Ahmed and Khursheed had spent every waking hour of every day since Irfan had left checking every news channel to keep up with what was happening across the border. Looking for any group of young jihadis that had been caught or killed. Any news of skirmishes with the Taliban, of bombings carried out by the Americans, anything at all that showed the faces of young men near or across the border. Praying, begging, that none of the faces would match that of their son. Ahmed recalled wondering at some point if he'd even be able to recognize Irfan's face if he saw it. But none of that mattered now. Irfan was back. He had come home, and all the sadness, the heartache, the anger, the anxiety of the last three years was gone. It had gone out through the gate as Irfan came in. Ahmed and Khursheed could finally let go of the breath they'd been holding for so long.

When Sameer came home from school that day, Irfan sat silently in the living room, listening to Khursheed describe, with great detail, the Quran khwani she was holding at their house the very next day to celebrate Irfan's homecoming. She fell silent as Ahmed walked into the living room hand in hand with Sameer. Irfan stood up immediately, staring hard at the boy staring back at him with a mixture of shock and confusion on his face.

'Sameer,' said Ahmed quietly. 'Don't you recognize your own brother?'

Irfan gave a faint smile and took a step forward, and Sameer tore his hand out from Ahmed's, turned around, and ran up the stairs.

'Sameer!' cried Khursheed, rushing to the staircase to go up after him.

'Leave him.' Ahmed gripped her elbow gently and pulled her back. 'He'll come on his own. He's just shocked.'

It wasn't until after the Maghrib prayers that evening, when the family was sitting down for dinner, that Sameer slowly came down the steps and hesitantly approached Irfan, his eyes cast downward.

Irfan smiled and placed a hand on top of the boy's head. 'Asalam Walaikum,' he said. Sameer mumbled a response, still staring at Irfan's feet. 'You won't believe the stories I have for you,' Irfan said as he crouched down in front of Sameer. 'But maybe you're too old for my stories now?' Sameer looked Irfan in the eye, taking in the thinner face, the full beard, and he threw his arms around Irfan's neck and buried his face into his shoulder. The boy's hot tears ran freely down his face as Irfan wrapped his arms around his little brother, holding him close as he cried.

'I thought you were gone forever!' the little voice sobbed.

Irfan held him tight and kissed the top of his head, and gently spoke into Sameer's ear. 'I'm back now, Sameer. I could never leave you forever.' Irfan consoled Sameer until the boy finally let go, his eyes red, cheeks stained and sticky with tears, and nose running.

'You're not going to go back, are you?' he asked.

'No, Sameer. I'm not going to go back. I'm staying right here.'

Khursheed's eyes met Ahmed's as they both watched their sons interact with one another, as Irfan finally managed to coax Sameer to sit down next to him and have his dinner. She smiled but said nothing as she watched him start piling biryani onto the boy's plate.

After his first bite, Irfan closed his eyes and sighed. 'Amma,' he said as he opened them, 'I missed this more than you will ever know.'

She smiled and leaned over the table to put a hand on the side of his face and pinch his cheek. 'I cannot put into words how light my heart feels now that you're home, beta.'

For weeks after Irfan returned, their home was the center of a seemingly unending celebration. For two weeks, there were nonstop visitors to the house. First came all the neighbors who arrived with their arms weighed down by gifts and decadent dishes they usually saved for special occasions like Eid or khatam-e-Qurans. The men, especially some of the older ones who had gone to Afghanistan themselves in the time of the war against the Soviets, presented Irfan with new, hand-woven ajraks and crisp shalwar kameez, pakols and bejeweled Sindhi caps. They gave him small leather pouches full of money. The oldest man in the neighborhood, Pir Baba, (named after the centuries-old Sufi who was said to be a direct descendant of the Prophet PBUH himself), gifted Irfan a beautiful dagger that had three emeralds embedded in its hilt. The sheath was a beautiful jade green, and the men all passed it around the room carefully, marveling at the craftsmanship. Ahmed quickly took the dagger from Irfan's hands, mumbling about putting it in a safe place. 'You can't keep things like that out of his hands now!' laughed the men. 'He's become a man!' They all sat around, talking about the politics of the West and discussing what the outcome of the war would be. All questions seemed to be directed Irfan's way, and any answer he gave was met with slow nods of contemplation. As if every word he spoke was a piece of sagely insight.

Everyone would pray together at these gatherings, the women in one room and the men at the neighborhood mosque. And afterward, copies of the Quran would be passed out at the house, and again, in separate rooms, the men and women would all sit around and read to themselves for about an hour, thanking the Almighty for bringing the young man home safely, praying for him to be rewarded for his actions in the name of Islam, and begging for a swift end to the ongoing war.

When the days of neighbors dropping in came to an end, it came time for the family to visit. Aunts, uncles, cousins, grandparents, great-aunts, great-uncles, twice removed, thrice removed, all filtered in and out of the house as they pleased, all bearing gifts and stories of how they'd last seen Irfan when he was 'this big,' and how he was unrecognizable now. A shining young man at the peak of his life. More than a few distant aunts shoved their daughters forward pointedly, and Irfan would shyly mutter a 'salaam' while simultaneously looking for the quickest way out of the room. Kids ran through the house, and although Sameer played with them, he also did his best to stay as close by his brother's side as he possibly could. Smells of food and chai constantly wafted out of the kitchen as Khursheed heated any number of the dozens of gifted dishes. Irfan didn't have a moment to himself until his Rubina Khala and her family finally left. The next morning, when he came down for breakfast, Khursheed and Ahmed were sitting at the table, a pot of chai between them, talking in low voices. They looked up as he came down, and Khursheed poured a cup out for him.

'I want you to shower and put on the clothes I ironed for you after you have breakfast. They're on my bed.'

'More guests?' Irfan asked as he sat down and pulled the cup his way.

'Yes. Mariam Auntie and her family are coming.'

'Which one is she?' He glanced up at his mother, who was carrying her cup over to the kitchen.

'Oh, you know. She's got that daughter—what was her name again, Jaan?' She turned to look at Ahmed.

'Falak,' said Ahmed with a smile.

Irfan looked from one parent to the other, realization dawning on his face. 'No.' He pushed his chair back as he said it. 'She's the one who you introduced me to in the courtyard last week. The woman that brought the pan full of sweets!'

Khursheed shook her head. 'I told you he'd react like this.'

'Like what? I'm too young to get married!'

Ahmed placed a hand on Irfan's arm and said quietly, 'And who said anything about getting you married? We just want you to consider it; no shame in that. I've taught boys younger than you who were engaged.'

Irfan stared at Ahmed and gently pulled his arm away. 'I'm not them,' he said simply.

'Irfan, please. Just meet the family, won't you? You don't have to decide today; just keep an open mind. There's no shame in meeting the girl, is there?' pleaded Khursheed.

'How do you know she'll even like me? Does she even want me right now?' asked Irfan.

'We don't know,' said Ahmed simply. 'And if either one of you, or both of you, rejects the proposal, then that's fine. Nobody's getting forced into this. There are worse ways to spend the day than meeting a pretty girl, beta.'

Irfan stood there a moment, mulling it over, and finally he spoke.

'You promise you're not going to force me into anything?'

Khursheed smiled. 'We aren't tyrants, you know. There's just so many mothers interested in my brave and handsome son, I have to consider some of them, don't I? I want grandchildren one day.'

Irfan pulled a face and shook his head. 'Fine, fine. I'll meet them.'

'I told you he'd be sensible,' said Ahmed pointedly, and Khursheed shot him a look that made him chuckle.

After Irfan had eaten his breakfast and gone to shower, Khursheed busied herself in the kitchen. As she washed the dishes, put another paratha on the tawa for when Sameer woke up, and began getting out ingredients for the meal she'd be cooking later that day for the guests, she felt her mind start to drift toward the anxiety-inducing truth behind her reason for inviting the proposal. She knew it was the same thought that Ahmed had in his mind as well, for the two of them lay next to each other in bed every night and talked about it until sleep came to them. They were both afraid that, for one reason or another, Irfan might go back.

Something had changed in her son. She had seen it in the weeks since he'd come home: fleeting glimpses of loneliness in his eyes, of pain. Something was gone, and it had left him empty. At times she could barely recognize the young man in front of her. He would look up at her with that slimmed face, the rough beard, those piercing eyes, and she would feel as if a stranger had wandered into her home. Ahmed had expressed similar feelings to her a few nights before, about how sometimes when he reached out to place a hand on his son, he would touch a body he didn't recognize. Irfan had always been relaxed under his father's hand. Now, every inch of him was coiled up, as if he were ready to burst—as if, when he was touched, it took him a moment to remember where he was and whose hand was on him. The two were terrified at the prospect of losing their son again, and so they hoped maybe a family of his own might fill that new void in him. Maybe, just maybe, the connection they'd lost with him could have opened up room for a deeper connection with another.

Later that day, Falak and Irfan sat silently across from each other in the living room as their families interacted. Ahmed nudged Irfan with his elbow at one point to remind him to say 'salaam' to Falak. Other than a few quick glances at each other, they didn't interact at all. The talking was done by the parents, and Falak's aunt and uncle, who had also accompanied her and her parents. They asked Irfan about his schooling, what he liked, disliked, if he had played any sports. At one point, Falak's father, Osman, brought the conversation to politics and the war. He looked Irfan in the eye and said, 'May Allah protect the sons of this land from all of the foreign devils.' Irfan smiled politely and nodded at the older man's prayer. Khursheed and Ahmed asked Falak the same questions, but her mother, Mariam, rattled off all the things Falak could do before the girl could answer for herself.

'She can cook dishes from every region in Pakistan! She can sew as well! And my girl is very, very highly educated. Mashallah! Mashallah! A history student! How many girls have you heard of majoring in history, Khursheed Baji?'

'Not many,' admitted Khursheed with a polite smile.

They stayed for lunch, which was rice with steamed peas and spiced mutton. Sameer ran around the table with Falak's younger brother and sister the whole time, the three children only pausing to eat when grabbed by a parent to have a spoonful shoved into their mouths. The guests left after having a few cups of chai. By then, the sky outside was tinted peach pink, and Osman stood up and announced that they had to leave so he could be home in time to say Asr prayers. After the requisite pleas of 'stay a while longer,' Khursheed and Ahmed finally agreed, and everyone moved to the courtyard to say their goodbyes. After many more compliments on Khursheed's cooking and a half-dozen promises to come back soon, Falak and her family left.

Two more meetings between the families took place, almost identical to that first one, with Irfan and Falak barely exchanging any words. Until finally, on their fourth visit, Osman cleared his throat pointedly and Ahmed put a hand on Irfan's shoulder.

'How about you two go and talk in the other room?' said Ahmed, nodding in Falak's direction.

'Um—' Irfan looked from his father to Osman to Falak, who looked just as confused as he felt.

'Go on, get to know each other,' Osman said. Khursheed and Mariam nodded as well, giving encouraging smiles. Falak shrugged and stood up, smoothing out the front of her patterned tunic and re-adjusting the blue scarf draped across her neck and shoulders. Irfan cleared his throat and stood as well, holding the door open for her as she walked past him and into the dining area.

'Leave the door open a bit!' called Khursheed from the living room. Irfan stepped out and pushed the door nearly closed behind him.

The parents busied themselves with small talk after Falak and Irfan went into the other room, but Khursheed kept one ear cocked in the direction of the door, and she could hear them talking quietly. She was acutely aware of the fact that Mariam was doing the same thing she was. After nearly twenty minutes, Osman stood up and straightened the hem of his kurta. 'We should be leaving now,' he said. 'We will stay in touch and hopefully see you again soon, inshallah.' And then he stuck his head into the other room to tell Falak that they were leaving.

Once the goodbyes had been exchanged and Khursheed and Ahmed had seen the family off, Sameer curled up on the couch and fell asleep. As Khursheed and Irfan were picking up the trays from the living room and carrying them into the kitchen, she asked him, 'What'd you think?'

Irfan was quiet for a moment, pretending to not have heard. Then, without looking up at her, he said, 'I'd like to see her again.'

The grin on Khursheed's face might've been visible from miles away.

PART SEVEN
IRFAN

Chapter Twenty-One

After he came back home, things passed by in a blur for Irfan. Even years later, he could recall just how quickly he met Falak, fell in love with her, and married her. He hadn't been sure what to make of her at first, the first two times they met with their families speaking for them. But when at last they were left alone to talk, she surprised him, and he found that he wanted to know more about her. Even years later, he could recall that first conversation as vividly as if it had just happened. He remembered Ahmed suggesting that he and Falak speak with each other in private, away from the eyes of their parents. They hadn't even looked at each other as they quietly made their way into the next room.

Falak pulled the chair out at the far end of the table, sat down, and placed a hand on the side of her face, staring at the cups of fine china stacked upside down on the kitchen countertop, tracing the carefully drawn floral designs with her eyes.

'Erm, do you want a cup of chai?' asked Irfan awkwardly.

She turned to him and shook her head. 'No, thank you.'

Irfan nodded, and then pulled out the chair at the opposite end of the table for himself. Once he was seated, he cleared his throat and looked at her, doing his best to maintain eye contact without really making eye contact by staring at the bridge of her nose.

'Well, you've finally managed to look at me for more than two seconds.' She smiled shyly as she spoke, as though taken aback for a moment by her own comment.

Irfan blinked twice and then laughed nervously. 'I'm sorry. I just don't know how to act in there with them. It's like they expect us to start swooning if we sit next to each other long enough.'

'And right when it happens, a sitar will strum, and a modernized version of some old, romantic folk song will play.'

Irfan laughed again. 'That's right. As all the great romances go.'

'Someone's parents have to disapprove first, though,' Falak said.

'That's true,' said Irfan. 'I don't think it'll be mine. They seem to love you. Unless, of course, you reveal some plan to murder your future mother-in-law.'

Falak shrugged. 'Maybe that would do it. Or I could just let slip that I used to be in a relationship. And that this search for a husband was my parents' way of bringing it to an end.'

Irfan finally made true eye contact, holding her stare as a heavy silence hung in the air for a moment. He couldn't be sure if she was serious or not. She had no reason to tell him this, and yet, he felt like she wasn't lying.

Falak, on the other hand, despite her unwavering look of seriousness, was mildly panicked on the inside. She couldn't tell what had compelled her to say what she had said, but it was too late to take it back now. Any of the other suitors her parents had introduced her to might've left right then, or reacted with shock—maybe even anger. She wouldn't have dared to say what he had just said to any of them.

But Irfan did not do any of those things. He just seemed confused. Finally, he spoke: 'Well, they might not throw a party over that news. But I can't see them thinking it makes you a bad potential wife,' he said.

'Maybe they wouldn't react harshly if you told them about a girl you had been with, but people react differently when it's a girl that's had the oh-so-secretive chakkar before marriage. I'm supposed to have been chaste and hidden away while waiting for you, or whatever other man I was bound to be married to.' Falak leaned back in her chair after saying this, eyeing Irfan carefully, trying to gauge his reaction.

He considered her words for a moment or two before leaning forward and speaking in a quiet voice, so any of the eavesdropping adults in the other room wouldn't hear what he was saying. 'Whatever I decide about you, or any girl my parents invite over, will not depend on what she has done in her past. Things like that are not my concern. And as for my parents, I can promise you that they have accepted people far worse before now.' He stopped talking abruptly after saying this, realizing that he was referring to himself and remembering exactly what he was hinting at. But at Falak's questioning look, he found himself unable to stop himself from continuing. 'I—erm, I know I've done worse. They wouldn't reject you for a little romance, so feel free to go into that room and tell them. And as for me, like I said, I've done worse. I wouldn't have any room to judge you for that even if it bothered me.'

There was a hand-carved wooden coaster on the table in front of Falak. She traced the inner pattern of it with the tip of her finger. 'Thank you,' she finally said. 'If you don't mind my asking . . . what have you done?'

'I'm sure at some point in the time you've spent coming and going from here that someone has mentioned where I was until recently. There's a reason my father isn't boasting about my education in there, you know,' Irfan said.

Falak smiled and said, 'I've heard about a half a dozen rumors, yes.'

'You don't believe them?' he asked.

'Should I?' she responded calmly.

'If I answered that honestly, I bet you'd ask your parents to leave right now and never come back here again,' said Irfan.

'Well, I won't push you to tell me. But I'm almost certain that you're wrong about that.'

Irfan searched her eyes for some sign of a lie; something deceptive, or a sign of the curiosity everyone had been showing since he came back— the kind that made him feel like an animal in a cage. A dozen gazes inspecting his body for any sign of his participation in the so-called 'holy war.' But he couldn't see that in her. Perhaps she was just good at hiding it. Or, a small voice in the back of his mind whispered, perhaps she was genuine. Finally, he smiled at her.

'Maybe next time. I'm not sure I could find the words to talk about it all right now anyway.'

Falak smiled back and said, 'What makes you think there'll be a next time?'

Before Irfan could answer, the door to the other room opened and Osman stuck his head in. 'We're leaving now, beti,' he said to Falak.

Over the course of the following month, they met eight more times. Each meeting was like the last. The families would sit together at first, conversing politely, sipping tea, while Irfan and Falak interacted silently with quick glances and shy grins, trying not to be embarrassed by the fact that their families were staging such a show just for them. And then, after a while, they'd both be allowed by the adults to go into the next room together with the door slightly ajar and left alone to talk for a while.

Irfan learned that Falak was not just a history major, but an art history major with a concentration in the artwork from the Golden Age of Islam. Her favorite painting was an illustration from the poet Nizami's Khamsa, depicting the ascent of the Prophet to Heaven on the back of a buraq. 'My mother doesn't deem it as impressive to tell people that her daughter is studying centuries-old paintings,' explained Falak.

'I find it very interesting,' said Irfan, and when she laughed and told him not to tease her, he said, 'Truly, I do. I'm not trying to tease you.' At this, Falak stared at him, looking as though she were about to say something, but instead she gave a shy smile and changed the subject. Irfan learned that her favorite colors were navy blue, seafoam green, and orange. Her favorite foods were chicken korma and palak gosht. And she preferred coffee to chai.

'The only reason I've been drinking it at all is to not come off as rude to your parents!' she said when Irfan made a face at this revelation. 'What would your mother say if I turned down a cup of chai?' she asked.

'If it's the kind she's given you so far, nothing. But if she uses that old samovar of hers to brew some Kashmiri chai and you turn that down, she's likely to call a firing squad on you.'

'I will keep that in mind!' laughed Falak.

Slowly, Irfan told her things about himself as well. She learned that his favorite meal was chicken karahi, or a hot paratha with a cup of chai. His favorite colors were red and yellow, and he considered maybe one day becoming a teacher, like his father.

'Admittedly, everything I've done recently might have ruined my chances at achieving that goal,' said Irfan. They were sitting next to each other at the table now, no longer on opposite ends. She sat a few inches away, two half-finished cups of chai in front of them.

'It's never too late to go back and finish school,' Falak pointed out, and then she paused before saying, 'You know, you've still not gone into details about what really happened to you.' Irfan's face fell a bit and Falak immediately regretted saying what she had, until she reminded herself that this was a man she could potentially marry, and it was only fair that she have some insight into what he was really like instead of trusting the rumors that were flying around. 'I'm sorry,' she said. 'I don't mean to pressure you. But I would like to know what the truth is. It would help me understand what you're like. I don't need explicit details, but I want to know what happened.'

'I don't blame you for wanting to know, so please don't apologize,' said Irfan. 'I've heard enough of the outlandish tales about myself down at the mosque when I've gone to pray. Things about me facing off against an American battalion on my own, and that's how I got wounded and sent back home.' Irfan gave a wry smile as he said this. 'I suppose the stories are important, aren't they? They take away from the gruesome reality of it all. Why talk about complexity when you can talk about heroes and villains? It's much easier to narrate a grand, holy war than it is to narrate hours spent watching the sands of a desert blistering in the sun. And it's much nicer to hear about young idealists gaining great strength and glory from the Almighty Himself in the heat of battle, instead of hearing about how the young idealists were most likely ripped to shreds by their enemies dropping air strikes and firing tanks, unloading with weapons we don't have.'

Falak listened to him silently. When he didn't continue, she asked, 'So, what does all of that have to do with you?'

Irfan stared at her a moment. 'Well, I fell for the stories too. I thought I might do some good over there. Perhaps I'd be the deciding factor in some great battle. Maybe my presence would be one that was remembered. We are so good, because we are who we are. And they, the Americans, the British, all those western men, are so bad. Because they are who they are. But now, I know it's not that simple. I wish it were black and white, but it isn't.' When she didn't say anything to this, Irfan added, 'I'm trying to tell you, in so many words, that I'm no hero.'

Falak smiled at this. 'Well, I certainly don't see you as a mythic figure, Irfan. But it does take a certain amount of bravery to go and fight for a cause you believe in. To fight armies that are dropping into a land they don't belong to, so they can punish the people who live there for crimes that they didn't commit.'

'I agree, it does take bravery to do that. And those men certainly don't belong there doing what they're doing,' Irfan said with a nod. 'But how much bravery would you say it takes to run away from that fight?'

A thick shroud of silence hung in the air for what seemed like hours after the words left his mouth. The shock of hearing himself say the words out loud for the first time added a warped effect to the room in Irfan's mind. Falak was stunned.

'I—what? What do you mean?'

'I mean exactly that, Falak.' And now that he'd said it, it seemed impossible to keep the rest from coming out. 'The man I followed, who led the group that I was a part of—a man called Nadir Malik—well, he was a story unto himself, one told by the people who followed him, and the ones who had known him in one life or the other. He was a ghost story, an untouchable creation—half man, half angel, you would think.' Irfan paused and smiled to himself. 'It's what I thought, anyway, what I believed. What we all believed. But now I know, he was nothing more than a fanatic. Maybe he'd been fighting things for too long. What he went through in Kashmir, maybe that's what broke him. Or maybe he got involved for good reasons but unknowingly, with the wrong people, like I did. I don't know. But I know that I probably did more harm to the people in Afghanistan, Mussalman or otherwise, than helped them. Which wasn't what I wanted to do, but I guess it's easy to forget what you want when you've bought into all the propaganda that's come your way. I realized it eventually, of course, the first time we encountered Americans and fought them. In a small town near Kabul. We were staying in the town's mosque, and they got us. Someone in the town told them about us, and they boxed us in, and we fought them, just like we'd been training to do. Like we'd all been hoping to do . . .'

Irfan's voice slipped, and he clenched his fist, taking a breath before continuing: 'I saved an American. Well, he was as good as dead anyway, so I didn't really save him, but I tried to help him. I tried to make his dying a bit easier. We'd both been hurt—we had been blasted away from the fighting by a grenade. And I watched that American boy's eyes as he died right in front of me. I felt everything leave his body while my hands were on him. I felt him die.'

Falak's mouth was slightly open, and she licked her lips and closed it, then inched her hand a bit closer to his before saying, 'You said you got hurt. . . . Is that why you came home?'

He shook his head.

'No. We did some things I couldn't agree with. Don't ask me what they were right now; I can't bring myself to talk about them yet. I can't do that. But, in short, I wanted to leave afterward. I couldn't do it anymore. It's not what I said to myself at the time, I simply questioned how I felt about it all. But looking back, I wanted to leave. And Nadir found out. He did not take to the idea very kindly.' Irfan let those words sit in the space between himself and Falak for a moment, between their hands, which were so close to each other now. 'He tried to kill me for it. Would've been a successful kill too, had a man named Bashir, who had become my friend, not saved my life. He killed him, I think. Nadir Malik, I mean. I don't know. We left. And somehow, Bashir got me back across the border and into one of the hospitals in Peshawar, where they were helping people return.'

Irfan's voice cracked, and he fell silent, staring at a spot on the table. Falak waited for him to continue. Irfan cleared his throat before speaking again. 'It's been strange to come back . . . to all of this, to everyone saying I'm a hero. Saying they pray for me now, treating me like I've seen some great big something . . . and I haven't. I don't know how to say that to them. I haven't even told anybody how I got hurt.' He looked up at

Falak after saying this. 'Amma walked in on me coming out of the shower last week, and she saw the scars on my side. I thought she was going to faint. But even then, she didn't ask how I got them. Neither did Abba. All anybody knows is that I went, I was gone for a few years, and then I got hurt and came back. To them, that means what I did was right. Allah was on my side; that's why He brought me back. But what if that's not how it happened? What if the injury, and nearly being killed, what if that's what He willed instead? To punish me for everything we did?'

Irfan's eyes held Falak's as he stopped talking. They were red and brimming with tears. She could see a vein throbbing in his forehead. How long had he been waiting to say all of this? How long had it all been festering inside of the man? A matter of inches separated their hands on the table, and very gently, Falak closed the distance. She slipped her hand into his and squeezed his fingers. 'If you were meant to die for anything, you would have, Irfan. Maybe the remorse you felt in your heart is what prevented that. Or maybe it really is something as simple as that man, your friend, deciding he didn't want to see you killed. I don't know. But you made it out. You don't have to keep punishing yourself for it. It doesn't do anyone any good.'

'What good was it for me to come back, then?' Irfan asked bitterly.

'Well . . . maybe, if you want to make up for some of it, you can start by moving away from it and teaching others to do the same,' she said. 'Other boys like you, ones who are in danger of being swept up by the same tides. Or worse.'

Irfan said nothing to her at first, but after a moment or two, he clasped his fingers around hers and returned the gentle squeeze she had given him.

Falak smiled and said in a soft voice, 'Thank you for telling me the truth, Irfan.'

'Still sure you don't want to leave this potential engagement behind while you can?' he asked without looking up at her.

'I think I want to stay a little while longer, actually,' she said.

Within the next three weeks, after two more meetings, Falak and Irfan approached their families together and told them that they wanted to marry each other. The mothers cried and embraced each other, congratulating one another on their new bond. The fathers stood straight backed and proud, wiping the tears from their eyes, and Osman hugged Irfan tight, clapping him on the back proudly. 'My daughter couldn't have found a better man. May Allah bless you both a thousand times over, Ameen.' Ahmed kissed the top of Falak's head and placed his hand there, conferring all the prayers and blessings he could onto his future daughter-in-law. After that afternoon began the task of keeping the two away from each other until the wedding. It all happened fairly quickly, but it seemed like a slow process all the same.

A dictator had awoken in Khursheed, and she went about the house cleaning and decorating a new room every single day, chasing Sameer around whenever he got in the way of her work and whacking the boy upside his head before shooing him outside. The guest bedroom was stripped down and scrubbed by a team of maids. It would belong to Irfan and Falak now. Any guests could use his old bed in the room he shared with Sameer. A new bedframe and mattress were purchased and set up in the room. When Irfan groaned in response to Khursheed asking him what color sheets he thought Falak would like best on the new bed, she yelled, 'It's YOUR marriage I'm thinking about! YOUR wife! Did I raise a donkey? Use your brain and give me a proper answer! I'm not doing this for my health, you know!'

Two to three times a week, Osman, Mariam, and two of Falak's male cousins would bring some of her things over from their own house to be set up in her future home. Some of the items included a large chest full of her clothes and jewelry, a beautiful, handcrafted rosewood dresser, a matching armoire, and a few boxes of books.

'She wouldn't hear a word about leaving these behind,' said Osman as he set one of the boxes of books down in the living room during one visit.

'It's not a problem. She can bring as many books as she likes,' said Irfan before Ahmed or Khursheed could respond.

Osman grinned and bowed his slightly. 'I'll be sure to pass on that message, beta.'

The dress for the walima was brought over, a magnificent sunflower color with a matching veil. It shimmered under the light as it was passed around carefully for everyone to admire. Irfan's clothes were chosen with the help of Ahmed and Osman both—they decided on a beautiful black sherwani and maroon pagri, with a matching maroon ajrak to drape over his shoulders. His clothes would match her maroon lengha, kameez, and veil.

All of the planning, booking a hall, arranging a caterer, inviting guests; all of the formalities of exchanging gifts between the families; all of the meeting of grandparents and aunts and uncles and cousins before the wedding; all the anticipation and nervousness and excitement that built like steam in a boiling kettle in both Irfan and Falak; it all led up to a weekend that went by in a blur.

The nikkah ceremony took place after the Jummah prayer on a chilly Friday afternoon. Everyone was thankful for the cool weather, as there was no guarantee the power wouldn't go out in the wedding hall. They all wanted to avoid heating up in their nice clothes, make-up, perfumes, and colognes as much as possible. The hall had generators, but all the better to have the weather in their favor as well. Once the prayer hall cleared out that afternoon, a clean white sheet was drawn through the middle of the hall all the way to the door to serve as a partition and, very slowly, the guests began to file in. The men on one side, the women on the other, with Irfan and Falak in front of everyone else on both sides. Falak was flanked by Mariam, Khursheed, and her grandmothers. On the other side, Irfan entered with Ahmed, Osman, an uncle, and Sameer, who had wedged himself between Irfan and Ahmed. The boy clutched Irfan's arm as he walked, staring up at his older brother with a mixture of awe and amusement.

A few dozen more people filed in on both sides, all the women and girls whispering with excitement, many of them taking time to blow gently in Falak's direction or whisper a prayer, warding off the evil eye. The men on the other side mumbled to each other, some of them telling jokes, but most tried to remain stone-faced. The festivities would come later, but this was the serious part: the signing of the marriage contract, which would make the bond official in the eyes of Allah.

Once everyone was seated, the doors were closed and the mullah cleared his throat. He began with a small prayer and stated that he would first ask Irfan if he approved this union, have him sign the contract, and then go to the other side and see to Falak. Irfan was convinced that the whole room could hear his heart thudding against his ribcage as the mullah asked him three times if he approved of the union. 'Qabool hai . . . qabool hai . . . qabool hai,' and then he signed, and his witnesses, Ahmed and Osman, signed as well.

For some reason, as he watched the old man walk over to the other side of the partition, Irfan imagined for a moment that Falak would change her mind and revoke her approval of their union. That she would run out, and he would be left sitting there sweating in his fancy new clothes surrounded by dozens of confused people. He was so lost in this thought that he almost didn't hear her voice speak quietly, yet firmly, on the other side: 'Haan ji, qabool hai . . . qabool hai . . . qabool hai . . .'

There was a pause, during which she signed the contract, along with Khursheed and Mariam, and then the voice of the mullah cut through the silence: 'Mubarak ho!'

The celebration that followed took place in a banquet hall the next street over. It was decorated with strings of red and gold lights hanging low from the ceiling. Garlands of dried jasmine and lilies were woven around the white pillars. The tables were all decorated with maroon tablecloths and centerpieces of bright marigold bouquets on each table. A lavish, high-backed sofa was placed at the far end of the hall, and that was where Irfan and Falak sat side by side. Her, with her head slightly bowed, a smile plastered onto her face the whole time; and Irfan, straight backed and tall, staring out at the people that filled the room.

Khursheed had burst into tears that afternoon when Irfan came down fully dressed for the ceremony. His face had not looked so bright and happy in years. The cloud that crept over his features so often since he had come home was not there that day. At one point, when they had a moment to themselves where someone wasn't running up to take a picture with them, Irfan leaned over and whispered playfully to Falak, 'Sure you still want to stay? Can't be too comfortable in that dress.'

She giggled and whispered back, 'I'm sure. Are you sure? Everyone expects you to be my husband now.'

'Well, I already said the words. Might be a bit complicated undoing it all at this point.' They both chuckled, and Falak reached over, using the sleeves of her dress and the commotion in the room as a cover, to intertwine her pinky with his and give it a squeeze.

When the time came to send off the bride, everyone in the room made a path, and Falak was helped off her perch by Khursheed and Mariam. Both women were crying. Ahmed and Osman flanked Irfan as he and Falak slowly walked side by side out of the hall. Both fathers were crying as well. More and more people surrounded the procession, walking with them, and someone's outstretched arm carried a copy of the Quran over the heads of Irfan and Falak, casting the protection of the holy book over the newlyweds.

Falak and Irfan were pressed so tightly against each other that he was able to take her hand in his and guide her out of the hall to the waiting car. Her head was bowed, and her eyes blurred with tears. The large hem of her lengha made it difficult to walk in the small crowd. Once they were at the car, Falak turned around to embrace her parents, both of whom ran their hands over her head and cried as they held her. Then they hugged Irfan, both kissing their new son-in-law on the cheek. Khursheed helped Falak into the back seat of the car, making sure her veil wasn't ruined as she bowed her head, and lifted the lengha so it wouldn't be trapped in the door. As Irfan bowed his head slightly and got in after her, he cast one last look behind him at the wedding guests before someone closed the door behind him.

Irfan's family would meet them at the house, but for now, he and Falak finally had a moment to themselves. The driver had the radio playing a famous Bollywood love song. He congratulated the new couple and then turned his attention to his driving. Irfan glanced at Falak, whose face was still covered by her veil. He could still hear her softly crying, so he reached over and took her hand in his again, squeezing it lightly. Her hand remained in his until they were finally alone in their new bedroom later that night.

Life for Irfan improved after his marriage to Falak, and it showed. His mood and demeanor changed greatly. He smiled and laughed a lot more and spent much more time with his family. He and Falak made it a point to take Sameer on an outing every weekend. Maybe to the Air Force Museum, or to a cinema to see the newest Bollywood hit. Or maybe just for a nice lunch or dinner out somewhere. Sometimes, after he came home from the mosque, there would be a gray cloud hanging over Irfan's face, but it would fade quickly once he saw Falak, who would come up to him with her scarf wrapped loosely around her head and, if nobody else was around, lean against his chest and push herself up on her toes to kiss him sweetly on the mouth.

After a couple of months, Irfan began working as Ahmed's assistant at the university, while simultaneously re-enrolling in classes so he could take his exams. Falak encouraged this, and every night after dinner, they went up to their room to finish their homework together before going to bed. She helped him with the things he didn't understand, patiently explaining things he had forgotten in the years since leaving school and now had to relearn as an older man.

Sometimes, Irfan would wake up in the middle of the night, pouring a cold sweat, having heard Nadir's voice yelling in his dreams, telling them to shoot first always. To stain themselves with the blood of their enemies, as that was the purest way to enter the afterlife. He would wake with the image of blood pouring out of the Afghan man's head where his eyes used to be still clear in his head, or the sound of the young American boy, begging him in an odd mixture of Pashto, Urdu, and English to get help while black blood poured out of his mouth and filled up the empty space around them, like a thick ocean to drown in. His side would sear with pain, as if the old wounds had been reopened, the blade digging itself into his flesh anew. On most nights when this happened, Falak would wake with him, and she would hold him until the trembling stopped and he caught his breath enough to explain what he had seen. She would listen, and once he finished, she would reassure him that it was in the past now. That he had to start forgiving himself. He was far from all of that now; he had been a different person then; he had been with different people. He hadn't been with her, or his family; the people who loved him. 'Come to the present, jaan,' she would say. 'Nobody can hurt you here. You are stronger than you think. And if they wanted to come after you, they would have to go through me anyway.' And then Irfan would laugh, rest his head on her shoulder, and wrap his arms around her, holding her close until they both drifted off to sleep again.

But some nights, Falak did not wake with him. She would be too deep in her sleep, and Irfan, trembling, would slip out of bed and leave their room to go out onto the terrace. He would stand there, bare-chested against the night winds passing through Karachi, cool in the autumn and winter months, and hot in the spring and summer, and close his eyes. He would stand there like that until the ringing in his ears that combined with the sound of Nadir's incessant preaching and the drone of gunfire quieted. Until the unending blazing desert and bloodied bodies flashing on a reel behind his eyes faded into a canvas of black. He would think of Falak or imagine himself as a teacher one day. He'd imagine Khursheed and Ahmed looking at him with tears in their eyes once he saved up enough money to buy them a new home. All of this would help reduce the searing pain in the old wound to a dull throb.

That's when he would head back inside, and instead of going back to his own room, he would open the door to Sameer's bedroom and slip inside. Very quietly, he would press his lips to the top of his younger brother's head as he slept. And he would whisper a dozen quick prayers, willing with all he had that the boy would not fall into the same spiral that he had. The war was still raging, more and more boys were falling into delusion every day, and Irfan could only stand there and try to pass all the good will he had in him on to his brother, casting it, in his mind, as a shield against everything that might harm him. On these nights, Falak would find Irfan an hour or two later at dawn when the call for Fajr sounded, fast asleep on the floor next to Sameer's bed.

Chapter Twenty-Two

In the summer of 2007, two weeks before Operation Sunrise, an old friend visited Irfan at the university .

He was now working as an assistant to the head of the Islamic Studies Department, as well as teaching his own poetry classes in the evenings at the library. Ahmed was the head of the Political Science Department, and he was pushing for Irfan to transfer to a university in Lahore the following year, to pursue his master's degree and start teaching full time. Falak had recently been hired by a private benefactor in Clifton to arrange his art collection to be displayed for his international partners. They were planning on having a child soon; perhaps sometime in the next two years, after Irfan graduated and they could decide on whether they wanted to move to Lahore or not.

The visitor came as Irfan was packing up his things for the day, getting ready to go home for a late lunch and a quick nap before coming back in the evening for his class at the library. There hadn't been a knock, but he noticed the shape of a person in the doorway out the corner of his eye. It only took him a moment to recognize who it was.

The face was harder, and the body broader than it had been years ago, implying a tense strength coiled underneath the light shawl and dusty kurta. His hair was long and disheveled under the black topi on his head, and there were streaks of the faintest gray running through it. The beard on his face was much thicker than it had been the last time Irfan had seen him.

Bashir stared at Irfan, and Irfan stared back, each man taking the other one in, before Bashir bowed his head slightly and spoke in a hoarse voice: 'Asalam Walaikum. Do I have your permission to come in, Teacher Sahib?' Irfan returned the greeting, then nodded, and Bashir stepped into the room. The tough effect of his face melted away as he smiled at Irfan, and then took a step forward with his arms outstretched. Irfan smiled back and hugged him, feeling the strong arms wrap themselves around his back and clap him hard on his shoulders. 'You've moved up in this world,' said Bashir as they pulled apart.

'If I have at all, it's only because of you,' said Irfan. They spent some time in the classroom, filling each other in as best they could about all that had happened since they had last seen each other. When Irfan told Bashir he had gotten married, Bashir's face glowed with happiness, and he hugged Irfan again.

'I hope to meet her one day,' he said.

'Why don't you come over for dinner? You can meet her; you can meet my whole family. They'd love to meet you.'

'You've told them about me?' asked Bashir.

'I've told them about my friend who saved my life, yes.'

At these words Bashir fell silent, and he stared at Irfan. 'You wouldn't have needed that at all if it hadn't been for me,' he finally said.

'You didn't know how they would react. We all fell under Nadir's manipulation. I might've done the same thing you did had our roles been reversed.'

Bashir winced at Nadir's name. He hadn't heard it spoken aloud in years. 'You know how many others like him are there?' he asked. Irfan shook his head. 'There's dozens. Maybe even hundreds. I thought I had maybe ended something when I killed him. For some time, I wasn't even sure he was dead. I thought maybe those stories about him were true, and he would recover and tell the rest of the Sons what happened. I kept waiting for them to find me. But I heard through some connections of mine that the legendary Ghost of Islam was found dead some years ago. A hundred or so American soldiers lay dead around him, but he had finally been killed. Along with some of his men.' Bashir smiled at these last words as he spoke them. 'The stories never end, do they?'

Irfan chuckled at the question. 'No. But we never stop believing them, either.' He then sighed and said, 'You know, I was afraid of the same thing for years. When I woke up in that hospital in Peshawar, I was afraid that maybe someone would hear about what happened. That someone would be tipped off, and they'd come for me then. I worried about the same thing once I got back home. For some reason—and forgive me for this, please, Bashir—I even considered that maybe you would have another change of heart and tell them where they could find me. Sometimes, I still wake up from nightmares that involve the Sons of Islam breaking into my home and punishing me for my apostasy.'

Bashir nodded his head slowly. 'It seems like a lifetime ago that we thought we would change the world with them. We thought somehow, the task of bringing back seas and rivers that had run dry fell on our shoulders, and the future depended on our actions.'

The distant memory of Bashir's dream of bringing back the ancient waters that must have carved the caves they sheltered in, that first night in Afghanistan, sprang to the forefront of Irfan's mind— along with something else. 'You said you heard about Nadir through your connections,' he said. 'What did you mean by that?'

Bashir's face tensed up again. He glanced around quickly, and then looked at Irfan again. 'Let's get some chai,' he said quietly. 'There's something I must tell you.'

A little while later, the two sat across from each other in Salim's tea-shop. Irfan introduced Bashir to Salim, the old Afghan man who owned the shop, and who had become famous in Karachi for his especially delicious chai and food. He had always been good and kind to Irfan and his family, bringing over a box of sweets himself when he heard that Irfan had come home. Irfan had cried himself to sleep that night, wondering how he could have done what he did in the man's home country, how he found the nerve to watch Salim's countrymen be killed and burned in front of him. In another life, any one of them might have been Salim himself. But Salim had never held it against him. In fact, he made it a point to always give free chai and snacks to Irfan or anyone else from his family when they dropped in. On the rare occasion he could be forced to take their money, Salim would hang onto it, and later, whenever Sameer came into the shop with his school friends, the older man would slip the money into the little boy's hands and say with a wink, 'Pocket money. For being such a good customer, zergai.'

After assuring Salim that they didn't need anything else and would most definitely tell him if they did, Irfan and Bashir were left alone at one of the corner tables to talk. As he sipped his chai, Bashir looked around and took note of the bustle inside the shop, the noise. It ensured that overhearing them would be very difficult.

'The chai is very good,' he said to Irfan, who nodded.

'It's the best I've ever had,' he responded. 'Now, what is it you wanted to tell me?'

Bashir stared at him before speaking. 'I didn't seek you out on a whim,' he said at last. 'I did it because I was hoping you'd help me with something. Earlier, when I mentioned having connections, I meant people who are still fighting that old fight.'

'Talibs?' asked Irfan.

Bashir shook his head. 'No. Well, not all Talibs. Some are. Others think they are. And some think the era of the Taliban has died and we need something more. All of them, however, have the same goal. And they follow the same ideals, more or less.'

'The same ones we did under Nadir?'

Bashir jerked his head in a noncommittal way. 'Some, yes. Others are worse, more deluded. After I got you back to Peshawar, I went into hiding for a while. I was able to get by on the story that we had been attacked by American forces and barely gotten away, but that many of us were killed and our group had broken apart. I was taken in by people who supported the cause, or I'd find a place in a mosque or a madrassah to stay for a while. Eventually, once I'd healed and was sure that nobody from the Sons of Islam was looking for me, I stopped running. And I finally had time to take it all in. Everything we had done, everything you said to me the last time we spoke in that truck. I realized you were right; our way hadn't been the way, and I came to terms with the ugly truth; we most likely did more harm than good. I fell ill after this dawned on me. Very ill, Irfan. For about a month, an old maulvi took care of me in his own home. He had a place set up for me in the back of his house. That's where he kept me. He would clean me himself; he would feed me. When he wasn't home, he would have his daughter give me medicine from behind the curtains surrounding my bed.

'I thought that maybe the man somehow knew who I was, that he supported what I had done. But after some time, I realized he did not know or care about any of that. He saw me as a person in need, and he decided to help me until I could take care of myself again. That is the route that might've been effective, had we taken it. But once I healed, I realized that I could still try and make up for it all. I could help people get away, the ones who had fallen into it. The craziness of it all, the delusions, just like we did. I could get into their groups and get them to walk away. I still had my mettle, whatever it was worth, and nobody living knew what really happened. This was something I could use to my advantage. That's what I've been doing for the past few years, Irfan. That's where I get those connections I mentioned earlier. Sometimes it only takes a couple of months, sometimes it'll take even longer. But there are more young boys who are willing to stop the violence than one might think. They've been brainwashed. Torn apart from every angle. The beliefs they hold are strong, until they actually have to spill blood. When they see that for the first time, it shakes them. Enough for them to sometimes reconsider what they're doing.'

Irfan listened closely and hung onto every word that came out of Bashir's mouth.

When he paused to sip his chai, Irfan asked, 'Sometimes?'

Bashir nodded. 'There have been times when I've failed to sway them, and they've exposed me as a kafir to their superiors.' He smiled wryly. 'I've had a few more close encounters with that beast of Death since I last saw you. This body of mine has more scars than I'd care to count. I'm sure you understand.' He tipped his head toward Irfan's side as if he could see the scarred flesh under his shirt.

Pressing his arm insecurely against the old wound, Irfan spun his cup slowly in his hand for a moment, and then asked the question that had been pressing on him: 'What does all of that have to do with me? How could I possibly help you in that?'

Bashir cleared his throat before answering. 'Well . . . I'm sure you've been keeping up with the news. You see everything that's been happening in Islamabad for the past year and a half, I take it?'

'Lal Masjid,' Irfan grunted. A mosque in the capital city, known for raising boys who would grow to become holy warriors, had been responding to pressure from the government by setting its students loose on the streets. They'd taken it upon themselves to forbid barbers from shaving men's beards and held mass burnings in the streets of books, CDs, posters, DVDs, tapes, and anything else they deemed blasphemous. Tensions had been rising, and everyone felt that soon, Pakistan's government would have to take action.

'Yes. That's where I've been for nearly a year now. But things are getting worse. The tension, it's like you can taste it in the air. Something is about to happen, something big. The military can't stay quiet much longer, and neither can the recruits in the mosque. Someone is going to strike in a big way, and when they do, it's going to blow up in everyone's faces. There are a few boys there who want to leave. They have wanted to for months. And there's never been a better time. The men of action are distracted, preparing for some sort of confrontation with the State. They won't notice people leaving as quickly as they normally would. Fifteen boys. Fifteen, and I can't get them out alone. I've arranged for eight of them to get to Peshawar, where a maulvi has agreed to take them on as volunteers in the mosque. Two of them I've arranged to go to Lahore, to stay with the old maulvi who helped me. His daughter has since been married, and he has extra room in his home. He needs someone to help him around his house. That leaves five young boys, Irfan—the oldest one only fifteen years old—whom I need to get to Karachi. I've arranged for them to have work at a restaurant until things settle. They can go home after that. But I need someone to accompany them on the train here. . . .'

Understanding flooded Irfan's brain before Bashir stopped speaking. 'You want me to do it,' he said quietly.

'I don't know anybody else in Karachi, Irfan. Nobody I can trust enough for this. Besides, seeing you would help them. They would see there is a life beyond it all. One of them might see that he can be a teacher sahib.' Bashir smiled as he spoke these last words.

'I can't come back to all of that, Bashir. I'm not like you. I appreciate what you're doing, but I have a wife. I want to have a child of my own soon. I can't go back to all of that.'

'I'm not asking you to,' said Bashir. 'I'm not asking you to join me on my travels and leave your family behind. I'm asking you to help me this once—that's all. If you choose not to, I can't say I won't be disappointed, but I'll find a way to do it. And you will still be my friend, my bhai. But take some time; think about it. I can leave you my number, and if you choose to do it, you can take a train up to Islamabad and call me. We can go from there. You would be saving boys younger than you and I were from something worse than they could ever imagine. It might even help you forgive yourself.'

'I—' Irfan started to say, but Bashir held up a hand to stop him.

'You don't need to explain. I'm not accusing you. Whatever you feel in your heart, Irfan, I feel it in mine as well. But doing this helps. Maybe not as much as I'd like it to, but little by little, it helps.'

Bashir pushed his chair back and stood up to leave, and Irfan stood with him.

'You're going already?' he asked. 'You should come for dinner, at least.'

'The next time I see you, I will come with you and have dinner at your house. I will meet your whole family, and we will talk for much longer,' said Bashir with a smile. 'Here.' He pulled out a pen and scribbled a phone number down on a napkin. 'If you decide you want to do it after you've given it some thought, call.' He pressed the napkin into Irfan's hands and hugged him, giving him a peck on the cheek before letting go. 'It was good seeing you again, Teacher Sahib.' Irfan smiled and watched as Bashir rewrapped his shawl around his shoulders, salaamed at Salim as a goodbye, and walked out of the shop.

Bashir's words rang truer than Irfan had expected. Two weeks later, more than a year of rising tensions between the Lal Masjid and the Pakistani military came to a head. No longer could accusations of being 'too soft' on militants from international outlets be tolerated. The army's Special Service forces flooded the city overnight, setting a curfew and making it clear to the inhabitants of Islamabad that something big was about to happen. The siege began the next day, July 3, with fire exchanges between the forces of the army and the young militants inside the complex. The militants, however, were few compared to the hundreds of innocent members living inside the madrassa who were caught in the crossfire. Irfan's train arrived in the city the night before the fighting began.

'The man saved my life,' he had explained to Falak while packing his bag two days earlier. He had only told his family that he was going to help an old friend with some business in Islamabad, and they had believed him. But later that same night, he told Falak who the friend was, and what the business was.

'With everything going on right now, you have to go?' she asked.

'Everything going on right now makes it more important that I go, janan. The man saved my life,' he repeated. 'The least I can do for him is this.'

'Are you sure this isn't you somehow trying to make amends for the past? To try and bring some sense of peace to yourself?' she asked.

As usual, what Falak said rang true, and Irfan paused what he was doing to look at her. Since he had spoken to Bashir, that old guilt had reared his head in him once again. He hadn't felt it for a while. It remained in the shadows of his being, occasionally surfacing in the form of a bad dream, or in the middle of prayer. But since seeing Bashir again, it had begun to gnaw at him, and he realized that he hadn't completely absolved himself of it yet.

'It might be a bit of that as well,' he said at last.

Falak bit her lip nervously and placed a hand on the side of his face.

'Then go. But please, come back whole.'

Irfan smiled and kissed her hand.

'Pray for me like you always do, and I will.'

Chapter Twenty-Three

When the army surrounded the mosque, Irfan was inside with everyone else. He and Bashir were trying to gather the boys who were headed to Karachi.

'This is a suicide mission,' whispered Irfan furiously as a crowd of students pushed past them, the older ones chanting their outrage and rushing to the windows and doors to barricade them and peer outside.

'All the more reason to get the boys out, fast,' responded Bashir. Their urgency did not help them, since negotiations between the army and the leader of the mosque had failed that day. They remained trapped inside. Amnesty had been promised to students who left the mosque—no harm was to come to them, and they might even be given money or granted admission into schools for a real education. But many of the boys were still too afraid to go. Gunfire was exchanged at intervals, and a few explosives were set off by the army. At some point, the boys Bashir and Irfan were trying to get out of the mosque—without attracting the attention of either the people inside or the army—decided to join the fray. Those students who weren't simply trying to escape unharmed had taken up arms and exchanged fire for a few days with the units surrounding the mosque. Some were killed, while some were caught and taken into custody.

Nearly twenty-four hours into the siege, Abdul Aziz, the head cleric of the masjid, was caught trying to sneak out, wearing a burqa. Hundreds of the students surrendered after that, yet some still remained inside, unwilling to give in, or perhaps unaware of the fact that the man who led them had fled, abandoning them and leaving his family and the rest of the people in the mosque to their fates.

Irfan wanted to leave as well, but Bashir was adamant that they stay, afraid that they would be arrested or killed if they tried to leave now.

'Stay here until all of this ends,' he said. 'You can say you were taken hostage. You have no ties to us. To any of this. Nobody's even seen you in this city before. Inshallah, we will all make it out of this, and then you can go home.' If anyone noticed Irfan's new face there, they didn't say anything. They probably assumed he was a recent member of the mosque, or a friend of someone's who sympathized with the cause. On the seventh day of the siege, the army finally stormed in. The main building of the complex, along with the whole city of Islamabad, became a warzone.

As he raced across the mezzanine on one of the upper levels, Irfan saw soldiers barricaded in the courtyard, engaged in a shootout with members of the mosque. Gunfire cracked from every direction, shattering brick and tearing through flesh as people charged through the courtyard. There were screams of pain, of prayer, shouted curses and cries for mercy, all flying through the air.

Irfan followed Bashir, who had drawn his gun now as he raced down to the lower levels, joining many of the young people loyal to the mosque. Some were armed, others were not.

'The bastards will kill the kids!' roared Bashir as he raced down the hall, firing off a shot through a cracked window without pausing to see if he hit his target.

As Irfan and Bashir went lower and lower, the sounds of gunfire from below got quieter. They did not know that the ground floor had been cleared by the army, or that the soldiers were now trying to move up, their progress slowed by the young men firing at them from the minarets of the mosque. As Irfan and Bashir reached the end of one hallway on one of the lower levels, they saw a group of people running toward the other end.

'Bhaiyon! Bhaiyon! They've gotten in! They are coming up! We must get away!' yelled one of the men as he passed. Bashir grabbed Irfan and ran after him. They took one of the back staircases that led directly to the basement, which was almost entirely closed off with sandbags. Three armed men were standing outside clutching their rifles tightly, and they pointed them wildly in Bashir and Irfan's direction as they approached.

'Let us in! The army has worked its way inside; they're headed here now!' Bashir yelled frantically at the men, hoping that they would recognize him.

Two of the sandbags were moved aside, allowing just enough space for the door to open a bit and for Bashir and Irfan to slip inside. The door was shut and locked behind them. The room was windowless and dark—the power had been knocked out, but lanterns illuminated the swarm of bodies packed into the room. Some of them were armed, and all were facing the doorway. A collective set of prayers was being recited by everyone in the room.

Bashir turned to look at Irfan in the dim light of a lantern. He took his cap off of his sweat-and-dirt-stained head, taking a moment to wipe it on his chest before saying to Irfan with a nervous chuckle, 'I'm sure you never thought you would be back in all of this again.'

Irfan opened his mouth to respond, but the sound of his voice was drowned out by an explosion that rent the room. Before he was blasted off his feet, Irfan lunged and tried to throw his arms around

Bashir in an instinctive attempt to grab him and drag him to the ground, to protect him. He felt his body connect with something, though he couldn't be sure what it was as he was sent flying off his feet.

Searing heat and blinding pain wrapped a cloak around Irfan's whole body as he flew through the air and collided with another body, and then the stone wall. From what seemed a far-off place, Irfan felt the back of his skull crack as his body crumpled against the wall and slid to the ground.

His eyes were open, he could feel it, but there was nothing clear to see. Dark shapes, bursts of light and color. No sound either, just a high-pitched ringing echoing in his ears. Somewhere off to his side, he felt his own mangled hand grabbing at something solid. A part of a person; maybe Bashir, hopefully Bashir. He mustered all the energy he could to cast his eyes down at his own chest, to try and look through the blurred shroud that had settled over his eyes, and even through the shadows and the pressing darkness, he managed to somehow see the blood pooling out over his chest. Something had been blasted into his body—a few shards of debris. The leaking wounds seemed to glow under his weak gaze. He could see them quite clearly now. And then, he rolled his head back to rest on the shattered floor of the room. Someone might have fired a few rounds through the doorway; a few bullets might've pierced his already broken body; but he did not feel them. The dull, throbbing pain that had enveloped his whole being just moments ago seemed like a memory from years past. A soundless prayer rose from the depths of his throat and reached his blackened lips. The whisper in his mind spoke the words. And in the final vision, Irfan saw himself standing in a field of light. Falak was in his arms, kissing him on the mouth, whispering soothing words in a musical language he could not understand. Sameer was much older now, smiling at his brother, and Khursheed and Ahmed stood a few feet away, beaming, hand in hand.

I came back to you, said the dying whisper somewhere in his mind, speaking to Falak in the vision. I came back like I said I would.

Perhaps he would meet her again in another time.

The thought brought peace to Irfan as he let out one final breath, and let the black shroud wrap itself around him completely.

ABOUT THE AUTHOR

Abu B. Rafique was born in Los Angeles, California, in 1995. His family moved to the Northern Virginia area when he was four years old, and they have been there ever since. At a young age, Rafique had a passion for reading and storytelling, although it wasn't something he considered as a serious pursuit until he got to high school. After graduating from Lake Braddock Secondary School, he enrolled in college but left after three semesters to pursue a career as a writer. At age twenty, he self-published his first collection of short stories. His short stories have been published in India, and his poetry is published in a number of Middle Eastern literary prints.

CPSIA information can be obtained
at www.ICGtesting.com
Printed in the USA
LVHW030023161221
706193LV00004B/61